RUSHERS
AGAINST
SOONERS

Pushing their horses to the limit, the Woodrowe clan, led by Grand the younger, his mother Miranda, and Tony Girondin, topped the last rolling hill and there below was Tandy Creek, running between wide green meadows.

And there, to their unbelieving eyes, was a freshly cut stake carefully marked. They saw next the campfire down by the creek under a cottonwood. No man alive could have beaten them here from the starting line and found time to plant his stakes and build a campfire.

"Sooners," said Tony Girondin. "Damned cheating, thieving Sooners."

And then they saw the man, huge, red-bearded with strange fiery eyes—Glendower, their sworn mortal enemy—holding them in the sights of his rifle, unable to believe his luck, his chance to fulfill a lifelong dream of vengeance . . .

THE
LAND
RUSHERS

Elizabeth Zachary

A Dell/Bryans Book

Published by
Dell Publishing Co., Inc.
1 Dag Hammarskjold Plaza
New York, New York 10017

Dell ® TM 681510, Dell Publishing Co., Inc.

ISBN: 0-440-06022-2

Printed in the United States of America

First printing—October 1979
Second printing—March 1980
Third printing—October 1980
Fourth printing—June 1981

THE
LAND
RUSHERS

Part One

Part One

1

He bought the girl just after crossing the Red
River to the northeast of Denison at Colbert's
Ferry. He paid two beeves for her. She was a tiny
little thing made up mostly of eyes and ebony hair
which, when loosed, fell to her little girl's buttock. By day it was plaited Indian fashion to
hang down her left shoulder. Seated atop a raw-
boned cow pony she looked the child she was.

"Rupe," his foreman asked, "what the hell you
need a little nigger gal for?"

"She speaks the language," he said.

"We'll be out of Chickasaw country in a matter of days," the foreman said.

"Speak one you can handle the other," Rupert

9

said. "Chickasaw, Choctaw, near enough alike, the tribes being pretty closely related."

But that wasn't the reason. And, at first, it wasn't even the fact that she was female. It was just that she was available. It was just that he was not actually blue but in a helluva fix. It was that it appealed to his sense of irony. The war had been over for over four years, a war in which he'd fought, allegedly, to free the Negroes, although that was not the real reason for it all, and he'd never owned a slave, never wanted one.

She had enough Chickasaw blood and, far, far back, enough white blood to free her hair of kinks and let it cascade down in inky waves. The whites of her eyes were that gleaming purity of health, in spite of her squalid upbringing. Her skin was soft and not yet touched by weather and time, a combination of the best of three races, darker than Indian, lighter than the face of her half-breed parents. When he bought her she was stinking dirty, but he remedied that by dousing her, wailing, kicking, clawing, into the chill waters of the Blue River, where he lost fifty beeves.

She spoke a smattering of English. "Where you take me?" she wanted to know.

"Far away," he said.

She looked up at him from those huge eyes, pupils black as soot behind long, thick lashes. "What you do me?"

"You palaver with Choctaws, other Indians," he said. "You help me."

Fifty head drowned in the swollen Blue, and hardly begun. Two-hundred-and-forty miles as the crow flies from the Red to the new railhead in Chetopa, just over the Kansas line from the

Cherokee Nation. Twelve men and a cook, counting himself. And now a thirteen-year-old girl.

Rupert Glendower was a tall man who looked older than his score and four years. Leaned by the years in the saddle, during the war and before and now afterwards, he was dressed in faded Union blue trooper's trousers tucked into riding boots and a sweat stained buckskin shirt. Unruly auburn hair poured from under the blackened sweat band of his wide-brimmed hat. The gun at his side was Union issue, a cavalryman's revolver. He had had several occasions to make use of it.

Considered handsome by many, he had a sharp Scot nose, pale blue eyes, a face already weathered and seamed by the elements, naturally fair skin baked to a sorrel brown by the Texas sun. And he was, he would have admitted wryly, plain loco, mad, crazy. Twelve riders and a cook and a teenage girl and two-thousand head of Texas longhorns headed up the East Shawnee Trail, the old Texas Road, where every drive since the end of the war had met with varying degrees of disaster.

Two-hundred-and-forty miles as the crow flies, much more when you took into account the endless hills and brush and forests of knotty oaks. A steer gets lost and you can waste a day. Already the herd had slowed from the open country pace of twenty miles a day to a torturous ten or less, winding in and around ridges, scattering into the trees; and it was a wet spring. The condition of the Blue where he lost fifty head told him what was ahead.

As the weather warmed and the rains continued he began to wonder seriously where he'd acquired the arrogance to think that he could succeed where others had failed. His herd was not even the best of stock. They were two-dollar beeves, drouth-starved, skinny, spooky, off and running at a bolt of thunder, the passing of a coyote.

He put the girl on the chuck wagon as they left the narrow eastern protrusion of Chickasaw territory. He didn't really need her to talk to the Choctaws. Many of them spoke some English. With others sign language would suffice. No language necessary when the smiling bastards deliberately stampeded the herd and then, still smiling, came back with groups of beeves asking for a reward for rounding them up. But they worked cheap, and they were better than the out-and-out raiders who spooked small groups of animals into the woodlands and disappeared with them. And when smiling Indian cattlemen added his own beeves to their herds that, too, was part of the price he expected to pay. All he had to do was get one-thousand reasonably healthy animals to Kansas. There he'd fatten them on good Kansas corn and put them on the rails and they'd bring eighty to ninety dollars a head in Cincinnati. He'd put his gold into a bag and hit the rails himself, all the way to California and to hell with Texas and neighbors who couldn't forget that he'd fought with the hated Blues during the war.

That was not what he would really have liked to do. What he would have liked, loved, gloried in, was riding back to Texas with a few good men to kill every Reb bastard in the area, for most of them had been present, recognizable in spite of their hoods, when his house and barns and stables went up in flames and he found himself tied to a tree with his shirt ripped off and felt the sting of their lash.

But, hell, you can't kill the whole State of Texas.

The Choctaws were no better than the Chickasaws, thieving varmints all, but, by God, didn't they live in a splendid country, all green with spring and running with fine-looking streams and off to the east a range of low mountains with inviting, pine-clad slopes.

The weather was good, for a change. The herd was being moved slowly through an area of new grass. Wouldn't hurt a thing to let them continue to eat, put some pounds on those boney ribs. He put the girl on a pony and rode with her to the east, into the mountains, found a stream as cold as the first blue norther of a bad winter and clear as a lady's looking glass. It was good to be away from the herd, from the eternal dust and the constant sounds of hooves and lowing and the shouts of the riders. He lay on new grass and looked up into a sky decorated with white, fluffy clouds. The girl sat beside him, clad now—he'd burned her filthy black, ankle length dress—in buckskins begged from the smallest man in the crew. She'd used his knife and a needle to make them fit better. He did not speak.

"Mr. Glendower," she said, breaking a peaceful silence filled with the hum of working bees and the call of a distant mocking bird, "I your woman?"

He lifted his hat a bit and looked at her. Woman? Hell, she was a child. He grunted.

"I be your woman, you want," she said.

He leaned on one elbow, looked at her musingly. She had been one of a dozen or so, small, wild eyed boys playing with bows and arrows, sticky-haired, snot-nosed little girls, a couple of sullen older teens both male and female. Her father had dickered, but not for long. As the foreman asked, why the hell did he need a little nigger gal? Two beeves.

Thing was, she was as much his as any pre-war slave had been the property of a white plantation owner. Ironic as all hell.

"Going for a swim," he said, rising.

She clasped her hands to her arms and shivered. "Cold."

"Be good for you."

He felt a little uncomfortable, undressing. He turned his back, felt the warm sun on skin which had not been exposed to the air in weeks, smelled himself. Well, he'd kill two birds with one stone. He tossed his clothing to the girl.

"Wash," he said. "There." He pointed to a little pool downstream. She picked up the clothing and went to the water and began beating it with stone on stone, rinsing it up and down in the water. He waded into the larger pool upstream, whooped with the icy bite of the water, rubbed himself vigorously with sand and, feeling refreshed and smelling much better, came out of the water to jump up and down until he was dried and a bit thawed out. The girl had hung his clothing on a bush. It moved slightly in the gentle breeze.

He sat on a sun-warmed rock and watched her plunge her hand into the water and come up with a crayfish. When she had several she came to him, pulled off a tail and shelled it, extended it to him.

"No, thanks," he said.

She ate it raw. "Good." She extended another to him. He opened his mouth. The meat was chill, chewy, tasting like raw fish.

"I cook, you no like," she said.

"Take all day to catch a bite," he said. "No, we'll eat when we get back."

She sat, knees on chest, arms around knees. "Much man," she said, nodding.

He self-consciously closed his legs.

"Wynema be your woman, you like," she said.

"That your name? Wynema?"

She smiled. White teeth, pink tongue, eyes atwinkle.

It came over him suddenly. He'd never been much for the women, not enough time, shortage of women on the battlefields, like Shiloh. Couple of hot-blooded Mex girls when he was a kid. But he knew it, remembered it, felt his face flush with it.

"Take off your clothes," he said, his voice gone hoarse.

She smiled. She made a ceremony of it, taking a long, long time to remove the only two garments she wore. Shirt being opened a thong at a time and, at last, two little mounds, half-lemon sized, dark circles, nipples engorged, a tiny waist, the navel an intriguing indentation. She had trouble with the piece of rope she used as a belt and he was just before taking his knife to it when she solved the knot, opened the britches, began to push them down.

Thirteen? Thirteen going on thirty. Dusky

breasts and areas of smooth skin, lithe arms, a barely developed bush of black hair emerging, a mound made prominent by her thinness, but, as the trousers dropped and she stepped out of them with an age-old grace, she was, by God, a woman, young, but shapely, eternal in her beauty and in the effect she had on him.

"Get the blanket," he said.

She swayed toward the grazing horses, tiny, small hips and buttock, little hand-sized mounds clenching and unclenching. She spread the blanket and sat on it, lying on one elbow. He was having difficulty breathing. He went to her. Her skin was smooth and warm, the air around them bracing in its coolness. Her hand went between his legs.

"Much man," she breathed. Fingers knew him expertly, sent shivers down his legs. Impatiently, he pushed her back, put his weight on her, sought her mouth hungrily and was met by openness, wetness, an active tongue.

"Where you learn all that?" he asked sharply, pulling back.

"No talk," she said, putting one hand over his mouth. It smelled freshly and cleanly of the crayfish. Then she removed it, inserted it between them, positioned him, her legs opening to take his body, twice her size.

It did not even occur to him, at first, that she was not virgin. That realization came later, when he remembered the ease, the sliding burst of goodness, which was the entry. And then he was wrapped in her small arms as she crooned an ancient song of pure lust into his ear, the sighing, moaning, muttering ecstasy of woman fulfilled. She was a tiny bundle of dynamite, the explosive force of her knowledge, her skill, her willingness, creeping into his bones and there to explode like a ten inch shell.

She sat, legs open, scarcely developed bush wet. "Now I your woman," she said.

"T reckon so," he admitted.

"Now I get new clothes."

"When we get to Kansas."

"Now you tell cook I no wash dishes."

Well, when they get uppity you have to do something. He turned her over his knee and from dynamite she became panther, scratching, screaming, until the force of his blows reddened the small behind and she, at last, subsided into child-like sobs.

"You do as you're told," he said. But the feel of her under his hand, ah. Once again she was dynamite in the clean, crisp air, in the pleasant warmth of the spring sun.

Later he carried her, squealing, into the icy water.

As far as Rupert Glendower was concerned, he'd gotten two things out of the war other than a scar and some bad memories, his gun and his tent. It was an officer's one man tent, easy to pitch and small enough, when folded, to take up little room on the chuck wagon. In that tent, as the herd moved slowly to the northeast, he was able, for long, sweet hours, to forget drought-stricken beeves, Indians, raiders, swollen rivers, the endless miles ahead. He was in the tent, with Wynema, when, an hour after sundown, he heard the foreman's voice calling him. He left her reluctantly, telling her to stay right there, that he'd be back.

"Man out here wants to talk to you, Rupe," the foreman said, as he stepped out, buckling his belt.

A full moon gave light which was augmented by the glow of a nearby campfire. He saw a big man, a white man, straddling a fine-looking horse. The saddle gleamed silver trim in the flickering light of the fire.

"What can I do for you?" Rupert asked. There were two Indians sitting horse behind the white man. They wore white man's clothing. Choctaws.

"Your name, sir, is Glendower, I believe."

"You are correct, sir. And may I ask yours?"

"I am, sir, Caleb Woodrowe."

"Pleased to make your acquaintance, Mr. Woodrowe," Rupert said. "Now what is it I can do for you?"

"It seems that you're grazing your animals on Choctaw grass," Woodrowe said.

"It's here for the taking," Rupert said, spreading his hands. "We'll be moving on. Grass grows back."

"This is new grass," Woodrowe said. "We've been holding our own stock off it, waiting for it to be fit for grazing. Your herd won't leave much."

"You say *we*, Mr. Woodrowe," Rupert said.

"I speak for my friends and my relatives among the Choctaw," Woodrowe said. "And we're going to have to ask you to move your herd."

"Glad to oblige," Rupert said. "We'll move 'em out first thing in the morning. Unless you and your Choctaw friends would like to lease me a bit of land for grazing on the way through."

"I'm afraid that's impossible," Woodrowe said. "The problem is, you see, that this grass is needed for Choctaw beeves. It's not for leasing."

"Well, if that's the way it is, that's the way it's gotta be. We'll move out in the morning."

"There's one more thing," Woodrowe said. "We're going to have to ask you to swing to the west."

Rupert's face when blank. He'd been keeping a friendly half-smile on his face. He had enough trouble. He didn't want more.

"The problem is," Woodrowe said, "you Texicans don't realize that this is settled country. Not like it was back before the war. We're farmers, cattlemen. You're headed right for farmlands and you know what beeves do to freshly planted crops."

"How far to the west?" Rupert asked.

"I would suggest that you swing to the northwest and hit Creek territory up around Little River."

"Sir," Rupert said, "you know that will add a hundred miles, maybe more. Take a look at my herd. They weren't in the best of shape when I left Texas with them and the trail hasn't done them much good. I'll be willing to pay for any damages to crops."

"With what?" Woodrowe asked. "Starved longhorns?"

"I think we can reach an agreement."

"Mr. Glendower, I sympathize with your problems, but we can't just sit still and allow you to drive two-thousand head through our farms.

You'll find some decent grass to the west. You might have some trouble with the Creeks, but you'll have them to face either way. What I wonder is why in the world you didn't take the herd up one of the western trails, where it's standard practice to lease grazing."

"I'm going to be frank with you, sir," Rupert said. "I've got my back to the wall. This herd is all I've got. I'm aiming to be the first drover to hit the new railhead at Chetopa, get the top prices. I'm not begging, Mr. Woodrowe, but if I take this herd off to the west, add a hundred miles to the drive, I'll lose more than half of them in the woods to Indians and raiders."

"I'm sorry," Woodrowe said. "We've got our crops to think about. That's the way it's got to be." He kicked his horse, pulled reins, turned. The two Choctaws stared at Rupert for a moment, then followed, taking dead eyes and expressionless, hateful faces out of Rupert's vision.

It was reflex action which sent Rupert's hand to the grip of his holstered gun.

"Well, Rupe," the foreman asked. "What do we do?"

He stood there with his head lowered for a moment. "Do as they say," he said, "move 'em out to the northwest."

"You said it. We'll lose half of them in the hills."

"Not if we don't go into the hills," Rupert said.

"That sounds like trouble," the foreman said.

"We'll start out early, before light. Move off to the northwest, then swing 'em back. We'll be through before they can stop us." No Indian-loving white man and no number of Indians were going to turn him into the western hills. If a few acres of corn were trampled, then he'd pay.

"What if they try to stop us?" the foreman asked.

"We've got twelve good men," Rupert said.

"Damn, Rupe, they've got a whole Indian Nation."

He chuckled. "There is no such thing as an Indian Nation. They've got a bunch of people who haven't fought anyone since Hernando de Soto whipped them good down in Mississippi three hundred years ago. They won't fight."

Wynema was waiting, huddled against the chill under a blanket. She threw it off when he came into the tent on his hands and knees, crawling to hold her close for a long time before he undressed.

Caleb Woodrowe watched the herd in the moonlight from the brow of a low hill for a while before he loped toward home, swaying easily in the saddle. Chota had a meal waiting for him.

"Any trouble?" she asked, in unaccented English.

"He seems to be a reasonable man," Woodrowe said. "Do any business today?"

"Slow," Chota said. Her hair was in two braids which touched her generous breasts. She wore his favorite dress, satin and lace. Black and white. She was tall for an Indian woman, graceful, holding her forty years well. He drank from a wooden bucket, using an enameled dipper, the water drawn fresh from the well on the back porch, cool and clean. During the meal she talked of her day watching store. She liked the work. The store had made enough money so that she didn't have to work, but she enjoyed spending her days there. It gave her a chance to see all her friends, to help them in the selection of a bolt of calico for new dress, just the right glass beads to go with it, to talk and gossip and drink coffee.

The meal finished, he pushed back. "Mail?"

She looked at him with a little smile. Her dark skin gleamed smoothly in the lamplight. She shook her head.

"Seems to me he could find time to write one letter," Woodrowe said gruffly.

"He's probably busy," Chota said.

"Busy," he spat. "Painting pictures? Squaw work."

She lapsed into Choctaw. "For which he is paid much money. For painting the likenesses of the fancy women of San Francisco he is paid much money."

She slept with her arm thrown across his chest. He lay awake and his thoughts went back in time, to the time long before the war when, as a young man, he'd trekked westward from Ft. Smith into this beautiful country of the Choctaws, a guest at first and not abusing the honor, learning, just letting the days slide past, nothing more pressing than to see what was over the next hill. She was over one hill, young, slim, vital. He broke bread in her father's house and did not want to leave, even though her father was dead set against his daughter, although one quarter white herself, marrying a white man. For days it was a guess as to whether they would kill him or accept him.

As a member of the tribe by marriage he was allowed to own property, to do business. He opened the store and he'd been there, at a place

called Crossroads, ever since. There he'd aided
in the birth of his son and there he had grieved
at the death of his second child, a girl. And they
had gradually accepted him, began to come to
him for his slowly given but well thought out
opinions. Trouble was, they didn't always listen,
and they shouldn't, not always. They were men.
They had their own lives. Like men, they made
mistakes, listening to the wrong voices in the time
of troubles, remembering the wrongs done to
them and to all Indians by the Government of
the United States, casting their lot with the Con-
federates. Well, they'd paid for it when all previous treaties were abrogated.

"Having sent men to fight against us," the
victorious Union said, "you have made invalid all
our solemn agreements."

He was there. He heard the Creek, John Harjo,
speak: "My heart fills with joy when I see you
here, as the brooks fill with water when the snows
melt in the spring; and I feel glad as the ponies
do when the fresh grass starts in the beginning of
the year."

He remembered well the tone of the old Creek
leader's voice, and the words, old, simple, delivered in a measured and dignified language. And
the words, the simplicity of them, the truth of
them, illustrated the problem. The Indian simply
was not yet suited to meet the white man head on
in competition.

"There has been trouble between us," old Harjo
said. "Young men have danced the war dance
with your enemies. But it was not begun by us. A
long time ago, in our ancestral homelands, you
sent the first soldiers against us. In all the memory

of the Indian there is no time when you did not make sorrow in our camps and there were times when we, like the buffalo bulls when the cows are attacked, went out to kill and hang scalps in our lodges, for we were not then weak and blind like the pups of a dog when seven sleeps old. We were strong and far-sighted like grown horses. The white women cried and our women laughed."

Poor old duffer, at one with the past, thinking it only yesterday when the Creeks fought, and a Creek hadn't fought in centuries, not to amount to anything. Fighting was left to the plains and western tribes and not even the wild Apache could be expected to fight against superior weapons and overwhelming numbers forever.

Once again, after the war, the Great White Fathers in Washington looked at the Indian problem and the outcome was as expected, another land grab. The entire Nation was in chaos. There had been no huge battles in Indian Territory, only an endless series of running fights and skirmishes in which women and children were killed, horses and cattle run off, families separated. With the exception of an immediate battle site in the South, no area had suffered more than Indian Territory during the war.

And now that the war was long over the pressures were going again, from the east, the south, the north. Two-and-one-half-million soldiers in both blue and gray had been demobilized and they added to the natural and inevitable westward push, seeking new opportunity, new land. And there was no good land left except that land, that choice and often cruel land which lay east of Arkansas, south of Kansas, north of Texas.

The problem presented by the drover was a minor one compared with what the Indian Nations would face in the future. Caleb Woodrowe knew that the immediate small problem with the drover could be solved, but men like the Cherokee, Boudinot, and the whites, they were creating problems which would not be pushed aside. Caleb often spoke at the councils of the Choctaws, spoke slowly and thoughtfully and wisely against Boudinot's view that the welfare of the Indian could be best served by making the Territory an integral part of the United States, by opening all of the Territory to white settlement. One only had to look at conditions within the various Indian Nations to see what would happen. Not even the Choctaws, the most advanced of the so-called Five Civilized Tribes, with a long history of dealing with the white man, were ready for that.

In his heart Caleb Woodrowe felt more Indian than white. He had come to love the Choctaw country as his own, had no desire to emulate the more powerful Indians and build his own empire within the Nation, bewailed the fact that in a society where each had been equal at the time of removal from Mississippi things had changed until five percent of the Choctaws owned ninety percent of the wealth within the Nation. That, he supposed, was a part of the human condition. Men are not equal in ability, in greed, in cunning. If all the land and all the wealth were once again redistributed, within a few years the greedy ones, the cunning ones, would once again have accumulated the lion's share.

For himself, he was content. He had the store. It had produced enough income to allow him to send his son to a fine Eastern school. It continued to supply all his needs. He lived simply. His greatest extravagances were gifts for Chota, new bolts of brightly colored cloth for dresses, jewelry, things to make her life easier in the house. In only one matter was he discontent. He had wanted many sons, many daughters. It was God's will that he have only one living son and it was his eternal sadness to know that his son, instead of being in his own country to use his education in aid of his mother's people, was wasting his life drawing pictures. Pictures, for God's sake. A scribbler of pictures. A drawer of woman's faces. Ah, Grand, Grand, come home where you belong.

He was awakened before dawn by a pounding on his door. It was his nephew, son of Chota's sister, who nodded greetings.

"Many beeves," the boy said. "You come."

He dressed quickly and saddled the roan. Six Choctaw men had gathered on the knoll of a hill. In the open farmlands below the herd was moving, horns glinting in the first rays of the rising sun. He could hear the rumble of their hooves, muted by the plowed land, the shouts of the cowboys. He saw the man, Glendower, riding point, leading the herd directly through the community's corn fields. He spurred his horse down the slope to come in front of the slowly moving herd. Glendower saw him, but did not rein up.

He shouted, closing the distance. Dust was a low cloud over the herd. Glendower pulled up. Already the herd had demolished acres of John Moody's corn. Woodrowe's roan skidded to a halt in the soft, dusty earth.

"Turn that herd or we'll turn them for you," Woodrowe said.

"I can't let you do that," Rupert said. "We're going through. We're going right up the trail. Don't try to stop us."

Woodrowe, having left his instructions with the waiting Choctaws, waved his hat in signal. The men on the knoll came down fast and three cowboys on the flank of the herd rode to meet them. Woodrowe was shocked. They intended to fight.

"You damned fool," he yelled at Glendower. "You don't know what you're doing."

He pulled his gun and fired it into the air, kicking the horse into motion toward the leading edge of the herd. If he could get the herd turned, moving fast, perhaps he could avert violence. The cowboys would have their hands full with the animals. Longhorns were spooky beasts. He could turn them. He kept firing into the air, yelling, waving his hat. The leading edge began to falter, beeves behind them piling up, horns tossing. He felt a vast and terrible blow and jerked forward, managing to stay on the horse by grasping the horse's mane. He felt himself going black, knew the approach to a vast abyss, fought to stay in the saddle.

He didn't feel it when he hit the ground. In that eternal darkness he could hear the sound of the cattle. A rumbling, thunderous, somehow soft sound which told him that he had not turned them. They were coming down on him. He managed to open his eyes. They were moving, but directly toward him, the pressure in the herd urging the leaders into a run. He looked around.

John Moody's cornfield had been cleared on a flat stretch of ground, trees removed, rocks carted off to form a low wall on two sides of the field. Larger rocks had not been moved, and it was toward one outcrop of the soft sandstone of the area that he crawled, moaning involuntarily. His entire back was flaming in pain. He gained the shelter of the rock outcrop and they were upon him, in full panic now, bellowing, pushing, a constant rumble of hooves. He pulled his feet up under him as best he could, but he felt an additional sharp pain as an animal stepped on and broke the arch of his left foot. His overloaded nerves, finding the load of pain too much to carry, deserted him and the blackness came.

When next he knew awareness there was a distant rumble in his ears. He lifted himself on one elbow. For miles the crops were in ruins. The dust had settled and the distant rumble was the sound of the herd, moving northward. He fainted as he was lifted onto a horse.

Chota Woodrowe followed the doctor from the room.

"You are his wife?" the doctor asked. He'd ruined a good horse getting to Crossroads from Fort Holmes, on the Little River. When he arrived the patient was comatose.

He was Army, dressed in blue, dusty, back and underarms of the tunic wet with the perspiration of the hard ride.

"I can't tell you that it looks good," he said to the Indian woman.

Chota looked calm, her face Indian stoic. Inside she was weeping a deluge of tears.

"The thing is," the doctor said, "the bullet is lodged right up tight against the spinal cord."

"Will you tell me what you can, please?" Chota asked.

"It would be best to get it out, of course," he said. "But one slip and he dies, or, at best, he'll never walk again."

"And if you do nothing?" Chota asked.

"Men have lived with bullets in them." He shrugged.

"But you would advise taking the bullet out?" she asked.

"That's your decision, Mrs. Woodrowe," he said. "I want you to know the risks."

"I know my Caleb," she said. "He would say to you, do your best, doctor, and leave the rest to God."

2

A chill and damp spring fog rolled in from the Pacific, heavy, cool air finding a channel directly up the Golden Gate, spreading into the bay, building to hide the hills on either side of the Gate. Grand Woodrowe watched the fog march in from the bay window of his comfortable apartment on Nob Hill. It was as if someone, some great god, were pouring smoke into a container, the gateway to the sea the narrow mouth, the bay the spreading cavity of the container.

He had been working. Pinned to his easel, glowing softly in the failing light, was a water colour. A feather. Just a feather. It was small, the image, looking as if it had been etched in tiny brush strokes onto a four-and-a-half by ten inch piece of magenta-sized paper, a mere scrap, the feather nothing more than white and blue, curved gracefully, blowing in the wind of passage of a galloping pony. Below it, in tiny lettering, the words, *cast me in the wind.*

As the fog climbed the hill, began to close in the city, he looked at the thing, made a mouth of disgust. What did it say? Why had it emerged from his sub-conscious? A symbol? Feather. Indians. Indians. Feather. A Requiem for Black Kettle?

He shrugged, rose, poured wine into a fine-stemmed glass and stood in front of the bay window to watch the fog finish its conquest. Black Kettle. What had he to do with the savage and stupid tribes of the west? Still, there was a hint of sadness in the feather, so brave, so blue. Perhaps he had been thinking of the Cheyenne chief, begging for a guarantee of safety for his few remaining people, going into camp in heavy snow on the frozen Washita up in the Wyoming winter only to have the hero, General George Armstrong Custer come down on him like Byron's wolf on the fold, cohorts of the twelve Seventh Calvary not gleaming in purple and gold but in faded blue and frosted, dusty hats to catch the Cheyenne camp just waking at dawn on a cold, November morning, women and children, pushed to the last stand, firing upon the heroes of the Seventh, dying with their last remaining warriors. Adieu, adios, farewell Black Kettle. Gone to be a good injun. Along with the fourteen-year-old boy who, according to an account by the heroic Major Benteen, charged an entire Seventh Cavalry squadron singlehanded, ignoring Benteen's offer of conciliation, getting Benteen's horse in the shoulder, barely big enough to hold up the heavy revolver which he kept firing until the major shot him.

Cast me in the wind, the white wind which had blown from the far eastern shores all the way now to the frozen and once impregnable fastness of the plains. Elias Boudinot was right. The Indian could no longer exist as a separate entity. His time was past. He was, like the Etruscans, the Armenians, the ancient Greeks, the Romans, the Celts, a mere memory discarded on the scrap heap of history. Indian? Forget it. Listen to the wise ones. Cast yourself in the white wind and become a part of it, as he'd become a part of it, savoring the luxuries available, good wine, good food not cooked over an open campfire or, at best, a primitive wood-burning stove in the wastes of the last stronghold of Indianism, his homeland, the Choctaw Nation.

He looked around musingly, eyes having adjusted to the near darkness, to see his studio, a large room, well lit by day by the northern bay windows, by night by gaslight. Off the studio, sitting room, furnished in rich wines and blues, velvet, marble, rich woods. Nothing like it at Crossroads. But, thinking of home, he was reminded that he had not written in weeks. Now that the steel rails extended all the way across the empty plains mail service was excellent. In fact, his last letter from his mother had arrived in a matter of days, not the weeks which it once had taken, before the Central Pacific began building

eastward to meet the westward builders and drive
the now famous golden spike at some forsaken
place in Utah.

Have to sit down, soon, and pen a few lines.
Hated writing. What to say? Dear Mother, your
son, the renegade redskin, is dissipating himself,
still, in San Francisco, still earning his keep by
painting portraits of San Francisco's ladies. He
knew full well what the Old Man felt about that.

He had not been home since graduating from
college. Over four years. When last he saw the
Choctaw Nation it was still in chaos from the war
and his father had given him an extended lecture
on the necessity of his staying there to aid in the
recovery. No curses, no "never darken my door
again" speeches, just a cold and disappointed
man who watched him step aboard one of John
Butterfield's stagecoaches, making the first
through run since the start of the war, and begin
the long, long journey which led first to Boggy
Depot, then Preston on the Red River and from
there to El Paso and Gila Bend, Yuma, San
Diego, Los Angeles, and finally the city of the
Golden Gate.

A long time, four years. And he could still
remember how, on a cool, spring night, the whip-
poorwills sang from the brush, lonely, mournful,
and how, in winter, the entire world went grey
with only a cedar here and there giving a hint of
color. Winter was weeping time, with the great
masses of cold air moving down from the high
plains bringing a touch of the far north, the ice
plains of Canada, to the frame house and the
store building which, even then, had seen better
days. Choctaws wrapped in blankets, swaddled in

layers of white man's clothing underneath, the mixture of dress speaking of their unstable hold on reality in a world which belonged to the future, to the huddled masses of the old countries who were beginning to swell the white population and adapt quickly to the idea that the Indian belonged on the page of a history book.

Well, it was not his concern. He had more white blood than Choctaw blood. His mother was only three-quarters Choctaw, his father white, making him, what? A mongrel. Enough Choctaw to give body to his straight, black hair. Enough white to lighten his skin so that, if he cared to, he might pass as Italian. Not that he cared to. He was what he was, what? Three-eighths Choctaw? Never was good at math. Liked to read, liked the sonorous Latin which he'd studied in Philadelphia, liked to muse over history, knowing that it repeats itself. Knowing that only the accident of having oceans on either side saved the American Indian from becoming a discard centuries earlier.

How many peoples, since the beginning of recorded history, had met the fate which was slowly but inexorably overtaking the Indian? While his remote ancestors on his mother's side were killing buffalo with crudely fashioned flint arrow heads and claiming as their main accomplishment the fashioning of clay pots, the Etruscans, for example, worked in gold. Where were the Etruscans?

Well, he was locked into a straight trail to the blues. He poured more wine, walked into the sitting room, lit gas jets and was cheered by the glow of them, took down Livy from his well stocked bookshelf and lost himself in it, was brought back from distant time and far places by a quick little knock.

She wore a street dress of dull green silk which spoke of money. Her mantilla was trimmed with black lace. A pert little bonnet trimmed with roses perched atop her raven tresses, which were arranged in braids and pinned close at the back, crimped at the front, parted and drawn back above her ears, the ends making lovely little finger-puffs in front of the little bonnet. Her voluminous skirts brushed the toes of high heeled walking boots.

"Miss Miranda," he said. "What are you doing here?"

"May I come in, please?" Her voice, although it contained the energy of her youth, was ladylike, soft.

"Of course," he said, opening the door wider and gesturing with his right hand. But he looked up and down the steeply sloping street.

She laughed. "Don't worry, no one knows I'm here."

She carried a carpet bag. "May I?" he asked, reaching for it.

"Yes, it's heavy as the devil," she said, "since it contains all my worldly goods." She laughed again. "Or at least as much of my worldly goods as I cared to bring."

He stood, the carpet bag in his hand. She looked at him, somewhat impishly. She removed her gloves casually, flinging them onto the back of an overstuffed chair, opened the mantilla and let it follow the gloves. The dress had a respectably high bodice, fitted her form, surprisingly mature for one so young.

"I am, of course, delighted to see you," he said, "but—"

"But?" She swirled to seat herself, arranging the skirt. "I ask you only for a place to sleep the night."

He tried to hide his frown. He placed the carpet bag on the floor near the door, walked to stand looking out the window. The fog and the night had closed in. Far down the street one single gas light was a diffused glow.

"You never did tell me how you came to have such a *grand* name as Grand," she said, after a long silence.

"You would have to ask my mother," he said. In the name of heaven, what was he to do? The girl was pure dynamite. One thing he could do, and do quickly, was walk to the studio and don his dark blue coat over his white waistcoat. At least then, if irate brothers or outraged mother appeared suddenly on the scene there would be no hint of impropriety on his part. But merely having the girl in his quarters was bad enough.

"Now, young lady," he said, reentering the room, "I think it's time for explanations."

"You called me Mindy," she said, with a wicked little smile on her full lips, "when you kissed me in the sun room. Sweet Mindy, if I remember correctly."

Yes, he'd done that, foolish as it was, carried away, for the moment, by her beauty.

"All right, Mindy," he said. "Are you in trouble?"

"That depends upon your honour, sir," she said. She had a way of being sarcastic without being overt about it. He made an impatient gesture with his hand. "Don't worry, as I said, no one knows I'm here. No big brothers with horse whips." She dampened her lower lip, full and kissable, with a pink tongue. "Although you're quite large enough to take care of yourself."

"Thank you," he said. "Mindy, have you had a fight with your mother?"

For a moment, and a moment only, her face hinted at a deep sadness, but she brightened quickly. "Not a fight," she said.

"What, then?"

"Will you let me sleep here?" She smiled. When she smiled she was not a sixteen-year-old girl, but a mature woman. "I can sleep quite comfortably here on the sofa. I won't be any bother. Then I'll be gone in the morning."

"Mindy, I think you should go home."

"I would," she said, smiling mysteriously, "if I only knew where it was."

Well, she'd had a spat with her mother, that was all. She'd get over it and she'd go back home and the last thing he wanted was to have Liberty Lee and her two rather large sons coming down on him. Liberty Lee was not a woman to be trifled with. Beautiful, mature, she was softness built around a tooled steel backbone. He knew something of her, having spent weeks in her home painting the huge portrait of her which now graced the wall above her mantle. During that time he'd seen the powerful men come and go, had listened as she conducted her business while posing. Money, power, she knew the language of both, and her son could well be, one day, the governor of California. Black Irish with an Irish temperament. He'd done two portraits while in the Lee house, and now, with the daughter of that powerful house seated, calmly and comfortably, on his sofa, he wished he'd done only one, or none, for the second had been of the girl who looked at him with amused, curled lips as he wrestled with his problem.

She had posed for him in a ball gown of white Chambray gauze trimmed with white satin folds and blond lace, hair done simply. Black hair, black as the sepia he used in his work, eyes of the deepest violet, a color which had given him considerable trouble, exposed forearms of an alabaster whiteness, neck slender and delicate, adorned by a choker with an expensive cameo resting in the pulsing hollow of it. She had been, by far, the most beautiful woman he'd ever painted, more beautiful, in her youth, than her mother, and more forward.

"You are part Indian," she'd said. "Have you ever scalped a man?"

"Not since I grew out of my rebellious youth," he said.

"Do you have captive white squaws in your lodge at home?"

"Squaws heap trouble," he said.

"Squaws follow you," she said. "I've heard talk."

"Lies, my dear young lady, all lies. I care only for my work."

"My mother says that Mrs. Goldini would say differently," Miranda said, with a smirk. "Do you really like the pudgy Italian type?"

He could feel himself fighting back a blush. Mrs. Goldini, *schlocko holani,* as his Creek friends would say, horse manure. Was there really talk about him and that woman who had practically thrown him down upon the carpet of her expensive parlor?

"Methinks that is a subject which is me own business," he said, apeing the accent of his British literature instructor at school in Philadelphia. "Now, if you will, Miss Miranda, just shut that beautiful mouth. I am working now on your lips."

"Did you work on Mrs. Goldini's lips?" she asked suggestively.

"Quiet, please," he said.

She was not the first to make suggestive remarks. While having one's portrait painted, if the artist were a careful workman, one spent long hours in the artist's company, looking directly at, in Grand's case, a handsome, swarthy, rather worldly-looking face peering around and over an easel. Under the proper circumstances, although he was not a man to take undue risks, he did not object. But to have a sixteen-year-old girl flirting openly with him there in her mother's sitting room, big brothers coming and going at odd times, made him slightly nervous. But when and where had he ever seen the match for that graceful curve of neck, that perfection of skin which was somewhat dark and touched by natural rosiness at the cheekbones? And then, to confirm his stupidity, he'd kissed her. Lightly at first and then, as her arms went around him, wetly, deeply, sinking into her femininity, savoring her fragrance, knowing only the feel of her through the silken gown.

"Mindy, sweet Mindy," he whispered hoarsely, "go away. Go away now. The portrait is finished. I must go."

And go he did, running for his life. A woman who had, according to gossip, changed her name from O'Lee to merely Lee because she felt that Irish were common people would not take lightly to her daughter being kissed by a man with an even more common blood, in the view of most whites.

Now she was in his apartment, making cryptic statements about not knowing where her home was. He had neither the time nor the patience to try to figure it out. He had an early appointment. "Mindy," he said, "don't think I'm turning you out, but you must go. Your mother will be worried. How did you get into town?"

She shrugged. "I walked and then rode on a produce wagon."

He groaned. "Mindy, I will go out, find a carriage. You must go home."

"If you put me out I'll merely have to go to a hotel," she said.

He shuddered. San Francisco was becoming more civilized, but a hotel was still no place for a girl of Miranda's age and position.

"Will you tell me why you have run away from home?" he asked. "Perhaps I can be of help."

"Only if you promise I can sleep here, on your sofa."

"All right," he said. "Perhaps that will be necessary. We'll decide after you tell me your problems."

"You promise in one breath and take it back in the other." She threw herself down, skirt folding down to show the shape of her legs. "If you're kind, you'll furnish me with a pillow and a quilt. If not, I'll have to make do with what I have."

He bolted the door carefully. If worse came to worst, if irate relatives came pounding on the door, there was the back entrance to the studio. He turned down the lights, covered her with a quilt. She murmured thanks and he left the darkened room to pace the floor in his bedroom. Once he peered into the sitting room. She was sleeping, making a little buzzing sound through her lips. Resigned, he made himself ready for bed. If she were true to her word and left in the morning, no harm done. Beautiful as she was, he was not responsible for her. Perhaps he would notify her mother, if he could think of a way in which to do so without incriminating himself, for merely having the girl in his bachelor's quarters overnight would qualify him, in the eyes of some, for horse-whipping or tar and feathers.

He dreamed. The Goldini lady, not at all pudgy, merely soft, full, mature, almond skinned, was in his bed, warm limbs over his, hands working to lift his nightshirt and bring a response which was immediate, intimate, loving, rousing. He moved and his hand could feel her, all softness and woman heat, belly pressed to his hip, inner-thigh over the front of his thighs, heat there where her secret places pressed. It was so real, so vivid.

He awoke with a start. Total darkness. It was not a dream. She was there. He put his arm around her and there was something wrong, but he didn't realize it until his mouth closed over hers and he smelled the lingering fragrance he'd smelled once before, when he kissed Miranda Lee in her mother's sun room. He jerked away, pulling down his nightshirt, dislodging her hand which clasped his manhood. He leaped from the bed and put match to a gas jet. She lay, hair fanned out on one of his pillows, a smile on her face.

"It was cold on the sofa," she said.

"Get up, get dressed," he said.

"I've never seen a man in a state of arousal," she said musingly. "See how it makes the night-shirt stand out."

He held a hand before him. He was aroused, for truth.

"Grand," she said, "don't fight so. I've decided that I'm going to be your woman."

He groaned. "Miranda—"

"Come to bed, darling," she whispered, extending her arms. The sheets fell away, exposing twin mounds of incomparable beauty.

The smart thing to do was to get dressed, pack his things, get as far away from San Francisco as he could. But, in all logic, the damage had been done. In the eyes of irate relatives, he would be as guilty, having been in her bed, she totally naked, as if he'd gathered the fruits of the unexpected windfall. She sat up, arms extended, waist a tiny thing, breasts heaving, lips wetted and parted slightly. No inexperienced sixteen-year-old, that. She'd been there before, and why not take advantage of the situation? She was offering herself freely.

With a sigh, he removed the nightshirt, stood before her, chest muscles hard and firm, taut belly, long, muscular legs. Her eyes widened. And then he was moving toward her, throwing aside the sheets to stare, in the rich glow of the gas-light, at her nudeness, rich, ivory, unblemished. He gathered her into his arms.

"Now that's more like it," she said, and those were the last words she spoke. Now he was using a different language, knowing her with his finger-tips, his lips, his cheeks as he pressed them to the heated softness of her breasts.

After her initial aggressiveness, he had ex-pected more of her, but she lapsed into accep-tance of his advances, breathing growing more hurried as he progressed to more and more inti-mate areas of her lush, young body. And when, at long last, he positioned himself, entered her heated slickness with one long, deep push, he came to her without love but with a passion which was shocked into fear by her outcry. A swift, sharp, expressive cry which, combined with her tightness, her involuntary shrinking away, over-come quickly by a thrust of loins, told him the truth. Too late, too late, into it, needing her, holding her wrapped tightly in his arms and owning her as only a man can own a woman, feeling the tenseness gradually leave her body, showing her, with his hands underneath her full rump, how to respond, and in the end knowing the always ego pleasing pleasure of her wild re-lease when her body became taut, lifted, fought and pressed and squirmed and a surprised and pleased moan of pleasure accompanied her in-terior spasms.

He lay beside her, her head, hair slightly dampened by their exertions, on his shoulder.

"Why, Mindy?"

"It was quite wonderful," she said, in a sleepy

voice. "Not at all what I expected. Ever so much nicer."

"Why, Mindy?" he asked harshly.

"We injuns must stick together," she said.

"Explain, please," he said.

"May I stay with you?"

"You're with me, aren't you?"

"May I stay?"

At the moment, there was nothing to lose. "Yes."

"Not forever," she said, her voice sounding as if she were near tears. "Just until you get tired of me. Then I'll go."

"Blast and damn," he said. He sat up, looked down. She was, indeed, weeping. He put on his nightshirt went to the kitchen and brewed hot tea, came back to find her lying there, eyes wide, staring at the ceiling. She took the tea.

"Now," he said. "Tell me."

"I don't want your pity," she said.

It was too much. He had no idea what had happened, but it could not be all that tragic. Her playacting, her overplaying of some imagined wrong, perhaps from her mother, had brought her, virginal, into his bed, had resulted in a rather spirited deflowering. That much could not be changed. The small spot of blood on his sheet was there. Of course, she could, in future, manage to place a small spot of blood on someone else's sheets if she were cunning enough—but he knew. She had been truly virgin.

"Hell, yes, I pity you," he said. "Miss Miranda Lee, daughter of one of the more influential women in California, heiress to riches, pampered, dressed in a gown which cost more than some men earn in a year. I do pity hell out of you."

"If you're going to be mean, I won't tell you," she said, pouting.

"I won't be mean. I will listen."

"My brother saw you kissing me," she said.

"Oh, God," he groaned.

"Oh, he didn't blame you," she said. "We injuns are capable of the lowest and most immoral behaviour."

"You keep saying that," he said. "It is not amusing."

"I heard him," she said, her voice low, her face strained. "He said, well, what do you expect, knowing what she is?"

He began to think that perhaps it was a bit more serious than he had thought. He took both her hands in his. "All right," he said. "Go on."

"He said that blood would tell, that I'd never be any good, that I would bring only shame to the family."

"Why?" he asked. "Why did he say such things?"

"Because I am not Liberty Lee's daughter," she said. She was going to cry. He couldn't stand seeing a woman cry. He took her in his arms.

"It's some mistake," he said.

"No, they discussed it fully. Mother—I mean, Mrs. Lee, she defended me. But she admitted, not in so many words but in the context of the conversation, that I was not her daughter."

"Why do you think you're part Indian?"

"My father, Danny O'Lee." She could not speak coherently now. "Some woman. Part Indian. Notorious, my brother said."

"There, there," he said. "There, there." He was patting her gently on the back. "And then you ran, without even talking to her."

"I never want to see any of them again."

"Now is that fair?" he asked. "You haven't given her a chance. She loves you. You can tell by the way she talks about you, by the way she looks at you."

"Yes, I suppose so," she said, through tears. "And that's one reason why I won't see her again. I won't do that to her, for she has been won—wonderful to me. I won't remind her by my presence, ever again, that her husband betrayed her with a common whore."

"You don't know that. You merely overheard part of a conversation."

"But my dear brother made it quite clear, and she didn't disagree with him, not about that."

"I think you should at least talk with her," he said.

"No." She pushed away from him. "You won't tell them where I am. Promise me that."

"I won't cause you more unhappiness," he said. "I promise."

But he did not promise that he would not talk with Liberty Lee. She was most surprised when he was announced, but asked him in. She was the grand lady, seated in a thronelike chair.

"Mr. Woodrowe, how pleasant," she said. "Is there something I can do for you? I've already recommended your services to several of my friends."

"As a matter of fact," he said. "I've come about your daughter."

She went stiff. "What do you know about Miranda? Have you seen her?"

"I know that she is quite upset by something she heard, or imagined she heard," he said. "Shall I go on?"

"Please," Liberty said, her remoteness gone.

"I must explain that we became quite friendly during the time in which I was painting her," he said.

Liberty's face reddened. "We will not go into that."

"In my foolishness I kissed her once, twice if you count a small break in the middle of the kiss. I'm not sure why she came to me. She said it was because, and I quote, we injuns must stick together."

"Oh, my dear God," Liberty said. "Where is she?"

"I have promised her not to tell," he said. "I will, however, do my utmost to persuade her to come back and speak with you. I'm sure you want that."

"Of course," she said.

"Is it true, then, what Miranda overheard?"

"Without knowing what she is supposed to have overheard, I can't say."

"That she is not your true daughter, but the result of a liaison between your late husband and some woman of the world," Grand said.

"She heard that," Liberty breathed. "Oh, the poor child."

"It is true, then."

"It has been a heavily guarded secret, known only to me, until I took my eldest son into my confidence for legal reasons," she said. "Oh, how dare he?"

"But the damage is done," Grand said.

"Will you ask her to come to me?"

"I will."

"Tell her that it doesn't matter. Tell her that I love her very much, that she is as much my natural child as either of my sons."

"I will, Mrs. Lee."

"Thank you. When will I hear from you?"

"As quickly as possible."

What in holy hell had he gotten into? On the trip back to the apartment he mused about the possible consequences of the heated night in his bed which had ended in more passion with the rising sun and resulted in his having missed an appointment to speak with a possible patron.

Miranda was dressed in a simple little house dress when he reached his apartment. He told her, as completely as he remembered, her mother's words. When he finished she was weeping softly.

"It changes nothing," she said. "I knew she'd feel that way, but it isn't fair to her. Oh, God, all these years. How she must have suffered."

"She will suffer more if you don't return to her," he said.

"Can't you see?" she asked earnestly. "She doesn't deserve more unhappiness. I will be doing her a kindness to get out of her life and stay, for by my mere presence I remind her of—of—"

And no amount of persuasion could alter her decision. In the end, the discussion was brought up short by the arrival of the telegram informing him that his father was in critical condition as the result of a gunshot wound.

"I have to go, Mindy," he said. "You understand. He's my father. He may be dying."

"Of course," she said.

"You can stay here as long as you like," he offered.

"No."

"What will you do?"

"I'm going with you," she said simply.

"I can't let you do that," he said.

"With you or without you, I'm going. To Kansas. There's where it happened. Where my mother—that notorious woman, had her affair with my father. Perhaps she's still there."

"There would be no gain in seeing her," he said.

"With or without you," she said.

During the long night on the train, over mountains and across deserts and into the warm late spring of the middle west, he came to accept his decision and, indeed, to be happy he had decided to let her accompany him.

3

It was not the first time he had shot a man in the back. Once, with the grey clad lines almost on them, they'd stood, smoke making the scene like something out of hell, yells, fear, the screams of the badly wounded, and the line of grey had turned and pump, fire, pump, fire, before they could regain safety, he'd seen at least three of them fall directly in front of his sights. But it was, somehow, different to see the big white man pounded forward over the pommel of his saddle. He told himself, as he leaped into action to try to use the momentum of the stampede to his own advantage, to move the herd rapidly past the Indian community, merely another aspect of the battle for survival, for what good would he be, what would he have left, if he lost the herd?

He was right about the Choctaws. They did not fight. The men riding down from the hill were pushed aside by the bulk of the panicked herd and then, with freshly planted crops being ground into nothing under the thousands of hooves, they were in the clear and a quick estimate told him he'd lost only a few beeves. He pushed them hard all day and kept men on the lookout. No problem.

The problem came just before sundown when they were trying to bed down the herd, get them settled in for the night. It came in the form of a U.S. Deputy Marshal and a dozen mounted Indians. He didn't know the white man was a U.S. Marshal until, backed by an uneasy contingent of his riders, he approached the group and saw the badge gleaming.

"Rupert Glendower, you're under arrest." The man was built on thin lines, had a weathered face, did not look too impressive, but Rupert had learned long since not to judge a man by his looks alone.

"On what charge?" he asked. "If it's the matter of crop damage, I'm willing to make restitution."

"On charges of attempted murder," the Marshal said. "For the shooting of Caleb Woodrowe."

"I didn't even fire my gun," Rupert said. "Woodrowe rode in front of the herd, which his men had stampeded, and fell. That's the last I saw of him."

"Well, we'll let the courts decide," the Marshal said. "I'll be taking your gun."

He hesitated. If he were taken away from the

herd he had scant confidence that the men would persevere, get them through. "Marshal, let me take the herd through. I'll turn myself in in Chetopa."

"We're impounding the herd," the marshal said, "until the claims of damage are satisfied."

Shoot his way out? The Indians were armed, but he was sure they'd give way quickly if he managed to kill the Marshal. He gauged it, considered it, saw a tensing of the Marshal's lips, the taut readiness of him. The man had not drawn his gun. But he was a soldier, not a quick draw artist. Maybe he could talk sense to the man, settle the claims. He was sure that no one had actually seen him shoot Woodrowe there in the dust and confusion.

He moved slowly, lifted the gun from its holster by two fingers, extended it. The Marshal made a motion and he tossed it over. "Come along," the Marshal said.

"My herd—"

"As I say, they're impounded. You'll have a fair hearing."

The girl, Wynema, had pulled her horse close in, was listening with an impassive face. Feeling as if all were lost, Rupert kicked his horse into motion. The girl followed.

"Where do you think you're going, gal?" the Marshal asked.

"I go with Mr. Glendower," she said.

The Marshal smirked at Rupert. The shame of it burned Rupert's face. "Mite young, ain't she?" the Marshal grinned.

They rode toward the northwest, toward the cavalry fort at the junction of Little River and the South Canadian. In the darkness Rupert could, by turning his head, see that the Marshal was riding close behind. The finality of the situation began to hit him. Locked up, he'd be at the mercy of the Federal officials, men who were instructed to help keep order in the Choctaw Nation, to keep undesirables out, to work closely with Choctaw leaders. A fair hearing? Not a chance.

He timed it well. It was his only choice, after all, one last chance to salvage something. A quick and decisive move, then run the herd all night, get them as close to the Creek border as possible. Use the last of his gold to bribe Creek officials.

In order to keep him in sight, the Marshal was keeping his horse's head on the flank of Rupert's roan. He poised himself, launched himself backward, turning, putting feet on the saddle and kicking off to take the Marshal by surprise, his weight and momentum knocking the man from the saddle. They rolled together on the dew-damp ground. The wiry Marshal, although an older man, was tough. It took application of a fist sized rock to his temple to still him. Then Rupert took both guns, felt the Marshal's pulse to be sure he was alive. He damned well didn't want to be hung for killing a lawman.

The herd was being picketed by Choctaws, but these were not battle-wise plains Indians. He had no trouble slipping past, losing himself in the herd, making his way to the campfire where his riders were bedded down. He woke the foreman.

"They take your guns?" The foreman nodded. "Where are they?"

"Can't say, Rupe," the foreman said.

"Here," Rupert said, giving him the Marshal's gun. He woke two of the better men, armed them with his Winchester and the rifle he'd taken from the Marshal's saddle boot. "They won't fight," he said. "Don't shoot to kill, just shoot to scare. Then we run these beeves, and I mean move 'em out."

"I don't think I want any of this," one man said.

"Double pay to anyone who sticks it out," Rupert said. "When we get to Chetopa."

Only the one man backed out. The others readied themselves. Rupert led the armed men through the herd and positioned them. One man stood by with the horses. The Indians seemed to be complacent, confident that there would be no trouble.

Rupert fired first, aiming close by the head of an Indian rider, knowing that the sound of the passing bullet would be a sharp, dull explosion in the man's ears. Nothing made a believer of a man quicker than a round passing close by his ear. The man's horse leaped and whinnied and then all hell broke loose.

The guards had been posted off away from the herd on a little rise of ground and as Rupert's men rushed for their horses they opened up with a will which made the little knoll light up with muzzle flashes. He heard a strangled yell, saw one of his men go down. The herd was snorting, pawing, lowing.

"Get to the horses," he told the foreman. "You and I will flank them and drive them off that hill."

They reached the horses together and mounted. Rupert led the way. The herd was moving now, the front runners already in full stampede. No way in the world to gather them all at night. Have to get the biggest group and run for it. He spurred around the slope, looking over his shoulder to see if the foreman was following, and saw that the coward had lit out in the other direction, riding hell-for-leather in the moonlight back down the trail toward Texas.

He fired a shot over the heads of the Indians on the hill, although he couldn't see them. They were lying behind rocks, in dips in the earth, but he got results. At least three rifles opened up his way. He could see the flashes and, once, heard that deadly *ziiiip* as a round went by close to his head. He looked for his men. He saw, in the dimness of the moon, three of them disappear over the crest of the rise to the north. Every last man was deserting him, running like rabbits simply because a few Indians knew how to shoot rifles.

He took shelter in the edge of the woods where he'd left the girl and cursed in a low monotone as the trail end of the herd disappeared. They were scattering all over everywhere, into the blackjacks and the low hills. It was over. With his men gone, with the Indians showing some spunk, he was whipped.

He found the girl, took her into the wooded lands, found a ravine where they spent the night without a fire, wrapped in blankets. He was awake at dawn. He made a reconnaissance ride, keeping to cover. He found a part of the herd two miles away, guarded by mounted Indians who kept their rifles in their hands. No sign of any of his men. He made a wide circle to the north, hoping to find some of them, saw more scattered beeves being rounded up by Indians.

There comes a time when a man has to admit that he's whipped. It was gone, all of it. They'd burned him out in Texas and now the Indians and their Indian-loving white friends had taken the rest, all that he'd salvaged from the ranch.

He rode back, keeping to cover, had to stay in hiding for long minutes while a squad of cavalry, no doubt send down from Fort Holmes, rode toward the remnants of his herd. So it had come to that. A man who had, only a few short years ago, worn the same blue, fought for his country, going against the will of the people of his own state, his own country, was now the object of a search by men in the uniform he'd worn so faithfully. Well, damn them all. He'd never expected to be treated as the conquering hero, but he at least expected a fair shake, and he'd been denied that because Uncle Sam was more interested in keeping his Indian "children" fat and happy than in seeing a man get a fair chance to drive a herd to the markets.

Now he was glad he'd shot the Indian-lover and wished that he'd killed more of them. As he rode back into the woods he felt pure hatred for all of them, the blue clad soldiers, the white Indian-lovers, the Indians, themselves.

But right now the first order of business was to save his own hide. He considered leaving the girl. She'd be taken in by someone. She'd be

dead weight in what would be a touchy ride out
of Indian Territory. But, instead of bypassing the
ravine where he'd left her, he rode into it, told
her to get mounted, led her toward the northwest,
in the direction which Caleb Woodrowe had
told him to take his herd.

Riding by night, holing up by day, he estimated that he was out of Choctaw land after
four nights of it. His estimate was confirmed as
they rode by day and saw no buildings, no farm
lands, no cattle.

He had chosen to ride to the westward to avoid
having to travel through the Creek and Seminole
Nations. By riding to the west, he would enter the
Unassigned Lands, supposedly unpopulated. He
knew that he might run into some few people,
illegal prospectors, Indians on the hunt, but he
doubted that word could spread into such thinly
populated country that one Rupert Glendower
was wanted for a crime back in the Choctaw
Nation.

The land was an endless series of rolling, tree-
covered hills. Travel was slow. The South Canadian was, fortunately, not in full flood at the
moment. When they reached it, and beat their
way through the thick brush and cottonwood
thickets the brown channel was only a hundred
yards wide, running down the middle of a gleaming, white, sandy river bed which, had it been
truly flooded, would have been impossible to
cross.

He entered the water on foot, exploring, being
very careful of his footing, always on the alert
for the sucking quicksands which could eat a

man or a horse in minutes. The footing was firm sand, and the depth, at mid-channel, wouldn't swim a horse. Safely across, he camped, dried his clothing, ranged out to shoot a jack rabbit for Wynema to roast over an open fire.

There at the very heart of Indian Territory, the Cheyenne and Arapaho lands to the west, Creek and Seminole to the east, Chickasaw to the south, he entered some of the richest looking country he'd ever seen. Dirt so rich that it would grow crops from pebbles, probably, timber for building, clear streams for water, open areas of grasslands for grazing. And it was all wasted, unassigned, not even used by the redmen, held in reserve for, perhaps, future occupation by some of the western tribes who had not yet quit fighting. Damned shame, he thought, such a waste.

It was a long ride, but not unpleasant. Once clear of the organized Nations, he felt a freedom which, at times, set him to humming as he rode along. He found himself chatting more and more to the girl, and at night, with a cheery campfire glowing, he was glad he'd brought her. Her wildness never ceased to inflame him. He put up with her constant claims of being his woman, did not think of what he'd do with her when he reached Kansas, thought more about what he'd do with himself. He had only a few dollars in gold. It wouldn't last long. He knew two things, war and cattle. Since there didn't happen to be a war, except with some of the renegade western tribes, that left one thing. And he would fall into a real case of the blues thinking of having to hire his body out as a cowhand for beans and biscuits

and a few meager dollars a month. There had to
be a better way than that, but he hadn't found it
when, after crossing the Arkansas just above the
Kansas line, he rode into the bustling little town
of Arkansas City.

The girl became an immediate problem. He
didn't care to become known as a squaw man,
much less a squaw man whose squaw was part
black. He made her wait on the outskirts while
he took a look at bustling streets of dirt, slab-
fronted stores, saloons, a frame hotel, farm
wagons and buggies and lean men on horseback.

Damn it, he felt responsible for her, and, moreover, he'd miss her. In the end, he used a part of
his scant gold cache to rent a one-room shack on
the northern edge of town. He took her there, told
her to clean herself up and wait for him, and
went down to a saloon. The raw whiskey burned
his throat and improved his outlook. He started
asking around about job possibilities. Kansas was
booming. The pressure of westward migration
was building the population of the state at a
fantastic rate and for every job there were three
men who'd like to have it. He found out quickly
that he was not the only one in a helluva fix. He
had another drink, standing next to a lank, odor-
ous man in overalls.

"Hard times for the white man," the lanky
man said. " 'Nuff land just across the line to give
all of us land, homes, give a man a chance to do
something instead of just letting it set there and
go to waste."

"Few Indians down there," Rupert said.

"Thieving savages," the man said. "What do

they do? Sit on some of the richest farm land in
the country, grow enough corn to feed their
horses and make some moon, beg off the white
man. And the worst of it is that right there in the
center of it there's land for the taking. More land
than the injuns will ever need, and what's it doing?
Just sitting there. Man ought to have the right to
go in and stake out a claim, before those mur-
dering savages out west realize it's easier to live
off the white man than to try to fight him and
they move in Apaches and the rest. Ain't right,
all that land going to waste, ignorant savages sitting on top of thousands of acres per man woman
or child."

Rupert agreed that it didn't seem fair, but he
knew that it might be tough to do anything about
it. The weight of the entire federal government
was behind protecting the land rights of the Indians. Tempting to think of going back and taking a little measure of revenge on the savages
who had taken his herd and were probably right
now dancing around campfires in high old merri-
ment while eating his beeves, but that was not
possible. Thing he had to do right now was get
some kind of job, or find some way to make his
purse a bit heavier.

He thought, during the next few days, of heading on west. California, maybe, but he'd planned
it another way. He'd planned to enter California
with enough gold to be able to live easy, maybe
buy some good land and grow fruit or something.
Going out there flat broke and ragged, he might
find himself picking that fruit for a living instead
of growing it, and he wasn't quite ready for that.

He kept asking around, found a couple of possibilities, but when he went to ask the jobs were
already taken. Meanwhile, after stocking the
shack with beans, bacon and flour and salt, he
was next to broke. When he was down to his last
dollar he was beginning to be just a little bit
desperate.

Wynema was happy, being his woman, living
in a real house, doing his cooking and his washing in an iron pot in the back yard. He made her
stay close to the shack, didn't want it known all
over town that he was living with a young mongrel wench, but she didn't seem to mind. She was
living better than she'd ever lived, didn't even
have the sense, he thought, to know that things
were rough.

He had to admit that the only bright spot in
his life right now was the time at night when he
crawled into bed with her and found that lithe,
small, slender young body always voraciously
eager for his attentions, and when he first thought
of a way to put a few dollars into his purse he
shook his head. Hell, for what she was, a child,
black and Indian, she was still his and although
he felt no deep affection for her, he did have a
certain sense of possession. But when he spent his
last fifty cents for sugar and coffee he had to
think about it again.

He went into the saloon and hung around until
he thought, by overhearing some talk and by siz-
ing up possibilities, that he'd found the right man.
The man had just come to town and was belting
down drinks as fast as he could, all the time talking in a loud voice how he was really going to

make some woman hump once he'd stoked his fires.

There were several places in town where he could have satisfied his desires, but Rupert had other plans. He made his way to the man's side. "Say you're about ready for some female action?" he asked. He had swallowed his pride. Hell, she was only a nigger gal. She wouldn't mind.

"You got any suggestions?" the man asked, looking him over.

"Young," Rupert said. "Not worn out."

"You're talking my language," the man said.

Rupert led him to the shack, opened the door. Wynema had his supper ready on the stove. She'd picked polk greens outside town and boiled them with potatoes and slabs of bacon.

"She's a nigger," the man said, halting just inside the door.

"Half injun," Rupert said. "Before you start yelling you just take a look."

"Rupe?" Wynema asked, looking at him wonderingly. "Your frin'?" Her English was improving a little, but not much.

"Yes," Rupe said. "You like make good time my friend?"

"I your woman, Rupe," she said.

"She ain't bad, at that," the man said.

"Please, Rupe," Wynema said, her eyes going wide.

"Two dollars. Silver or gold," Rupert said.

The man dug into his purse and handed over two silver dollars.

"You have one hour," Rupert said, taking out his watch and looking at it. Now, by God, he wouldn't have to sell the watch, and that was going to be the next thing before he had his inspiration.

"Rupe, no," Wynema said.

"You give him a good time," Rupert said. "Or I'll take the end of a rope to you, you understand?"

She backed slowly away, tears forming. "You hear me?" he asked, taking a menacing step toward her.

"You want this, Rupe?" she asked.

"Yes, damn it, I want it. You give him good time."

He walked. He felt strangely disturbed. He kept looking at his watch, and then he was standing outside the door. He heard her cry out once, and started to go in, but the hour wasn't up. When it was he knocked on the door. The man came out, buckling his belt. He went in. She was huddled under the quilt on the bed. She was weeping.

He walked to stand beside the bed. "He hurt you or something?"

She shook her head.

"Now it wasn't all that bad, was it?"

"Now I not your woman," she said.

"Sure you are," he said, feeling a hint of pity for her. "It's just that we're in a helluva fix, Wynema. We are going to have to work together."

"No more," she said, shaking her head violently. "No more your frins. All right?"

But he found two more that night and sent them in to her and then when it was late and there was only the one bed he had to force himself to get into it with her, feeling unclean. She was cringing on the far side and he did not touch her.

And the word began to spread. The thirteen-year-old girl up in Rupert Glendower's shack was well worth two dollars.

4

A train ride almost exactly halfway across the North American continent was not an adventure to be taken lightly. As Grand Woodrowe traveled toward the east with a sixteen-year-old girl who occupied an uncertain place in his life, the railroads were too busy opening up the empire of the west to concern themselves with service and comfort. Summer heat broiled the high deserts, dust swirled into the open windows, the smell of burning coal was always present and small clinkers and sooty smoke dimmed the whiteness of fresh linen almost immediately.

Grand, an educated man, had a certain awareness of overall conditions not common to the flood of people who were following Horace Greeley's advice. He was aware, for example, that he owed the small comforts of rail travel, which, in spite of its drawbacks was head and shoulders above the mode of travel which had taken him to California, the stagecoach, to public money. The right of way which stretched from the west coast through the high plains and the midwest had once, not belonged to, but had been used by Indians, had become, by the manipulations of various governments, property of Spain, France, then the young United States, was given without reservation to the rail builders. And for miles and miles and miles the emptiness, twenty sections, twenty square miles of land, had been granted the railroads for each mile of track. In addition there were public money loans, outright grants, and all in the name of allowing the growing nation, like a child put into an overcoat too large for him, to begin to fill the huge central portion of the North American continent. If the child discovered lice in the seams of the overcoat as he grew, he merely eradicated them.

There was time for talk, for merely thinking as the eye tired of the endless vista of desert, mountain, plain. He introduced Miranda to the writings of Bret Harte and Mark Twain, two men who were creating national interest in the far west. He tried to explain to her the forces which were in operation. The flood of immigration, slowed by the war, was in full spate again and a good percentage of the newcomers pushed west to join the flow of dispossessed Southerners, still suffering from the punative settlements forced upon them by the Union.

Miranda knew little of politics or national conditions, but welcomed his talk as a relief from her own private miseries. She clung to him, for she was young and so very much alone, leaving all behind her in California. Ahead of her was a future which was an unfathomable blackness and the only familar thing in her life was Grand Woodrowe.

To the north of them, a bloody, if scattered, war was in process. Since the Minnesota Sioux donned warpaint in 1862 and the Cheyenne followed suit to spread terror from Colorado westward, there had not been one year without an Indian uprising. The Sioux had made the Powder River Trail into Montana a bloody pathway and the treaties which had been made to allow building of the transcontinental railroad were often broken by both redman and white man.

Meanwhile, the entire nation was a cauldron. New advances in steel making were revolutionizing the industrial east. Hooded riders rode quiet, sandy roads in many southern states, fighting to rid the south of the type of government Lincoln had warned against. "To send a parcel of Northern men here as Representatives elected at the point of a bayonet would be disgraceful and outrageous," Lincoln said. His warnings, ignored, resulted in the old Confederacy being governed by northern carpetbaggers and fellow-traveling southern scalawags and Negroes who could not read.

The amended constitution guaranteed the Negro human rights, but in the main he was not ready to apply them. He fell swift victim to the nightrides of the Klan and stayed away from the polls in droves, the situation resulting in still another constitutional amendment, the Fifteenth, which specifically declared that the right to vote shall not be abridged because of race, color, or previous condition of servitude. Virginia, Texas, Mississippi and Georgia were forced to ratify the amendment as a condition for reentry into the Union.

As Grand and Melinda rode eastward, finding the comforts of Mr. Pullman's infant invention, the sleeping car, to be, at best, doubtful, the South still chafed under carpetbagger rule and once proud southern families, like the Indians, deprived of their land through confiscatory taxation and outright fraud, joined the flow of humanity toward the golden promise of the west, only to find the good lands taken, to find, as Rupert Glendower was discovering in Arkansas City, that life on the frontier was harsh.

Grand was convinced that white progress would, eventually, overwhelm even the warlike tribes, that the day of the Indian was past. He agreed thoroughly with a thoughtful article in the publication of his university that the thrust was westward, evidenced even by recent filings at the Patent Office. The Westinghouse airbrake would make rail travel safer. James Oliver's plow with its chilled steel moldboard would break the deep, black, age-old soil of the plains with ruthless efficiency. Refrigerated cars on the railroads would make the shipment of western beef more economical.

That all was not well in his country—he considered himself a citizen of the United States, not a Choctaw—was evident to him. As the South was being looted, with carpetbaggers using public money to furnish their offices with chandeliers costing six-hundred-and-fifty dollars, with sixty-dollar imported spittoons, President Grant's administration was engaged in its own plunder, with an official as high as the Secretary of War being impeached for accepting bribes.

None of this, however, actually touched him. He was not a rich man, but he had been well paid for his work of the past few years. In any center of civilization he would be able to earn good money with his talent. As one man, he was helpless to change anything, and he was not sure he would have bothered had he had the power. His main concern was to see his father, watch him into the grave or into recuperation, and return as swiftly as possibly to his apartment overlooking San Francisco bay. There, far removed from the turmoil of the rest of the nation, he would drink his wine, paint his pictures, and what? What about this young girl he'd taken under his wing, not exactly by his own choice?

"When you think of it seriously," he told her, "what has been changed by your accidentally overhearing what had been a well kept secret? Are you different? Are you not still the same Miranda Lee?"

"Don't make me try to explain it, please," she replied. "You can't possibly know how I feel. You know yourself, who you are. You know your father and your mother and your people."

"But you must have a goal," he said. "You must know where you're going. Do you?"

"I'd like to see her, to talk with her."

"She could be long dead, you know."

"There is that chance, of course," she said.

"You have no conception of the vastness of this country," he said. "Your father met her in Kansas. She could be anywhere, if she's still alive. Finding her will be impossible."

"Grand," she said, taking his arm as she sat beside him on the only slightly padded seat of the day coach, "I do have one goal. I want to please you."

"You have already achieved that," he said.

5

The Marshal of Arkansas City, Kansas was no Wyatt Earp, but then Arkansas City was not Dodge. There were no huge trail herds coming into Arkansas City with their riders, wild Texicans, seeking to enhance reputation by taking on a fast gun. Arkansas City was a farm town, wild enough, but since the Marshal was known as a madman who walked with a double-barreled shotgun cradled in his arms, there was only the usual amount of trouble, fights in the saloons, disputes over the women who seemed to appear, as if by magic, in all western boom towns.

Once the Marshal let it be known that he had a simple philosophy about law enforcement Arkansas City was a relatively quiet town. He stated

his philosophy by firing both barrels of his shotgun simultaneously into the mid-section of a cow-
boy who fancied himself to be a bad man.

"This here badge," the Marshal said to the
dead man in the dust, "says I don't have to fight
fair."

The Marshal was paid in silver and gold. He
took a pittance of silver from the Town Fathers
and enough gold from various other places to
ease the sordid life of a lawman and to allow him
to drink the best eastern whisky. In return for
the gold he had merely to look the other way in
some cases and no one seemed to mind. One of
his primary sources of gold was the hotel-saloon
which featured girls doing the French Can-Can
and other interesting movements in horizontal
positions. The owner of the hotel had an agreement with the Marshal. He had a law enforcement monopoly.

And now the newcomer, Rupert Glendower,
had two nymphs in the shack on the north edge
of town.

The second addition to Rupert's new profession was a sloe-eyed little girl, half starved when
he first saw her, slim, bones of her hips protrud-
ing, mound very, very prominent, making it seem
as if her flat, concave little belly and thin frame
were designed to accentuate the core of her sex.
She came out of the Cherokee Nation with a no-
good father whose weakness was the white man's
whisky and a mother who could have been called
a "pore devil" injun, being about a bale short of
a load. They came straggling down Arkansas
City's main street, the drunken father mounted

on a moth-eaten mule, the mother and daughter walking, and began to beg for food.

Business was good for Rupert. He had his own little silver mine in Wynema and she was beginning to take to the work, telling him to bring her only strong, young men, not old men who smelled like billy goats. Rupert had a new suit of clothes and money in his pocket and Wynema had two new dresses and some fancy underthings which she used to good effect when she had "callers". Her one complaint had been satisfied when Rupert swallowed his distaste and moved from his side of the bed to hers. He told his little gold mine she was still his woman.

He saw the little Cherokee girl and remembered how dirty, sticky haired, smelly, Wynema had been when he bought her down in the Chickasaw country. The little girl had, he saw immediately, potential. Prices were high in the town's one brothel and there were always men who would spend two dollars, even for an Indian, rather than have to pay much more for a hard-bitten, cold, often over-the-hill white whore. He bought the father a pint of rotgut and squatted beside him to talk.

"No sell flesh and blood," the drunken Cherokee said, and it took all of five minutes and another pint of rotgut to convince him to accept five dollars in silver and give his little daughter the chance to do something with her life, to live with the white man and do interesting work.

The girl had one of those unpronounceable Indian names. She spoke only a few words of English. He took her to the shack and had to whop

Wynema in order to convince her that the new girl would not take her place as his woman. He told her the girl would help in the work, take some of the load off Wynema, leave her more time to take care of him.

"I am boss," Wynema said.

"You're the boss. Up to you to get her cleaned up, feed her, get a little meat on her bones, teach her the work."

Wynema promptly lammed the other girl up beside the ear, thrust her, frightened, weeping, into a tub of scalding water where she was forced to scrub until her skin was truly red. Rupert named her Sarah. Repeated questioning revealed that she thought she was thirteen, Wynema's age.

Rupert watched the washing ceremony. Her breasts were smaller than Wynema's, scarcely formed. Being fully Indian, her body hair was almost non-existent. He told Wynema to go to the general store and buy the girl a dress, gave her money, sent her out. She looked at him suspiciously. When she was gone he walked to the cowering girl, who was trying to hide her nakedness behind a piece of toweling, jerked the cloth away, and examined her, feeling himself melt just a little inside. There was something about the very young ones, something defenseless and very exciting. It was like he had full power over her.

"You ever have man?" he asked. She looked at him blankly. He made an illustrative gesture with a finger poking into the circle of his thumb and forefinger. "You ever have man?"

Her eyes went wide. She shook her head violently.

"You like," he said, picking her up and carrying her to the bed. "You like fine. I show. You do what I show you. You understand?"

She lay, stiff and frightened, as he explored her. So small she was, so thin. He had meant to be kind to her, to relax her, but his natural urges, the feeling of being in complete control of her destiny, urged him on. She was still tense and frightened when he entered, causing her to moan in pain. He had just emptied himself into her when the door opened and Wynema came in, crying out at him. She leaped onto his back and began to scratch and hit him and he knocked her off to fall heavily to the floor.

"Crazy," he said. "How's she going to work if she doesn't know how?"

"I will kill her," Wynema said.

"You'll do no such damned thing," he said. He felt like kicking her where she lay. Crazy. But he had to keep her a little bit happy. "You're still the boss," he said. "After I teach her what to do you'll be my only woman."

"You promise, Rupe?" she asked.

"I promise."

He sent her out, gave her a dollar to spend any way she wanted, knowing that she'd blow it all on candy and come home half sick. He gave the new girl, Sarah, a glass of milk sweetened with sugar and talked to her gently, telling her what was expected of her, not knowing how much she understood, but when, aroused by the thin, naked body on the bed, he began to savor her body with hands and lips, she was not as tense. With his hand he coaxed her until there was an almost involuntary rise of her loins and this time, when he took her, she responded to his hand-pressures on her little backside and moved with him. When she cried out in surprise and goodness, he grinned. He found out she loved anything sweet and that was the way he trained her. When she was good she got sugar-milk and hard candy. When she was bad she got whopped. She slept on a bed by herself, a bed he had to buy so that both girls could work, separated from each other by a quilt hung from the ceiling. He was thinking about getting a better house when the Marshal came calling.

The Marshal came directly to the point. "There's them don't like your whoring out children," he said. "There's them don't like it a'tall. They don't like it so much that they want you to be elsewhere by the end of this very day."

"Marshal," Rupert said, "maybe we can work something out." Having been in the town for a while he knew the score. He put his hand into the pocket which held his purse.

"Son," the Marshal said, "you can't afford me. Best you just take those two little bangtails and find yourself a town which ain't already satisfied with what it's got."

"That way, is it?"

"No hard feelings, son."

"No hard feelings, Marshal. Been wanting to see the country anyhow."

"They's a train out in about two hours," the Marshal said.

"Going which way?"

"East."

Well, that wasn't bad. They were building rail over south of Chetopa. His two-dollar girls would do a good business around the work camps and in the boom towns which sprang up along a new railroad. Chetopa itself, being just newly a railhead, would be booming. Seemed sort of ironic, though, that he'd be going into Chetopa not with two thousand head of beeves, as he'd originally planned it, but with two young girls, one mostly black, the other all Indian.

He had money in his pocket. He put the two girls in a seat by themselves and moved a few seats away from them, settled in for the long ride. He thought about the hotel-saloon in Arkansas City and began to plan how, when he'd made enough, maybe after getting a few more girls, he'd build one somewhere which would make it look like the frontier saloon it was. His place would have a lot of red plush drapes, lots of polished wood and a rich-hued walnut bar.

He talked to a few people on the train. Funny, anyone who lived in Kansas seemed to be preoccupied with the Indian Territory. Favorite theme was good land wasted on no-good Indians. It no longer seemed to matter to him. What was past was past. He still wouldn't mind owning some of that rich dirt over in the Unassigned Lands, but he wasn't about to take on the combined Indian Nations to try to get any of it. He had his plans.

"They's talk," one grizzled old farmer said, "of formin' a army, goin' into the Strip and across it and jest takin' over the Unassigned Lands."

"There are soldiers in the Strip who'd come in and run you out," Rupert said. "Uncle Sam looks after his Indian children."

"No white man's gonna shoot another white man over some injun," the farmer said.

He amused himself for a while thinking about it, wondering what would happen if whites just went into the Unassigned Lands and took them. Would the soldiers shoot? Amusing to think about it, but he wasn't going to be the one to find out.

The town of Chetopa was, indeed, booming. The Missouri, Kansas and Texas Railroad had arrived there only in May. By previous agreement, the railroad which reached the border of Indian lands first had the right to build on into the Cherokee Nation, although there were many Indians who did not want the railroads. The Missouri, Kansas and Texas hadn't even waited for official approval of that right, but, after reaching Chetopa, had pushed graders and track layers down through the Cherokee Nation in a direct line toward the northeastern corner of the Creek Nation.

There were still a lot of unanswered questions, and the backers of the new line down the Old Texas Road were taking risks, because there was no certainty that titles to land could be cleared in order for the government to award the traditional twenty square miles per each mile of track to the company, but since J.P. Morgan himself, along with John D. Rockefeller, were among the promoters and stockholders, the risk was deemed mimimal. How could ignorant Indians stand against the wishes of the country and against such powerful men as Morgan and Rockefeller?

Chetopa was all optimism and boom. Money flowed freely. Irish and Chinese laborers, on their free time, came to appreciate the economy of the new service which Glendower brought to town, and by the time Grand Woodrowe and Miranda Lee detrained in bustling Chetopa, Rupert's business was three days established and he'd discovered that the railroad hotel served the best meal in town. There he first saw Miranda Lee.

As it had happened, Grand and Miranda's first good night's sleep in several days coincided with an unexpected night in the hotel for Rupert. There was a girl in the chorus line in the saloon who had caught his eye. He was thinking ahead to the time when he would have a string of girls and a place of his own. He had set up shop in a two room shotgun house, thrown together out of warped boards and corregated tin. The back room was, once again, separated by a hanging quilt, so that it was a two bed shop. The other room had a dilapidated wood-burner on which Wynema cooked. Things were going well, and the shotgun shack was plenty good enough for the clientele, mostly laborers. But the girl in the chorus line, ah. She was all white, lily white, and her gleaming, bare arms, her breasts pushed high into the revealing vee of her costume, started Rupert thinking. The end result was that he paid five times more for her than he charged for an hour with his two lithe, young gold mines. And it wasn't worth it, except for the insight he got into a line of the business he intended to investigate further. When he told her of his plans she laughed at him.

"Stick with your niggers and injuns," she said. "You're a little short of class."

He didn't hit her. The man who ran the store looked after his girls, and had two burly Irishmen to see to it that anyone who mistreated one of them paid dearly for it. He just kicked her out of the overpriced room, telling her that she could learn a lot from his injun and his nigger about being a woman, that he'd had more action out of a sheep. And it was true. All she did to earn her money was look lily white and lie there as if she had been bored stiff, which she probably was.

He went down to the dining room, after bathing her scent off him in a tub which was too short for his long legs, and found the place to be crowded, as usual. He got the last table, ordered steak and eggs, and was getting control of his anger when the most beautiful girl he'd ever seen came down the stairs and stood, all silks and raven hair, waiting to be seated by the uniformed waiter.

Grand had gone to see about arranging transportation to the south. He would meet her in the dining room when he'd checked on stage schedules. She felt rather wonderful. The morning had begun with a bit of good-spirited horseplay which ended in spirited love-making. There was a feeling of adventure in the town, so busy, so crowded, so vital, that she'd never experienced in the staid and settled town of San Francisco. She looked forward to seeing more of the country, to meeting Grand's parents, to seeing the Indian Territory.

Not having a table available was a minor nuisance. She smiled at the waiter and said she'd wait, that she wanted a table for two, would be joined shortly by a gentleman.

Rupert could not take his eyes off her. Her dark hair, piled atop her head, her lively eyes, her obvious good breeding, all appealed to him. He was dressed neatly and rather expensively in a waistcoated suit, shirt frilly and clean white, his hair tonsured by the town's best barber. Perhaps it was merely to prove to himself that the lily-skinned whore's opinion of him was wrong, perhaps it was the memory of grand southern ladies who, even in defeat, managed to look, always, so beautiful, so elegant, so self-assured.

He motioned the waiter to his table. He was halfway through his hearty breakfast. "Tell the lady that she's welcome to join me at my table, since there's no room elsewhere." He slipped the waiter a coin and watched with interest as he conferred with the beautiful young girl who looked doubtfully toward him. He half-raised himself in his chair, made a stately bow over the table, and waved his hand toward the empty chair across from him. Her doubt gave way to a smile.

He rose, bowed again. "Can't stand to see such a charming lady standing," he said.

"You're very kind," she said, seating herself. "I'll sit with you until there is another table, for I'm expecting my husband."

He didn't like the sound of the word, but there it was. Ah, well. He introduced himself. She, not fully prepared for her first experience posing as Grand's wife, said, "I'm Miranda Lee," without thinking.

"I'm charmed, Mrs. Lee," he said. "You will join me in coffee while you wait?"

She nodded. The hovering waiter soon was back with a cup of deliciously strong coffee.

"If I may say so," Rupert said, "you're not

the type of lady one would expect to see in a rail-road boom town. Is your husband with the rail-road?"

"Oh, no," she said. "We're merely traveling through."

"Ah," he said.

He was, she decided, exactly the kind of man one expected to see in the wild west, tall, strong looking, face weathered by the elements. With his neatly trimmed auburn hair and his tasteful clothing he was quite handsome. He talked easily, asking questions with a disarming ease, and she found herself talking about the long trip from California, how she'd ridden on a railroad which her own father had helped to build. He touched her family pride with his interest, and, once again not prepared for deceit, told him that her father's name was Danny O'Lee. She realized her slip immediately, but he didn't seem to notice. He had, of course, caught the slip. An O'Lee married to a Lee? Odd coincidence, he thought.

He seemed to want to drown in her violet eyes. Such was the youthful radiance of her face that he could not look directly at her for longer than a mere second. He had never been so bowled over by a woman. He wanted to keep her at the table forever, his steak and eggs forgotten until she said, "Please do finish your meal, Mr. Glen-dower. It would be a shame to waste something which smells so delicious."

"You're hungry," he said.

"I must admit that I'm famished," she said, with a little laugh.

"Then we will remedy that," he said, waving to the waiter. "Never fear, when Mr. Lee comes I will have finished and I will leave you in privacy."

She ordered, steak and eggs, laughing at herself to think that she was, always, a light eater. Something in the air, the clean early summer air, she supposed.

In her almost euphoric state of well being, basking without shame in the obvious admiration of a handsome man, she continued to talk, youthfully and enthusiastically, about how exciting it was to travel to such far places, to see different kinds of people, all the wild, beautiful scenery between Kansas and California, and when he, interested, polite, asked the reason for her travels, she paused for only a moment. She had to start asking questions somewhere.

"I'm looking for someone," she said. "A woman. Did you by chance know my father, Danny O'Lee, or hear of him?"

"No. I just came up from Texas a short while ago," he said. "This woman, a relative?"

"In a way," she said. "Actually, she was a friend of my father's."

"I see," Rupert said, his mind working, wondering. She was obviously a lady, richly dressed. It would be an intriguing story if he could get her to tell him all of it. She was intriguing in every way.

Miranda sat facing the entrance, which extended into the hotel's lobby. A flash of red caught her eye and she looked up, saw a dark skinned young girl in a red, feather-hemmed skirt which reached to her ankles and, at the top, exposed a large area of skin and the swell of two small but developing breasts. The waiter was standing there, as if to guard the dining room from the girl, who was obviously a mulatto. The girl was looking directly at her, waving one hand frantically. The waiter, frowning, moved toward her.

Wynema had been worried when Rupert didn't come home. She had minded the store, the two of them doing good business, hiding the silver dollars in a fruit jar under a loose board in the flooring between customers, and then she'd stayed awake for ever so long waiting for Rupe. She was awake just after sunrise and he still wasn't home, so she went out into the streets looking for him. She had some wonderful news for him. He would be so proud of her. She could not wait to tell him.

She knew that he drank and ate at the hotel, and, dressed in what she considered her finest, a dress which she'd picked out personally, she entered the hotel cautiously and saw his easily recognizable red hair in the dining room. She knew that she would not be allowed to enter. She didn't know that she looked to be exactly what she was in the red dress, but she knew that the color of her skin barred her from the fancy white places. That didn't bother her. Seeing Rupe with a beautiful white girl did. So, she thought, that was why he didn't come home.

She saw the waiter moving toward her purposefully and, at the last minute, dashed past him, anger overcoming her caution. She arrived at Rupert's table breathless, everyone in the dining room looking. She was hard not to see. Rupert, hearing the commotion, turned to look into her dark, angry little face.

"Rupe, you come," she said. "We talk."

Miranda, although surprised, looked on bemused as the man's handsome face went a deep shade of red.

"Get out of here, Wynema," he said. "You know you shouldn't be in here."

The waiter was coming, a fierce scowl on his face. For Rupert, the magic moment had been ruined. He had, he knew, been making a good impression upon Miranda Lee.

"Rupe, we have talk. Important," Wynema insisted.

And everyone in the place was looking. The girl across the table from him was smiling, derisively, he imagined. The silly little bitch had ruined everything. "I told you to get out of here," he grated between his teeth. "Now."

"Rupe, it's important," Wynema said, wanting to tell him the good news.

He hit her backhand, his knuckles leaving white marks on her cheek. The force of the blow sent her backward, to fall, catching herself with her hands before her rump hit the floor. With a gasp, Miranda leaped to her feet.

"How dare you?" she asked, shocked, seeing the expression of pain and humiliation on the small, dark girl's face, feeling an instant outflow of pity. She had never seen a man strike a woman before.

The waiter gathered Wynema by the arms. "Sorry, sir," he said. "Sorry for the bother. We'll see to it that she doesn't bother you again." He almost picked Wynema off her feet, his fingers digging into her arms, and hustled her toward the entrance.

"Rupe," Wynema wailed, over her shoulder. "Rupe."

Miranda was standing, pale faced, still shocked.

"I apologize," Rupert said.

"You struck her," Miranda said, in disbelief.

"She's my housekeeper. She's only a nigger."

"She is, sir, a human being," Miranda said.

The shock had worn off. People at other tables began to buzz, some to laugh. And to Rupert the laughter was cutting.

"You should be ashamed of yourself," Miranda said.

"Look, it's none of your business," he said harshly, wanting only to be away, to get away from the derisive laughter.

"It is the business of everyone when an innocent child is mistreated," Miranda flared.

People were still looking and the girl was talking loudly, loudly enough for all to hear. Rupert Glendower was not a man to take humiliation lightly.

"She's about as innocent as you are," he said. "You're no more married than I am. Your father's name was O'Lee and you say yours is Lee. I think you're just what my girl is, only a little more expensive."

She hit him before she thought, not swinging from the hip, for he would have been able to see her preparations and block her hand, but with a quick little jab of a slap which had about enough force to swat a fly, but made a sharp little explosion of sound. There was a gasp from watching people and Rupert's vision glazed with red. Be-

fore he thought he had his fist drawn back. No
one hit Rupert Glendower with impunity.

"Look, look, everybody," Miranda said loudly, "the big strong *gentleman* likes to hit women.
Now he's going to hit me."

He lowered his fist slowly, knuckles white with
the effort it took to keep from knocking the smirk
from her face. The slap, humiliation added atop
embarrassment, focused his emotions on her,
made her the symbol of all those in the dining
room who looked at him as if he were some kind
of animal.

"You will regret that," he said, through
clenched teeth. He left the dining room with his
head high, walking slowly, arms swinging, re-
trieved his hat and gunbelt, went into the street,
not looking back.

Fortunately for Wynema, his hatred remained
focused on the cool, beautiful white girl, the symbol of all those who looked down on him. He
entered the shotgun shack in a dangerous frame
of mind. Wynema, seeing the thunder on his
face, cringed away.

"Don't hit me, Rupe," she said. "I got surprise
for you."

Sarah was still in bed. Another girl sat, cowering, in a broken-legged chair near the wood burning cookstove which was fired up and dispelling
the early morning chill. The smell of coffee filled
the room.

"Lotus wants work with us," Wynema said.

He got his temper under control. The girl was
at least half Chinese. A rarity. Not many Chinese
women, only the coolies who worked the rails.

Darkness of skin indicated, perhaps, an Indian mother. He hung his hat on a nail and walked to look down at her. She was small, obviously young.

"You speak English?" he asked.

"A little," she said.

"Where are you from?"

"North," she said.

"That doesn't tell me a helluva lot," he said.

"I will work for you," she said. "I have talk with Wynema."

"Not until I know a little about you," he said. "Your parents."

"No one looks for me," she said.

"How did you get to Chetopa?"

"Man brought me."

"From where?"

"West."

"I thought you said north."

She shrugged.

"Get her out of here, Wynema," he said, turning away. "She's trouble."

"No, good girl. Want work," Wynema said. "Seneca mother, she say. Chinese father. Mother poor devil Seneca. Father leave, work railroad. Railroad man brought her Chetopa."

"Is that right?" He looked at her again. Not bad. Round faced but sort of pretty. Good little body, probably every bit as young as Wynema and Sarah.

"Got no mama, got no papa," she said.

"What you do for this man brought you here?" he asked.

She shrugged again. "Wash, cook, make good time."

"What happened to him?"

She shrugged. "Talk, damn it," Rupert said, "or out you go."

"Go back California."

He didn't like it much. But she was enough Chinese to appeal to the chinks who worked the rails. "All right. You work. You do as you're told. You take orders from me and from Wynema. You understand?"

"I understand. What I get?"

"Food, clothes, spending money. I take care of you."

She nodded. He told Wynema to clean her up and get her a decent dress. Hell, with three of them working, he'd be rolling in money. And the ease with which he'd come by still another recruit started him thinking. He had two things going for him, the youth of his girls and the cheapness of his girls. As long as men were building railroads there'd be workers who couldn't rake up the kind of money it took to go to one of the white houses. If he had five or six of them, he could afford a better place, have girls like that Lee wench who was no more married than he, girls for whom he could charge an arm and a leg.

He began to feel better. He went out, had a mid-morning drink. To show that he wasn't intimidated by what had happened, he had his drink in the bar at the railroad hotel. And he had his lunch there, saw the girl come in with a big, dark fellow dressed like a city dude.

"Who is the man with the dark haired young woman?" he asked the waiter.

"A Mr. Woodrowe, sir," the waiter said. The name had a familiar ring.

"What do you know about him?" Rupert asked.

"Not much, sir," the waiter said, taking the silver dollar with a quickness which was almost slight of hand. "Only that he was inquiring about transportation to the south, into the Choctaw Nation."

Bing. Woodrowe. Well, it was a small world, wasn't it? That white injun-lover down there, Woodrowe. This man going into Choctaw territory, also named Woodrowe. Looked Indian. So the high and mighty bitch was bedded down with an injun, of all things, and she had the nerve to look down her nose at him.

The way she looked at the injun sent cold shivers of hatred through him. Someday, someday, he'd make her remember how she'd spoken to him, how she'd slapped him in front of a lot of people. It was a small world, and someday they'd meet again.

6

"It was not a wise thing to do," Grand told her, with a smile to soften the reproof. "You must realize, my dear Mindy, that you are no longer in San Francisco, where a gentleman rises when a lady comes into the room."

"But he seemed so gentlemanly at first," Miranda said.

"Most of them are good people," Grand said. "They've left their homes in the east looking for better things. They're God-fearing Christians and eventually they'll have churches built one to about each section of land and uniformed policemen walking patrol. But right now the very elements which bring them also bring the lawless."

They were bouncing along in a stagecoach,

having left the rails at the bustling, brawling, filthy tent city which marked the end of construction. Their route was an old one, the same trail which Rupert Glendower had intended traveling with his herd, the Texas Road, with long days of travel through first, the Cherokee Nation and then the Choctaw country. At least for the time being, they had the bouncing, rattling vehicle to themselves, the rumble of the wheels, the hoofbeats of the horses, the creakings of the coach body forcing them to speak loudly, but still with no danger of being overheard by the driver and his helper, a half-breed Indian armed with a heavy shotgun.

"You're fortunate that there were so many people there," Grand said. "Otherwise you would have, no doubt, received the same treatment as the young girl."

"I can't believe men could do such things," she said.

Grand laughed bitterly. "Lady, you have no conception of what men can do when they are not faced with stern and immediate punishment."

Late spring was being kind to the Cherokee country. It seemed, to Miranda, to be so utterly peaceful. It was not what she had expected, and she voiced her surprise to Grand.

"I know," he said. "You expected to see herds of buffalo and wild Indians in breech-clouts riding ponies bareback." He smiled indulgently. "There are schools and churches here. These people, like the Choctaws, have been in contact with the white man for more than a century. They have taken well to his ways. They haven't mastered them, as you'll see, but they're not savages."

When they broke their tiring journey at Moskogee she saw tall, dark, strong men in morning clothes, women in brightly colored, gay dresses. Except for the color of their skin, they could have been any people, anywhere, but then she heard the soft, somewhat guttural sound of the language and realized the difference.

As the trip continued, Grand seemed to become more withdrawn. When, at last, he announced that they were now in the Choctaw Nation she saw endlessly rolling, wooded hills, blue sky, now and then a plume of woodsmoke from the stovepipe of a house built far from the road. Grand explained that the Choctaws didn't like towns, that a Choctaw town would seem, to the white man, to be a scattered settlement, with no house closer than a bowshot to another. However, he seemed reluctant to talk. Mindy, thinking it to be concern over what he would find at the end of the journey, respected his silences. She could not know that the main concern for Grand's moodiness was herself. When, at last, it was necessary for him to speak he did not know how to begin.

"There is something we must discuss," he said, not looking at her.

"Of course," she said.

"Our relationship," he said.

"I see," she said. "I have become a burden to you. I should have stayed in Kansas. After all, that's why I came east, to search Kansas for my—" She could not quite bring herself to say the word, mother.

"No, no," he said, somewhat impatiently. "I don't mean long range relationship." He paused. "Or do I?"

"What is it, Grand?" she asked.

"Perhaps I should stop in Eufala and marry you," he said musingly.

She was taken aback for a moment. Neither of them had mentioned marriage. She decided to treat it lightly. "Not, sir, a very romantic proposal."

"I'm serious," he said, looking at her. And he realized that he was. That first night, when she came into his bed, he took her without love, and he was not yet sure whether or not he loved her. Marriage had not been in his thoughts, either. But the days with her, the nights with her. Like some small, wounded animal she had sought warmth and comfort in his bed and he had taken her in, intending, at first, to offer only warmth and comfort. When had his feelings changed? They had. He knew that. He could not look at her without a surge of pleasure. Rather than becoming washed out, tired, she had blossomed under the hardship of travel. Her youth and beauty was a vibrant and almost palpable aura which flowed over him, leaving him the better for it.

He sighed. "I see that we will have to arrive at the subject with a brief trip around the barn. Let me state, first, that I consider myself to be my own man, a product of my background, of course, but above it, fully capable of choosing my own direcion, my own system of values. Secondly, let me say, my dear Miranda, that we are, as the saying goes, living in sin."

"You shock me, sir," she said, still trying to dispell his seriousness with lightness.

"Thirdly, although, as I say, I have my own values, there are others to consider."

"Ah," she said. "I think I am beginning to

understand. We have violated some tribal taboo?"

"Damn it, Mindy," he said. "I'm not the only Choctaw who can read and write and speak English."

"Sorry," she said.

"My mother is a devout Baptist."

"I am sorry," she said. "Now I do see."

"Perhaps," he said. "We've always been, ah, blessed by the presence of the missionaries. Most Choctaws are Presbyterian or Methodist, but the Baptists have recently become quite active and my mother found their teaching to be more to her liking."

"And Baptists are very moral people," Mindy said. "But, Grand, you don't have to marry me just to keep from shocking your mother."

He grinned. "Sounded that way, didn't it? But that's not it. Oh, I think we have to arrive at some story to cover our traveling together. It's not, my dear girl, a caving-in on my part. I don't feel sinful. But I will be in my mother's house. I am there seldom. When I am there, it does not harm me to conform, for a little while, to her beliefs."

"I can understand that," she said.

"It might be well, however, to consider marriage," he said. "The decision would be yours. You have much to consider. You're quite young. If I should gain old age, I would be a dotterer while you were still an active and beautiful woman. Moreover, the life of an artist is not the world's most secure."

"Neither of those considerations would give me pause," she said. "But, Grand, I pushed myself on you. I could not, in all conscience, allow you to sacrifice your way of life just to make me an honest woman. No, marriage is not necessary. We will find another way. I will not touch you, not even smile at you when we're around your family. In fact, you could find me a place, nearby, where I could stay."

"No. I will not leave you alone."

"Then, listen to this. I can act very young. I will act so young and silly that it will seem impossible for a man of your sophistication to be interested in such a young and trivial girl. We will tell them some of the truth, saying that I am the daughter of a patron of yours and that you are doing us a favor by combining your trip to your father's bedside with an effort to locate a lost family member of mine. Isn't that clever?"

He mused. His father would see through that in a minute, but his mother? It just might work. There was scant choice. He was not about to leave her alone. There were men in the Indian Territory who would pluck such a flower without a second's hesitation and, having despoiled, lose themselves in the hills and the emptiness. There was law in the Choctaw Nation, but it was inadequate to handle the problems. The Indian police and the Lighthorsemen did their best to maintain order, but because of treaty specifics they had no jurisdiction over white men. The long and always weak arm of U.S. justice had to reach out all the way from the Western District of Arkansas at Ft. Smith, in the form of U.S. Marshals, a few men trying to keep the law in thousands of square miles. When last Grand was in the Choctaw Nation, murder was commonplace, with as many as one hundred men dying with their boots on in one year. Armed gangs of whites made their thief runs from the wild seclusion of Indian Territory into the more settled areas of Kansas and Texas. The stealing of horses and cattle was commonplace, and, if detected, instantly punished by shooting or hanging. He doubted that the situation could have been cured in a mere four years, for the basic problem was still there, the reluctance of the Federal Government to allow the Choctaws to police their own land. To leave Miranda alone, or even with a family of Choctaws friendly to his father, was unthinkable.

In the end, he agreed with Miranda that they would tell the story she had concocted. Thus, he arrived at Crossroads feeling just a bit uneasy.

To Miranda, it seemed that the handsome Indian woman did not even look at her. Grand, however, caught the quick, appraising look which his mother bestowed upon the girl.

"So you have arrived," Chota said, in her slow but perfect English.

He embraced her, felt himself grown young again, remembered for vivid moments the smells of her, the softness of her breast, the love which he'd known as a child. His eyes were damp when he pulled away and introduced Miranda as "the daughter of a very dear and valued patron, traveling under my protection to attempt to discover the whereabouts of an aunt, who had fallen out of correspondence with the family."

"You are welcome," Chota said.

"My father?" Grand asked.

Behind them, the stage, having discharged only two passengers and picked up one, lurched into movement and, until the sound faded, she was silent. "He lives," Chota said.

"Then let's go to him," Grand said.

"One moment, my son," Chota said. "Please prepare yourself."

He looked at her for a moment, his strong white teeth chewing on his lower lip. "It is bad?"

"You will see," she said.

"But he does live? He will live?"

"If it is God's will, you will give him reason to live," Chota said.

Grand could scarcely restrain himself from crying out when he first saw Caleb Woodrowe's shrunken face, his emaciated body under a thin covering. The old man's eyes were closed, the lids seeming to be transparent. His face, once so robust, was wasted, baggy darkness under his eyes, his mouth thinned and downturned. As Grand stood beside the bed Caleb groaned in his sleep and made a fitful movement under the cover. Chota leaped to his side, wetted a cloth and soothed his brow with it.

The coolness awoke Caleb, lids fluttering. At first his eyes did not seem to focus, then they widened and he made a convulsive start, as if trying to sit up.

"Easy, easy," Chota said, pushing him back. "He is here. He will stay while you rest."

"Grand?" Even the voice was wasted, weak, a mere croak.

"I'm here, father," Grand said. He put his hand atop the crinkled parchment of Caleb's hand and pressed.

"Help me get out of this damned bed," Caleb said.

Grand laughed. "Sure thing. We'll feed you and

get some meat back on those old bones and then
we'll get you out of that bed."

"Damned women," Caleb said, but, so saying,
he lapsed once again into sleep.

Grand stood for a moment, a tear wetting his
cheek. Then he was pulled away by his mother.

"How long has he been this way?" he asked.

"For long weeks now," she said.

"The doctors—"

"Did what they could," she said. "The Army
doctor removed two things from him, the bullet
near his spine and—" She could not say it. Instead, she pointed. And for the first time Grand
noticed that at the foot of the bed there was only
one little mound, made by the toes on one upturned foot.

"When that happened," Chota said. "He decided to die."

As the day grew late, Chota's relatives came,
serious-faced, silent, courteous men and women
of various ages, the old men wearing faded and
dusty, dark hats often decorated with one or two
feathers, the women in their long skirts. The parlor of the Woodrowe house was filled with them,
the room dark, cozy, rich in reds and blues, velvet
upholstery on the settee and the chairs. Miranda
did her best to make herself unobtrusive. She
was seeing Grand with new eyes. He, dressed in
the finery of the city, spoke his native language,
showed the proper respect for the elder members
of the family, made small jokes and gifts of coins
to the wide-eyed and silent children.

The women brought food. Grand, being the
perfect gentleman, presented each new arrival in

turn to Mindy, and those who spoke English made polite small talk, asking if her journey had been trying, a few showing curiosity about the California lands far to the west. She sampled the food, being looked after, at the moment, by a tall and strong girl, a cousin of Grand's, called Ruth. There was a delicious pastry called *abunaha,* cooked corn beaten into dough mixed with pre-cooked beans, wrapped in corn shucks and boiled; *pashofa,* cooked meal mixed with chopped meat; *walusha,* grape juice mixed with meal and corn syrup; and, best of all, *bahar,* hickory nuts and walnuts pulped and mixed with cracked, parched corn, sugar and water. In addition, in the kitchen there were great dishes of venison, squash and fresh beans from the garden which had been planted just before the last front of the early spring.

It was a subdued but joyous festival, for, Miranda began to realize, the Choctaws had a sense of family as strong as any Irish clan, and the return of Caleb and Chota's son was an event which would, as one old woman said, her words being translated by Grand, be recorded in the history of the tribe.

As night fell and the kerosene lamps were lit in the crowded parlor, the Principal Chief of the Choctaws, Allen Wright, arrived in a handsome surrey pulled by two splendid bays and added great honor to the Woodrowe house by presenting himself to Grand in a pleasant and brief speech of welcome. Wright was a man of some education. He was dressed neatly in a black suit, vested, with white linen and a black bow tie. His thick, black hair was parted and combed neatly. He drew on the Bible for his greeting, saying, "Rejoice with me; for I have found my sheep which was lost, for this my son was dead, and alive again; he was lost, and is found."

The gathering would be remembered by Miranda as representative of the entire Choctaw Nation. There, under one roof, one family and close friends illustrated one of the problems which frustrated men such as Allen Wright, whose stated ambition as Principal Chief was "to lead the Choctaws in a rapid march to civilization". The niece, Ruth, attending school, learning the white man's rules, his culture, his language, represented one extreme. The older people, although dressed, mostly, in white man's clothing, represented the other. The older ones clung to tradition, wanted nothing more than to be left alone to continue their way of life. Wright, who had been chief during the difficult post-war years, knew that never again would the Indian be left alone.

Grand, knowing how proud his mother was to have the Chief a guest in her house, acted as host and talked with Wright, learning that, as he suspected, the problems were much the same as they had been when last he was at home. Crime was still rampant. "However," the Chief said, with a chuckle, "we have found that the surest way to decrease crime is to decrease the number of criminals." He cited the number of executions which had been performed during his administration—a show of pride which made Grand shudder. Underneath that veneer of civilization, he thought, there was still the primal man, the primitive who delivered eye for an eye punishment without a doubt of his right to do so.

After the departure of the Chief, the evening ended with the older ones, wrinkled old hags, tottering old white-headed men, harking back to legend, with tales of spirits and ghosts and witches, told in hushed voices, mostly in English for Miranda's benefit. Outside a wind had sprung up and to the northwest, the sky was dark with roiling clouds and lightning. The stories were so convincing that Mindy found herself drawing her shawl closer around her shoulders and looking over her shoulder toward the dark windows and the darkened corners of the room.

Grand had made two or three visits to the sickroom during the afternoon and evening, finding his father awake only once, exchanging a few words with him. Only a few remained when Miranda, in spite of her interest, simply had to go to bed. She was shown to a pleasant little room by Chota, leaving Grand with two of the tribal elders. It was obvious to Grand that the two had something specific on their minds, so he waited politely for them to get to it. When it came, he kept his face passive.

"Your father, Caleb Woodrowe, although not of the blood, is a brother."

"He has always been honored to be considered so," Grand said.

"Now he is confined to his bed."

"It is true," Grand said.

"And, thus, cannot represent our district, as planned, at the upcoming meeting of the Council at Chahta Tamaha."

"Ah," Grand said. Chahta Tamaha, Choctaw

Town, the Capital of the Choctaw Nation. "But there are other worthy men."

"Yes, we know of such a one."

Grand was silent. It was happening, and from an unexpected quarter. He was fully aware that he was a disappointment to his father and mother for leaving the nation, for failing to use his ability, his education to help his mother's people. He had expected, and had dreaded, to be reminded of his obligation by his own family, not by two elderly men whose ties were old friendship. He had his own plans. Seeing his father in his present state was, of course, very sad, but death comes to all. It was unfortunate that his father had been brought so near his end by violence, but violence was certainly not foreign to the Indian Nations. It was not his affair. He had chosen his way, and it did not include eating *abunaha* and *bahar* and living at Crossroads.

As he sat, moodily awaiting a renewed assault, his mother came into the room, looked questioningly at the two elders.

"You will tell him of the need, Chota," one said.

"I think he knows," she said. "They have spoken to you?"

Grand nodded. "Mother, there are others who are more familiar with the problems. I am, in effect, an outsider."

"It is in your blood," said one of the elders.

"It is only until your father is able to be up and around," Chota said. "We are a thinly populated district, a poor district. And the problems are many. You have been given a good mind, my son, a fine education. You know the mind of the white man. Thus, knowing both minds, the mind of the white and the mind of the Choctaw, you could speak well in this time of renewed trouble."

"I will leave when my father is recovered," Grand said. "Meantime, I will be by his side."

"I will be at his side," Chota said. "Your place is to fill his position while he is unable to do so. Did you not see the life which came into his eyes when he saw you? You will see it glow fiercely when he is told that you have shouldered his responsibilities."

He knew that he was trapped. He nodded. "Be it so," he said, "but only until he is recovered." Or, he thought, until he is dead.

His arrival had been timely. Upon his agreement, he was informed that the Council would sit beginning only two days hence. There was little time for preparation, but having discussed problems with the elders of the community, he rode to the Capital with the knowledge that the meeting would cover, first, the ongoing problem created by the building of the railroad, which would, it was estimated, be entering the Choctaw Nation within the next two years. The main concern was the insistence of the Government that the Choctaws give up twenty full sections of land to each mile of rail built, the practice which had been instrumental in encouraging the building of the transcontinental railroads. The Choctaws knew from bitter experience that one demand on their lands would be swiftly followed by another, and they resisted any attempt to reduce their holdings.

The deliberations of the Council were conducted in Choctaw and translated into English. Each session began with a prayer offered by a

member. The Council room was always full of
interested people. Since this meeting was a special
one, called to consider one problem, the opening
statement by Chief Wright was brief, and the
main topic came under discussion early. There
was little dissent to Wright's stand that the granting of such large amounts of land to the railroad's builders should be resisted by all possible
means.

How to go about resisting was the question,
and it was decided that coordinated action by all
of the Five Civilized Tribes would be desirable.
A delegation would be appointed to journey to
the capitals of each of the nations to coordinate
resistance. It was Chief Wright, himself, who
suggested Grand Woodrowe as the Chief Delegate to the Cherokee Nation. Grand accepted,
since it would be a matter of only a few days. He
could not help but feel proud that his father had
engendered such faith, such regard for himself,
that his son would be automatically accepted as
capable of following in his father's footsteps.

With each delegation named, the meeting
turned to other matters, one of which was the
always serious smuggling of hard liquor into the
Nation. Exposed to speeches which would have
sounded at home in the mouths of missionaries,
damnation of demon rum, open acknowledgment
that the Indian had never been able to handle
that aspect of white man's civilization, Grand
abandoned his seat. The serious business had
been concluded and he found himself involved,
against his will, in doing exactly what he had
never intended to do, entering into the hopeless
fight against the onrush of the great white wind.

During Grand's absence, Miranda found herself to be an honored guest in his father's home, so much so that she protested to Chota that there was enough work in the house for two women, that she would not allow Chota to treat her as visiting royalty. She pitched in with a will and, after some protestation, Chota accepted her help gladly. There was the store to be run, the invalid to be tended, the house to be kept, the meals to be cooked.

Initally, there had been an unexpressed tension between the two women, but it eased as Mindy showed her willingness to work. Although she was the daughter of a wealthy house, she had not been pampered, had been assigned her own household chores. Admittedly, the experience of washing clothing in a huge, black, iron kettle over a glowing fire of wood embers, the smell of strong lye soap tingling her nose, was not an experience which she would have elected to be a part of her daily life, but she did it and, hanging up the clothes on a fresh, breezy morning, she chatted with Chota, telling her about her desire to discover the location of the "missing aunt", about her life in California. In her turn, she asked questions about the Choctaws.

Chota Woodrowe, having been a student in the earliest schools set up after the Removal, spoke English when she had met Caleb, and he had helped her polish it, had helped and guided her in her reading. Although her knowledge of the outside world came from her reading, Mindy found her to be better informed than, say, the average San Francisco matron. She was quite impressed by Chota's knowledge of history and enthralled as she, gradually, insistently, drew out of the older woman the collection of legends, myths, and facts which made up the known history of the tribe.

Miranda was a child of her time and her opinion of Indians was formed, partially, by the press account of the "heroic" battles against the tribes of the west. Like most people of her time she considered the redman to be a brutal savage, capable of the most ingenious tortures and cruelties. It was a revelation to her to find an Indian, Chota, to be sensitive, intelligent, well informed, and concerned but, strangely, not overly bitter about the treatment of Indians as a whole by the U.S. Government.

Chota had been born in the new Choctaw Nation, but she had heard many times the stories of the Removal, when an entire tribe was forced to leave the lands of its ancestors. Miranda shuddered as Chota recounted, in a calm, non-censorious voice, the hardships of the migration, how many had died of disease and exposure, how, in the dead of a severe winter, a main body of the tribe had waded chest deep waters of an Arkansas swamp.

"But you, I mean the Choctaws, did not have to leave," Mindy said. "The tribe was given the choice of accepting individual land allotments in Mississippi and living as a part of society."

"That is true," Chota said. "And some few accepted the land and remained. And even as the main body of the Nation was leaving, the whites swarmed in, began to take the land of those who had chosen to stay by force. There are still Choctaws there. Now and again one of them, or a family of them, finds the way here, and we accept them, encourage them, for the white man's promise has never been kept. Those who stayed became less than slaves."

"Never?" Miranda asked. "A promise has never been kept?"

Chota laughed. "Are you familiar with a map of the Nation?"

"I have looked at one," Miranda said.

"In Mississippi, when the tribe agreed to the Treaty of Dancing Rabbit Creek, we were given lands in the west extending from Arkansas westward to the limit of the territory. This, mind you, was a solemnly negotiated treaty, and had been duly and formally signed. But even before the migration of the tribe could begin, the Federal men came to the tribe and asked that the Choctaws cede almost half of the new lands for the relocation of the Chickasaws. Can you imagine why a Choctaw said, at that time, that he had hoped to be able to set foot on the new land before being asked to part with it?"

"It does sound unfair," Miranda said.

"And so, the Choctaw was never to occupy that portion of his land, which had been granted to him forever, nor has he been allowed the use of another large segment of the original grant. Once again the men from Washington came, this time to offer money to lease another segment of our new land in which to settle other tribes of Indians, the Wichitas, the Kiowas, the Comanches and Cheyennes, warlike tribes which would not make good neighbors. And yet, we had to agree. And so, the Choctaw western land which once stretched westward for over four hundred miles had been cut to less than two hundred miles and this even before the resettlement had been effected."

"And now they want more," Miranda said. "Twenty sections for each mile of rail."

"And more, and more," Chota said. "There are those among us, my son for one, who think that it will not end until there is no tribe, until there is no Indian Nation, until those of us who are left live side by side with the white man and compete with him."

"*You* could," Mindy said.

"Perhaps. But the rest? A few, maybe. And then it will all be gone and there will be nothing left of the Choctaw but the names which he has given to the land, unless the whites decide to change them."

When Grand returned to Crossroads from the Council meeting, he found a different girl. She was wearing one of Chota's work dresses and was, raven hair protected from the sun by a concealing bonnet, working industriously in the garden, using a hoe to remove the new sprigs of grass.

"Ah, you've gone native on me," he said, having greeted his mother inside and having looked in on his father to find his condition largely unchanged.

"I don't mind," she said. "It gives me something to do, and, God knows, Chota needs all the help she can get."

"Chota, is it?" he asked, with a grin. "So there is a treaty of peace between the white woman and the Indian?"

"Your mother is a wonderful woman," Mindy

shot back, chagrined by his tongue-in-cheek attitude.

Grand laughed. "I should have known better," he said. "Leaving you alone with her. She's probably converted you totally to the cause of the noble redman."

"And why are you laughing?" she asked. "You went to the capital, didn't you?"

"Yes, and I will be going away again. This time into the Cherokee Nation."

"You see," she said. "You like to sound cynical, but deep down your heart is with them completely."

"Of course," he said. "I simply realize the futility of it."

"Grand," she said, pushing back the bonnet, wiping perspiration from her forehead. "It must stop somewhere. A promise must be kept sometime. There is a solemn treaty which states that Choctaw land shall never become a part of any state or territory, that it will be forever Choctaw. And now they're trying to take huge chunks of it to enrich already wealthy men who are building a railroad."

Grand smiled at her. "Yes, she has done a good job on you," he said. "Well, little one, we are here, and here we stay, for a while. While we are here we will do what we can."

7

It was good to be at home. The very fact that he thought of it in that context was a revelation to him. Only days in the Nation and San Francisco seemed to be far, far in the past. The quiet dignity of the old men made him want to get out his brushes. He came to the realization that he'd never drawn on his background in any of his work. But, yes, he had. In one little sketch which had proved to be somewhat prophetic, the feather. Cast me in the wind. The white wind was blowing, and already he was caught up in it.

The word of his involvement had spread rapidly, even beyond the scattered Crossroads community, and men came to him to express their viewpoints and to hear him speak. It was, to them, more than a mere life and death matter. They, too, felt the pressures, knew that to the north, in Kansas, white men grumbled about the rich and beautiful lands still held by the Indians. How could he express his convictions to such men? How to say, well, you can't fight it? He compromised by telling them, whenever he had the chance, to adapt more and more to the white ways, to educate their children in the lore of the white race, to study the white man, to know his greed, his skill in business, to be at least familiar with his technical advances.

He could not be convinced that things would change, that the few thousand Choctaws, in combination with the other Indians of the Territory, could block the onrush of the white waves. But at some point in time he became convinced that it was desirable to postpone the inevitable, to give the Indian as much time as possible to become capable of competition before he was tossed, headfirst, into white society without the protection of tribe, treaty, and his own traditions.

Caleb Woodrowe remained a very sick man, although, as Chota had predicted, the news of Grand's participation in the Council meeting seemed to put life into his eyes. During the days between the Council meeting and Grand's departure for the Cherokee Nation, Caleb seemed to rally. He insisted on being propped up on several pillows and from this half-reclining position he listened to Grand's account of the meetings and agreed with Grand's selection as delegate to the Cherokees.

Grand chose his time to bring up a subject which had been bothering him. He knew the basic facts about the incident with the Texican drover, but there had not been time nor opportunity to delve into it.

"Father," he said, "do you feel like telling me what you know about what happened to you?"

"Not much to it," Caleb said. "Some of the men and I went out to stop a trail herd being driven over the corn fields and first thing I knew I was down in front of the herd."

"But do you know who shot you?"

"Not for sure. The Glendower fellow was close by, but there were others. I heard several shots, including my own, trying to turn the herd. Certainly Glendower had the best opportunity, but I couldn't swear he did it."

Grand asked more questions, but Caleb simply did not know any more facts, and the conversation had tired his father. He left him to rest. At the first opportunity he sought out the men who had been with Caleb and questioned them about the affair. No one had actually seen the shooting. There had been much confusion, several shots, dust, milling and running cattle. The Indian lawman assigned to the Crossroads area could offer little more.

"We've made application to the whites through the agency," the lawman said. "But, as you know, we don't have the right to bring a white man back into the nation for trial. What we have wouldn't be enough to establish attempted murder, anyhow. Best we could do is charge him, or have him charged in a white court, with destruction of property. And we got the herd. Split it up among those who suffered damages, what was left of it."

"But," Grand said, "didn't he assault a U.S. Marshal in his escape?"

The Indian shrugged. "That's between the white men," he said. "Ain't no wanted posters out on him, I can tell you that."

Well, it had happened, a senseless incident of violence in a violent land. And Caleb Woodrowe was minus a leg, his health ruined, the bullet wound healing slowly, the danger of infection always present. It was gangrene which had cost him his leg. And his persistent refusal of an early amputation had prolonged the effects of it, further weakening his already bad condition. It was generally agreed that Caleb was much man to be able to live at all, considering his weakened state when the Army doctor finally, the patient in delirium, performed the amputation without Caleb's permission.

There was nothing to be done. There was one moment of bemusement at the smallness of the world when, while discussing his father's condition with Miranda, he mentioned Glendower's name.

"But that was the name of the man in Chetopa," she said. "The one who hit the little black girl."

And Grand remembered him, the auburn hair, the handsome face weathered and toughened, the strong build of the man. Grand was not a man of violence, but he would remember that face. Perhaps he'd see it again.

When it was time to go north, he suggested that Miranda remain at Crossroads with his mother. "No," she said. "I will go. I came east with a purpose, you know. There will be railroad

men there, since the line is being built into Cherokee country. My father was a railroad man. Perhaps there will be men there who remember him.
I have to start somewhere, Grand."

Although it was awkward, he agreed. The fiction of his being her protector on a journey approved by her mother had, apparently, satisfied
everyone, even Chota, although Grand sometimes
wondered how much he was fooling his mother.

Advance elements of the rail building effort
had already effected Muskogee, but the railhead
was still to the north, the effect of the invasion
having been to turn the small town of Chouteau
into a booming, sprawling, transient hellhole.
During his early talks with Cherokee leaders
Grand often heard the complaint that the railroad
was making the territory even more lawless.
Whisky runners smuggled their illegal goods into
the Cherokee Nation in the baggage cars. Gam-
blers preyed upon the workers. The criminals
were not within the jurisdiction of Indian courts,
and the nearest Federal authority was too far
distant to trouble them. However, the camp followers moved with the rails, and once construction was complete they would be gone. Now the
concern was to fight the breaking of still another
solemn promise, a promise which was only as
good as the faith of a growing young nation
would make it, to prevent the granting of alternate strips of land on either side of the track,
strips one mile wide and extending outward ten
miles.

In Muskogee, Grand learned that no less a
personage than the Secretary of the Interior was
making an inspection trip to the end of the rails

and, with delegates of the other nations accompanying him, he journeyed further to the north.

The meeting with the high government official took place in a private car in the heart of the brawling tent city of Chouteau and, although the Secretary listened carefully, the meeting was, of course, inconclusive. There were educated and articulate men among the delegates, but by common consent Grand was elected spokesman. It was he who pointed out to the Secretary that although the treaty of 1866 had implied that land grants would be made to railroads in Indian Territory, the treaty itself forbade such grants until or "whenever the Indian title to the land shall be extinguished by treaty or otherwise." Grand pointed out that the lands could not, under the treaty, be made a part of the United States except in the unlikely event that the Indians and their heirs become extinct or abandon the land.

"I understand that well, Mr. Woodrowe," the Secretary said. "We do have a problem, however. In order to bring prosperity and progress to Indian lands, the railroads are needed. And such is the cost of building that they must have proper compensation."

"Then, sir," Grand said, "such compensation must be agreed upon by negotiations between the railroads and the Indian governments."

"The treaty did promise them their reward," the Secretary said.

"It did not promise," Grand said. "Nor does anyone have the right to promise land granted to the Indian by treaty to anyone."

"Perhaps, sir, you know the intent of the Congress better than I," the Secretary said huffily.

"Well, sir, I can read," Grand said. He spread his hands, indicating the muddy, makeshift streets, the refuse, the patched and faded tents which spoiled the land. "And if this is progress—"

"A temporary condition," the Secretary said.

Another of the delegates brought up the subject of the crime which accompanied the rail building. The Secretary said that the Government had long wanted to place Federal courts in the Indian lands.

"But it is our land," the Cherokee delegate said. "And in our land we should have the right to enforce our laws."

"Not if the accused person is a citizen of the United States," the Secretary said. "Moreover, I think you overemphasize the crime problem. It is well known that there was great lawlessness among your people before the coming of the rails."

"Not our people," the Cherokee said. "Among the whites over whom we have no control, the men who come into our land to escape their debts, who flee punishment for crimes committed in the United States."

"Well," the Secretary said, in dismissal, "I'm sure that men of good will can solve all problems in time."

The Secretary was to change his mind about only one thing, the crime problem. That very night, as Grand and Mindy celebrated privacy, being alone for the first time since their arrival in the Indian Nations, by clinging and sighing and mingling their bodies in great hunger and eagerness, a murder happened just under the window of his sleeping car. And, as he discussed the shame of it in a hushed tone in the morning, a paymaster was robbed within two hundred feet of him. In great agitation—one of the bullets fired during the robbery having broken the glass in a window not ten feet from him—he telegraphed President Grant to send troops to protect the rail workers.

Although accomodations in the new and hastily built hotel were primitive at best, Miranda was happy. She went to Grand's bed with undisguised eagerness, having longed for days to have his arms around her, to know the strength and eagerness of his passion. On the day of his meeting with the Secretary of the Interior, Grand gave her strict orders to remain in her room, or at worst to venture no further than the dining room or the lobby of the hotel. She made no promise, but he took her silence to be consent. He had not been gone more than five minutes when she finished dressing and went downstairs into the lobby of the hotel.

The desk clerk was a harried looking middle-aged man with a prematurely white handlebar moustache. He listened impatiently as she explained that she was looking for railroad men who had known or had heard of one Danny O'Lee. As it happened, an official of the railroad had spent the night in the hotel and even as Miranda stated her problem to the clerk, the official came down to return his key to the clerk. The railroad man became instantly attentive, but his eyes dulled when she stated her desire for information about a man named O'Lee.

"Worked on the M. K. & T., did he?" the man asked.

"No. On the transcontinental," Mindy said. "I'm interested in finding men who knew him about seventeen years ago and afterwards."

The official frowned in thought. "Can't help you," he said. "Sorry." He turned to go, touched his hat brim, paused. "I just happened to remember." He looked at the desk clerk. "Isn't old John Warren working here?"

The clerk nodded. "There's a John Warren works at the Red Barn, down the street."

"Old John might be your man," the railroad man told Mindy. "He worked 'em all. Came to us from the U.P. Best section boss I ever had."

"You're very kind," Miranda said. She asked the clerk for the location of the place called the Red Barn.

"Well, you can't miss it," he said. "Just down the street. But it's no place for a lady, miss, if you know what I mean."

Outside it was a beautiful day. There were few women on the muddy streets, but she couldn't imagine anything terrible happening in broad daylight on such a day with so many people around. She held her skirts out of the mud and made her way among cargo wagons, riders, two or three stylish passenger vehicles, across the street and a block down. There were three horses tied to a rail outside a hastily constructed wooden building with a high, false facade. The front was painted barn-red and there were no windows. A mud-smeared boardwalk stretched only for the width of the building. She hesitated for a moment, and pushed upon the door to step into a dim interior, a small room with a settee, on which sat a man and a woman, the latter dressed in a revealing black gown which showed the upper curve of lush breasts. A bar ran down one side of the room. From somewhere above, the sound coming down a flight of not too secure looking board stairs, came the high, cackling laugh of a woman.

The woman on the couch looked up when Miranda came in, rose, after a long appraisal of the newcomer, swayed toward her. "You lost, honey?" she asked.

"I'm looking for a Mr. John Warren," Miranda said. "I was told he works here."

"He does." The woman, at close range, was not young. Her face was heavily made up. The gown was soiled, and there was the rank, acidic smell of too much drink consumed about her, a morning-after smell.

"I'd like to see him, if I may," Miranda said.

"Well, he'll be back in a minute," the woman said. She looked back over her shoulder as she walked back toward the man on the couch. Miranda stood uncertainly, ill at ease. Time seemed to stand still until, only two or three minutes later, a white-haired old man with a full beard came down the stairs slowly.

"Mr. Warren?"

The old man examined her. His eyes, although almost hidden by bushy, white eyebrows, were alert. "The same," he said.

"I'd like to talk with you, if I may," she said.

He nodded, walked slowly, but with dignity and straight, if stiff, posture, to stand behind the bar. She faced him across the bar.

"If you're looking for work you've got it," he said.

"No, no thank you," she said.

He shrugged. "Thought you had too much class for this place."

"As a matter of fact, Mr. Warren, I've been told that you might have known a railroad man named Danny O'Lee."

"Knew a lot of men," he said.

"He worked the Central Pacific," she said. "But he traveled a lot. A big man." She described her father, his job as she had heard it described.

"Got killed, did he?" the old man asked.

"Yes. You do remember him?"

"Could've been a hell-raiser. Yep."

"About seventeen years ago he was traveling in this part of the country. He met a woman. Would you know anything about that?"

"Seventeen years ago? I'd have been up east."

"But did you ever hear him mention a woman?"

"Child, if I tried to remember all the things these old ears have heard there wouldn't be room for it in my head. I didn't know O'Lee all that well. Knew him in the profession, that's all. Good man. Could hold his liquor. Remember one time in a blizzard, we was all barracked up and nothing to drink but rotgut so bad the Indians wouldn't touch it. All we had to keep us warm, though. Yep, he could hold his liquor. Took four days before they could plow the track and get it clear. Let's see. It was me and O'Lee and some dude from the office. I was just before leaving the C.P., as I recall. He was telling me I was making a mistake, that the future was in the west, not with the U.P. on the eastern side. We told each other a lot of lies and drank a lot of booze to keep from freezing."

"Did he talk about his past at all?" she asked.

Warren scratched his chin through his beard. "Seem to remember some talk about prospecting."

"Yes, yes," Mindy said. "He was a prospector, before he went to work for the railroad."

"Told him he was crazy, wasting time looking for gold in Texas and Indian Territory. He liked the country, though. Remember him talking about it as if it were God's own. Said some of the Indian country was real pretty."

"Did he mention anything at all about a woman?"

The old man chuckled. "Honey, when it's twenty below and you're snowed in you're gonna talk about women sooner or later. We talked about women."

"Do you remember any names?"

"Names? Nope. I probably told him about the girls worked in Kansas City. Things like that. He said some of the Mex girls in Texas were pretty hot." He fluttered a hand. " 'Scuse the language."

"That's all right. But he never mentioned a special woman?"

Warren reached under the counter and came up with a bottle. He splashed about an inch of amber liquid into a glass, offered it to Miranda and when she declined, he sipped it slowly. "Makes me think better," he said. "Strictly against the law. No booze in injun country. But then I don't think you'd turn an old man in."

She smiled. "Of course not."

"Special woman. Nope. Can't remember." He finished the whisky, taking small sips, his bushy brows lowered. "Kept talking about wanting to go back someday. Wanted to see a girl named Lilah." His brows shot up. "Well, by God," he said. "There's a name."

"Lilah? Was there a last name with it?"

"No, no. Not as I can recall. Just Lilah, in Texas."

"Where in Texas?"

"Can't say."

"Mr. Warren, did you get the impression that he had some special feeling for this Lilah?"

"Seems as how he did."

"Did he, by any chance, mention a child?"

Warren looked at her. "Ah, so that's it."

"Did you get the impression that she was, well, a nice girl or like the women you mentioned who worked in Kansas City?"

"Can't say one way or the other. It's the child you're looking for, huh?"

"Yes," she said, improvising. "Danny O'Lee was my father. We found out, after he died, that he had a child by a woman in this part of the country. We, the family, would like to find her, to help her if she needs it."

"Little lady," Warren said. "It's a big country and it's been a long time. And have you ever thought that you might not want to find this child, if she's still alive? Now I can tell a lady when I see one, and I think you're one. What if you find her working in a place like this or something?"

"Well, then we'd know, wouldn't we?" Mindy asked. "Is there anything else at all you can tell me?"

"Reckon not. Sorry I can't be of more help."

"You've been very kind. At least now I have a name, or at least a part of a name. I thank you very much."

The old man was pouring one more little drink when she started out the door, eyes squinted at the suddenness of the bright sun.

Lilah. Her mother's name could be Lilah. For the first time it all began to seem real. Until that moment, it had been something of a game. There were times, when she would awake in a strange place, she could not understand where she was and why she was not in her comfortable room at home. And then she'd remember the shock she'd felt when she overheard the conversation between her mother and her brother, or between the people she'd always thought to be her mother and her brother. Had she overreacted? What was it in her which had sent her, immediately, from her own home into the bed of a man she scarcely knew?

It was this last, when she thought about it, which helped convince her that she was not, truly, Liberty Lee's daughter. The speed with which she'd crawled into Grand's bed was in direct contrast with her upbringing. Oh, well, she knew that her "mother", Liberty Lee, had not been a model of purity. She was not blind. She knew that Liberty had been the mistress of a powerful man, but even that was within the character of Liberty. It was not on a par with, in a moment of self pity and shock, crawling into the bed of the first man she could think of. Why? Was it to punish *them,* Liberty and her brother? To convince herself that she was not what she had always thought herself to be? To confirm her bastard origin?

These thoughts and more flooded her, confused her, as she stood on the boardwalk letting her eyes adjust to the sudden brightness. The old man had asked her what she would think if she found the "child" working in a brothel. What would she think if she found her real mother in a soiled dress, her breath reeking of the previous night's whisky, her face heavily painted and wrinkled under the paint?

At that moment she realized that it was not important to continue her search. God, in spite of her waywardness, had been kind to her. Of all the men in the world she had crawled into Grand Woodrowe's bed, and there, scarcely knowing why she was there, she had found something. Herself? Well, perhaps not, not just yet. But she had found a kind man, a loving man, a generous and gentle man who, even if he did not love her, treasured her. Many, she knew, had less.

No, she would not continue the search. What would she do? He had mentioned marriage. She thought of being married to him, of helping him in his work, but what was his work? He considered himself to be an artist, and yet he was in a rag-tag tent town on the business of the Choctaws. Both had meaning. She knew little about art, but she had seen how her mother's face, how her own face, came to life on canvas under Grand's brushes. And her brief stay in Chota's house, her talks with that warm and wise woman had opened her eyes to the problems of the Indians.

She looked around her at the mud street, the hastily constructed buildings. An Indian family drove by in a flat bed wagon, the man tall and dignified on the driver's seat, the woman beside him, wrapped in a dark shawl, large eyed, solemn children in the bed of the wagon. A man on horseback was cantering slowly from a distance, coming in from the edge of town. From somewhere a mocking bird sang. In the distance there was the mournful hoot of a train whistle.

She was a sixteen-year-old girl far from home and suddenly she was lonely. Liberty Lee's face appeared in her mind and she felt the beginning of tears. She would wire her immediately. She had been very inconsiderate. Of course Liberty loved her, and she had, she was sure, hurt her badly. *Oh, Mother, Mother forgive me, for I am just a child.*

But no. Head up, back straight. Not a child. A woman. Grand's woman, and, if he wanted her, his wife. For out of the whole comic-tragic situation there was that, Grand. She had gone to him in desperation, with a scarcely recognized need to punish them, those who had deceived her, and now, with a mocking bird's song in her ears, the hot sun on her face, she was seeing Grand in a new light. And for the first time in her life, with a thrilling upsurge of emotion, she knew the meaning of the word love. Suddenly the most important thing in the world was to see Grand. She lifted her skirts to step off the board-walk into the mud and had to step back, as the cantering horse pulled up short, flesh making plopping sounds, hoofs soft thuds in the mud, and the man flung himself off. She started to walk around the horse.

"Well, well," Rupert Glendower said, pushing back his hat to show his auburn hair. "Look who's here."

She looked at him coldly, knowing now that he had been involved in the shooting of Grand's father. She nodded and turned away.

"Don't be in such a hurry," Rupert said. He moved swiftly to take her arm and turn her. "Going off duty?"

"Please take your hand off me," she said.

"Hey, look, we got off to a bad start," he said. "Let's you and me sign a treaty of peace."

"Please," she said, looking down at his hand on her arm. He removed it.

"When will you be back?" he asked. "I didn't know you worked here."

She flushed, realizing that he'd drawn the wrong conclusion about her being in front of the Red Barn. She started to speak, considered it to be a lowering of herself, turned with a flourish of skirts and walked swiftly away, booted feet slipping in the mud.

"My money's as good as any man's," Rupert called after her.

Not even the unpleasant encounter with Glendower could lower her spirits. After the initial flush of anger she put him out of her mind and went back to her thoughts, realizing anew that she had come to love Grand Woodrowe, eager to see him, disappointed that he was not yet back at the hotel. She waited impatiently and when he did return, at lunch time, threw herself into his arms.

"Hey, what's this?" he asked laughingly.

"I've missed you, that's what."

"And I you," he said, kissing her tenderly.

The meal was fried chicken and fried potatoes with cornbread, plain but deliciously cooked and filling. He told her about his morning, the unconcern of the Secretary of the Interior about the Indians' rights and the sudden preoccupation with safety after having been exposed to the crime in the tent city.

"We're going to have to stay another day or two," he said. "The Secretary has called in troops and I want to talk with the officer in charge. Perhaps we can convince him to help us, by driving out some of the criminal element. All the Secretary is worried about is protection of the rails and the workers. We want to see if we can get the Army to work with Indian authorities for a general clean-up."

"I don't mind," she said. "As long as I'm with you."

He looked at her strangely. "You've never said anything like that before."

"Grand, perhaps it's been because I've been too mired down in my own misery."

"What brought about the change?"

"Oh, a lot of things. I was thinking of how you took me in, how you understood, immediately."

"Purely selfish, lady," he said. "I'd have been a fool not to accept such a lovely gift."

"It's more than that, isn't it?" she asked.

He smiled. "You know it is. And when we have a bit of time we'll talk about it, now that you've brought up the subject. Meantime, I have a meeting to attend."

"May I come?"

He smiled. "I'd like nothing better, but the old ones might not understand why I bring a young white eyes into a meeting of men."

"Yes, I understand."

"I know it will be boring for you, just sitting around this room."

"I'll be fine," she said.

It was not until after he had gone to his meeting that she realized she had not mentioned having met Rupert Glendower, and a bolt of fear went through her. What if Grand met the man on the street? There was no proof, but everyone felt that Glendower was responsible, if not directly guilty, for the shooting of Grand's father. Would Grand do anything foolish? Glendower had a cold and reckless look about him. Grand, large as he was, wise as he was, was not a brawler or a gunfighter. He would be no match for Glendower.

She went down to the desk and had the clerk order a carriage for her. It took some time. Grand had not mentioned the site of the meeting, but it shouldn't be hard to find in a town so small. She asked the driver if he knew where the meeting was being held and he had no idea. She told him to drive toward the railroad. The general store which had been the center of the small town before the coming of the railroad was in that direction. There she could ask where the meeting was being held. She quickly learned, from the Cherokee who ran the store, that the meeting was being conducted outside town a few miles in the home of a rancher. She thanked the storekeeper and started out.

She did not recognize the girl at first, as she came into the store, but the dress the girl wore drew her eyes. It was black, cabaret length, out of place on the streets, the skirt decorated with feathers at the hem, the neckline low. It took a moment for the dark face to register, and then she knew that it was the same girl Glendower had brutalized in Chetopa. The girl did not look at her, but went directly to the counter to purchase candy in a brown bag. Miranda went to her carriage and was seated when the girl came out, stuffing candy into her mouth with fingers which did not look overly clean.

"Wait," Miranda told the driver, as the girl went off down the street. She watched, saw the girl walk into an area of tents, disappear into a large tent, the flap dropping behind her.

She did not want to go back to the hotel. The day was too pretty to be cooped up inside. "Do you know a nice road into the countryside?" she asked the driver.

The driver was a teenage Cherokee, cleancut, round-faced, mostly silent. "Yes m'am," he said.

"I think a drive in the country would be nice."

"Yes m'am." He slapped the horses into motion with the reins. The surrey wheels slipped and slid in the ruts as the vehicle jerked into motion. They were just even with the area of tents when she heard a series of screams and, from the tent into which the girl she'd seen in Chetopa disappear, a flurry of motion. A small Indian girl dashed out of the tent, pursued by the black

girl, who was wielding a riding crop. The Indian
girl was screaming as the lash struck her shoulders, bare above a dress which was more saloon
costume than street wear. The Indian girl ran
directly into the path of the surrey, so that the
driver had to pull up. There, in the middle of the
muddy street, she fell, and the black girl stood
over her, beating her.

"Whores," the driver said, spitting.

Miranda, without thinking, leaped from the
surrey and seized the black girl's arm, stopping
the blows. The girl screamed a curse.

"Stop it," Miranda said, fighting until she had
wrested the riding crop from the girl's hand.

"None of your business," Wynema said, then
her eyes went wide. "You," she said.

"Why are you beating this girl?" Mindy asked,
still shocked and angered. The driver had come
to her side. Wynema looked at her fiercely, spat
into the mud, stooped to seize the Indian girl's
arm and drag her to her feet. She said something
in an Indian language which Miranda did not
understand. The Indian girl looked at Miranda,
tears streaking her face, and broke into a torrent
of Indian which was cut off abruptly when Wynema slapped her. The Indian girl, Mindy
thought, could be no more than twelve.

"What is she saying?" she asked the driver.

"She say, you help her," the driver said.

Wynema tried to drag the girl away, but she
fought and jerked free, ran to Miranda, threw
herself onto her knees in front of her.

"Now you wait," Miranda told Wynema. "Just
you wait a minute. What is she saying? Tell me."

"She say they keep her, make her do bad

things," the driver said. "Come, madam. No place for you. They are whores of the man Glendower."

"Ask her if she is being kept against her will."

The driver spoke to the girl, nodded, turned to Miranda. "She say her father sold her to Glendower."

Miranda gasped. "Tell her to come with me," she said.

The driver ran a hand over his face. "Madam, best not to mix in this."

Miranda took the Indian child's arm. "Tell her I will take her to the authorities and get help for her."

"Madam," the driver said, nodding his head to indicate that she should look behind her. From the tent Lotus and Sarah, dressed much like Wynema and the Indian girl, had emerged, and with them were two other girls. Wynema spoke rapidly. The four girls approached. In the hand of one was a long knife.

The driver put his hand on Mindy's arm. "Madam, we go."

A buxom woman with hennaed hair emerged from the tent next to Wynema's tent. "What the hell's going on here?" she asked. Wynema ran to her, pointed back to Miranda. The woman walked purposefully toward Mindy. "Listen, honey," she said harshly, "butt out. This is none of your business."

"Madam, we go," the driver said nervously, as two men came from another tent and began to approach. He pulled Miranda's arm. The Indian girl was weeping silently.

"Tell her I will send help," Miranda said, and

the driver spoke to her, pulling Miranda toward the surrey. She looked back as the driver slapped the horses into motion to see Wynema and the others dragging the little Indian girl into the tent.

"Take me to the sheriff's office," she said.

"Sheriff not here," the driver said. "Have no say about railroad people anyhow."

"But those girls were Indian," Miranda said. "If they're what you say—"

"Whores," the boy said matter-of-factly. "Two dollars. Cheaper than whorehouse."

"They're just children, all of them. Something must be done."

The boy shrugged.

She was out of the mood to drive in the country. Back at the hotel she paced the room, angered and concerned. What kind of man was this Rupert Glendower, to prostitute children? She was still angry when Grand returned. She told him immediately that she'd run into Rupert Glendower.

"I heard that he was in Chouteau," he said.

And then she told him about the young girls, demanded that something be done. "They're Indian girls," she said, "all just children. Even if Indian law can't do anything to Glendower, it should be able to do something about the girls."

"Yes," he said. "I will discuss this, along with other problems, with the Federal Army Officer when he arrives."

"Grand," she said, "the black girl was beating the little Indian girl with a riding crop. It left great, red welts on her shoulders. She begged me for help."

"You will promise me this," Grand said. "As long as we are here, you will not go near that place, nor will you wander in the streets. You will promise me."

"I will promise you this," she said. "Unless something is done to help those girls I will personally raise holy hell. I will scream and kick and yell to anyone who will listen and I'll go all the way to Washington if I have to."

He smiled. "I can understand how you feel. I promise you something will be done."

A small body of cavalry arrived late in the day and went into field quarters on the outskirts of town. Grand went to the site and introduced himself, asking if it would be possible to have a talk with the Major who commanded the troop. The Major, veteran of the Indian fighting in the northern plains, had been in the saddle for most of the day. "What I want right now," he said, "is a decent meal and drink, not necessarily in that order."

"It will be my pleasure to supply the meal, if you'll join us in the hotel," Grand said. "As for the drink, being part Indian I won't assist you in breaking the law."

"Well," the Major said, "we can't have everything, eh?" He gave orders, instructing his junior officers to see to the pitching of tents and to setting up mounted patrols in the town and along the site of the rail construction, then followed Grand back to the hotel. He accepted Grand's offer to wash up in Grand's room, and it was there, with a blank face at first and then a wide smile which showed good teeth and seemed to stretch his sandy moustache, that he met Miranda.

"Major Tom Bedford," Grand said.

The Major bowed. "Your servant, m'am," he said. "Now I don't feel quite as tired as I did."

"You're very kind," she said, with a polite smile.

"I promised the Major a meal," Grand said. "Would you join us?"

"With pleasure," Mindy said.

Grand brought up the problems immediately, pointing out that the lawless element which came with the rails was doing great damage to Indian property and, often, to Indian persons. Bedford listened politely as Grand talked.

"I understand the problem," Bedford said. "The Secretary was quite upset about crime."

"Then perhaps we can all work together to do something about it," Grand said. "If the Army would work in cooperation with the Indian lawmen—"

"We will, of course, do all we can," Bedford said. "I must point out, however, that my orders are to protect railroad property. You know as well as I that the Army has no right to do anything in Indian Territory except keep the peace. I can't allow my troop to become, as it were, a deputy force for the Indian marshals. And if we start to act merely as a law-keeping body the first to protest would be the Indians. They're very jealous of their autonomy, as you well know."

"Yes, yes," Grand said. "But can we expect you to protect Indian property as well as railroad property?"

"Mr. Woodrowe, my orders are not to interfere in any way in the internal affairs of the Indian Nations."

"But if the criminal is a citizen of the United States you can act, can't you?" Miranda asked.

"Well," Bedford said, after a moment's thought, "it would depend upon the situation."

"Let me give you an example," Mindy said. "It has come to my attention that a white man, one Rupert Glendower, is keeping a harem of under-aged Indian and black girls, forcing them to perform acts of prostitution. I know from my own observation that at least one of the young girls is being kept against her will. Now it seems to me that this would be an excellent place for cooperation between Indian authorities and the Army."

Bedford shrugged. "On the surface, it would seem so, but I'd have to clear any action with the Colonel, up at the fort. Sad as it may seem, I was ordered specifically not to use Army force in any way except to protect railroad interests. It seems to me that the situation you mention has little to do with the M. K. & T."

"If it weren't for the M. K. & T. they wouldn't be here," Mindy said.

"Offhand," Bedford said, "I'd say it would be a matter for the Indian authorities."

"But they have no jurisdiction over Glendower," Grand said.

"And so you're going to stand by and let that man continue to make slaves out of young and defenseless girls," Miranda said.

Bedford flushed. "I have no other choice," he

said. He had not finished his meal, but he arose. "Now, if you'll excuse me, I must be getting back to my men."

"I'm sorry," Mindy said, when he had gone.

"We will do something," he said. "Let me speak with the Cherokees."

Mindy insisted on being present when, the Indian marshal having come back to town, the subject was discussed. The marshal was an older man with a dark, placid face. It was difficult to determine by his expression what he was thinking as Mindy finished her story and waited for his response.

"We can arrest the girls for prostitution," he said, at last.

"What?" Mindy exploded. "They're only children. They are not at fault. They've been forced into it by Glendower."

The marshal looked at her blankly. "We cannot arrest the white man."

"Isn't there anything you can do?"

The marshal was silent in thought. "There is a mission near Muskogee which accepts orphan girls. If we had a way of getting the girls away from the white man—"

"They're Indians," she said. "Can't you just go and get them?"

"This man Glendower," the marshal said. "He has a reputation. He is quick with his gun. There would be trouble, maybe killings. If we kill the white man then there is much trouble. If he kills me, that is much trouble for me."

"This is unbelievable," Mindy said. "You're not even moved to think that young girls, no more than thirteen or so, are being prostituted?"

The marshal shrugged. "In my life I have seen much which moves me. I cannot always remedy it."

"If there is no danger, if I can assure you that Glendower will not be present, will you take men and go get the girls and take them to the mission?"

"How can you assure me that?" the marshal asked.

"I will send for Glendower, tell him that I want to talk with him," Miranda said.

"No," Grand said. "I can't allow that."

"Here, in the hotel," Mindy said. "There will be no danger."

Grand looked doubtful. "This means something to me, Grand," Mindy said. "I saw that man beat the little black girl in Chetopa. I saw the black girl beating the Indian girl with a riding crop, and she fell to her knees in front of me and begged me to help her. We must help her."

"Yes, I suppose we must," Grand said. "Marshal?"

"I will send for Lighthorsemen."

When the Indian auxillary policemen arrived the next day, Mindy sought out the young Cherokee who had driven the surrey and paid him to seek out Rupert Glendower. The message she sent was to the effect that she'd like to discuss business with Glendower. He thought she was a whore, so let him continue to think it. Let him think that she was interested in going into business with him. And it would do no harm, since he had seemed to be attracted to her, to let him imagine other benefits of a meeting, so the word was, "Tell Mr. Glendower that Miss Lee wishes to discuss business and other matters. Tell him to come to my room at six o'clock." That gave the boy plenty of time to find Glendower and gave the marshal time to ready his forces to spirit the girls quickly out of the tent camp along the tracks.

Grand agreed to the ruse on one condition, that he be in the next room, the door unlocked, in a position to come to Mindy's aid if needed. He was with her as the hour approached, for the Cherokee boy had returned with a message from Glendower saying that he would come. Mindy was dressed in blue, had her hair done in large curls hanging from the main mass of it, which was piled high on her head. When the knock came, she called out, "One moment, please," and hurried Grand out of the room, closing the connecting door behind him.

Glendower was neatly and expensively dressed and smelled of bay rum. He had his hat in his hand. When she opened the door he stepped partially in, his pale eyes taking in the room at a glance. Seeing that it was empty, save for himself and Mindy, he smiled.

"An unexpected pleasure," he said.

"Please come in," she said. "May I take your hat?"

He handed the hat to her and she put it on the dressing table, turned to smile at him. "I'm afraid that I can offer only tea," she said.

"Sure," Glendower said, seating himself. She poured tea and handed him a cup and saucer. He had no difficulty with it. He sipped, looking at her over the rim of the cup. "Well, lady, you asked me to come here, so it's up to you to tell me why."

"I think we have interests in common," Mindy said.

"Such as?" he asked.

"As a matter of fact," she said, "I've been hearing about you all up and down the line. It seems that you've got yourself a fine business operation."

He studied her face. She felt ill at ease. She was not accustomed to lying. "What's that to you?" he asked.

"How many girls do you have?" she asked. "Five, six?"

"I'm afraid I don't know what you're talking about," he said. It seemed too good to be true that this beautiful bitch was coming to him.

"Oh, come now, Mr. Glendower," she said, with a little smile. "I suspected it when I saw you with the little black girl in Chetopa. As it happened, I've heard about your operation and, here in Chouteau, I had occasion to see the girls in the tent down by the tracks. I don't think we need to make pretense with each other. We each know what the other is, don't we?"

She had to keep him talking for at least a half hour, longer if possible. And he was not being overly cooperative.

"On my part, I've found it fine to be a solo act, up to now, but as you know, this is rough country. It's where the ready cash is, but it can be slightly nerve-racking for a woman alone at times."

"What about the Indian?" He smiled. "Your husband, wasn't it?"

"Oh, him," she said. "He ran out of money."

For the first time his smile seemed relaxed. "I can see how that would happen."

"As a matter of fact, I'm quite good at what I do," she said, "and what I do best is to make money disappear."

"Just what do you have in mind?" Rupert asked, his natural caution being overcome by the sheer beauty of the girl. He had not given up on the idea of having a fine establishment of his own, with red carpets and drapes, with polished walnut bars and plush sofas and chairs. With a girl like this one as the leading attraction it would be assured of success.

"I don't have in mind living in a tent," Mindy said.

"Of course not," he said quickly. "Listen, I have plans."

"I'd love to hear about them," she said.

He talked. He leaned forward in his chair and told her of his dream of having the finest house in the mid-west. She showed her interest by asking questions, and by making comments. Once he started talking she had only to smile and nod and prime him with small talk to keep him going. And when he finished and looked at her expectantly she smiled.

"I had something of the same sort in mind," she said. "At first I had hoped that I could do it alone, without a partner, but now that I've seen how things are, I know I need a good man."

"I don't know about this partner thing," he said, frowning.

"Perhaps partner is too strong a word," she said. "Let's say a co-worker, a protector, a man who can handle the business end of it and leave me to my specialty."

"Something might be worked out," he said. "Tell you what, let's you and me go down to the Red Barn, have a drink, and talk about it." He rose, as if he expected her to follow his suggestion without question.

"More tea?" she asked, holding up the pot.

"Let's go," he said.

"I think you're getting the wrong idea," she said. "I am not looking for a man to give me orders."

He flushed, but he sat down. "All right," he said. "Let's talk some more. What kind of business are you doing now?"

"Small and very selective," she said.

"Yes, be good to keep it that way. I can steer the right sort of pigeon your way and be on hand if things get bothersome. Follow the rails. It won't take long for us to accumulate enough to build a place. Meanwhile, we'll be plucking the cream off every boom town as the railroad goes south. I'll get you a place in each town. Hell, we can work Chouteau for another few months."

"Perhaps," she said. "But I won't be content to live in such places for too long." She was getting into the part. It was, she found, sort of exciting to pretend to be a whore, to play a part. But, still, she wondered how much time had passed, how much longer she would have to keep up the pretense.

"I think I can make it a little bit interesting for you," Glendower said. "I can be good to a woman when she's nice to me." He rose, came toward her chair. She felt an urge to shudder in revulsion when he took her hand, but she hid it and smiled up at him.

"Yes," he said, "you'll find out that I'm all right. It's just that you need to know me better."

"I'm sure we'll come to know each other well," she said, trying to withdraw her hand.

"No time like now to start," he said, pulling her to her feet and sweeping her into his arms.

She turned her face away from his kiss, not fighting, for she could feel the strength of him, but being limp, cold.

"Hey, come on," he coaxed, in a soft voice.

"Mr. Glendower," she said, "being co-workers does not entitle you to free samples."

He released her, his anger flaring. But, damn it, she was a high class piece of merchandise, exactly what he needed. Sooner or later she'd come around. Meantime, he could wait. But when the time came, when he thought it was time, she'd sing another tune. He'd make her squirm and beg.

"All right, *Miss* Lee," he said. "I'll respect your wishes." He walked to the dressing table and put his hat on. "When do we start? Tonight? I can send up a couple of good prospects."

"Not tonight," she said. Had it been long enough? Surely, surely it had. She could not stand to be in his presence much longer. Where he had touched her her skin seemed to be crawling.

"All right, when?" he asked, his voice hard and tense.

"We'll talk again tomorrow," she said. "At lunch."

"Why can't we settle it tonight?" he asked.

"Because tonight I have an engagement of my own," she said. "He's due here at six-thirty. Do you have the time?"

He took out his watch. "Almost time," he said, feeling a flurry of anger to think that she'd be in bed with another man, right there in that bed which was made up neatly now with a patchwork quilt atop. He told himself that it wasn't the first time and wouldn't be the last. And soon he'd be in her bed and then she'd see what a real man was.

"If you'll excuse me, then," Mindy said, feeling a vast relief. She took his arm and walked him to the door. "Lunch, tomorrow?"

"See you then," Rupert said.

8

Wynema was preparing the girls for the night's work. Some of them had to be reminded to bathe. The new one was still weepy and sullen and had to have a good talking to and a reminder, with the lash, that she had work to do.

"You don't work I take your hide off," Wynema said. "You work or run around in your bones with your hide off?"

"I work," the girl said.

When they were all ready, dressed in their finest, fancy underwear underneath ready to be exposed to give that extra little touch of sensuality, Wynema sat down and waited. Her Rupe was, she figured, right now making the rounds of the tent city, spreading the word. Not that it

needed to be spread much more. Wynema and
her girls were known up and down the line now,
and almost every night was a busy one. But there
were six of them now, and they could do business
with a lot of men, so Rupe should be out trying
to find new customers.

She heard a wagon coming toward the tent
and told the girls to be ready. She was standing
in the large tent, just inside the open flap of
entry. She peered out. A wagon with a canvas
cover had halted just outside. She stood in the
opening, the lamplight from inside lighting her
from behind, striking a sensual pose. She did not
realize anything was wrong until men came at
her from all sides, from around the tent, from
behind the wagon, one man jumping down from
the driver's seat, and even then, for a moment,
she thought that several customers were merely
arriving at once. But then she was seized and
men were pushing past her to seize the other
girls and she was screaming and cursing and trying to get out of the grasp of a tall Indian man
wearing a lawman's badge.

"There is nothing to fear," the marshal said.
"We have come to help you. You must all be
quiet."

Some of the other girls were screaming. Men
put hands over their mouths and carried them,
kicking and fighting, to the wagon, to toss them
roughly into the covered bed. Wynema skinned
one knee and came up spitting and fighting, but
two strong men were seated at the rear as the
wagon jerked into motion.

"Don't be afraid," the marshal told them.

"We're taking you to a place where you'll be well treated."

"You have no right," Wynema said. "Leave us alone. Let us go back to our home."

"The people at the mission will take care of you," the marshal said. "You won't have to be whores anymore."

"We don't want to go," Wynema screamed. "We want to go back to our home."

"I want to stay here," the new one said in Cherokee. "I do not want to go back to the tent." Wynema reached out and slapped her. The marshal hit her roughly.

"Just sit quiet," he said.

"Where you take us?" Lotus asked.

He told them again. He told them that things would be fine at the mission, that they would have plenty to eat and would be taught in the school. Meanwhile, he kept looking back. They were clearing the tent city, and there was no pursuit. He had not been in favor of the operation. As far as he was concerned, the little whores could have stayed with the white man. Small loss. As far as he could tell only two were Cherokee, and they had soiled themselves by sleeping with white dregs. The others? They had nothing to do with him. But the delegate from the Choctaw Nation had been quite excited about saving the little whores, and so it was done. He lit his pipe and leaned back against a stave. It was a long ride to the mission. Across from him his deputy nodded. The Lighthorsemen who had helped peeled off as they cleared the town. Now there was only himself, the deputy, and the driver.

Wynema tried to find a comfortable way to lie down. The bed of the wagon was slightly padded with empty feed sacks and the hard boards, accentuated by the bumpy road, seemed to make her bones hurt no matter which way she chose to position herself. She watched as the two men nodded on the makeshift seats which had been positioned on either side of the opening at the back of the wagon.

"Lotus," she whispered, putting her lips next to the girl's ear. "What you think?"

"I was in a mission school once," Lotus said. "They make you pray a lot."

Wynema kept watching the moonlit road behind them, hoping to see Rupert coming to fetch them home. When, after another hour, nothing happened, she nudged Lotus awake. "I go back," she whispered.

Lotus carefully raised her head. The other girls seemed to be sleeping. The two men sat with their chins on chest, either asleep or nearly so.

"You come?" Wynema asked. "Rupe be glad to see us."

"Naw," Lotus said. "Tired of banging. Hard work. Smelly old men. Praying not all that bad."

"You pray," Wynema said. "I go back with Rupe."

She poised herself, sprang into motion. She was vaulting over the tailgate of the wagon when the deputy was aroused and, acting swiftly, grabbed for her, catching the feathered hem of her skirt. Wynema, thrown off balance, fell heavily, hearing the material rip, and then she was rolling to her feet and running for the brush alongside the lonely road.

The deputy yelled out and the marshal came fully awake.

"One of 'em got away," the deputy yelled, leaping from the wagon.

"Which one?" the marshal asked, striking a match to look around inside the dark wagon. The five remaining girls were in various positions of surprise, one rubbing her eyes.

"Hold on," the marshal said. "It was the nigger. Just let her go."

The deputy climbed back into the wagon and it lumbered into motion. "Yeah, guess you're right. They wouldn't want her at the mission anyhow."

Wynema crouched in the brush and waited until the sound of the wagon had faded into the distance. Then she started off at a half-trot back up the road. It was almost dawn when she reached the tent on the outskirts near the tracks. She approached it cautiously and, finding it empty, went inside. There was no sign of Rupert, but that wasn't unusual. He slept at the hotel. She knew he would be at the tent with the morning to see how much money had been taken in during the night. She lay down, sore and bruised from her fall from the wagon. She awoke with Rupert shaking her.

"What the hell's going on?" he demanded. "Where is everybody?"

"Men come in the night, Rupe," she said. "Take girls away to mission."

"What are you, crazy?" he asked, drawing

back his fist. "What kind of lies are you telling?"

She clung to him, weeping. "No lie, Rupe. Cherokee law. Take all girls. I jump out of wagon and come back."

Rupert shoved her away. Once again the damned Indians. First his herd, his last nest egg, then his girls.

"Rupe, go get girls," Wynema said.

"Who were they, the men who came after you?"

"Cherokee. Marshal and Lighthorsemen."

"Not the white soldiers?"

"Cherokee," Wynema insisted.

Damn. The Cherokees hadn't bothered him before. They stayed away from the railroad people, and from the white camp followers. And then it hit him. That damned girl. He should have known. He'd heard that Grand Woodrowe was in town making palaver with the Cherokee over something. She was still Woodrowe's woman and his being summoned by her to her hotel room was a trick to get him out of the way. Otherwise there might have been a few good Indians around if he'd been on hand when they tried to steal his girls. He should have known it was too good to be true. He should have remembered the way she'd acted when he hit Wynema in the dining room in Chetopa.

"You stay," he told Wynema. He had to be sure. He rode at a lope to the Red Barn. The old man was behind the bar, sneaking a little drink. Rupert passed the time of day and then, without putting much emphasis on it, he said, "I thought I saw a girl I know coming out of here yesterday." He described Miranda.

Warren nodded. "Nice lady," he said. "Looking for some lost relative."

Rupert didn't push it. He first offered to buy Warren a drink, and was accepted, and then, after they'd shared a few, he brought up the subject again. It went with what he'd been told by the girl, herself, in Chetopa. She was looking for a woman who had been involved with Danny O'Lee some seventeen years in the past, and there was a child involved. Well, well, well. And the woman's name might be Lilah. Before he left he had it all, everything that old John Warren knew, and he was more convinced than ever that Miranda Lee was not a high-priced whore. And when he went to the hotel and asked if Grand Woodrowe was registered, and was told that yes, Mr. and Mrs. Grand Woodrowe were staying in such and such a room, the very room he'd been drinking tea in while his gold·mine was being looted, he went away with a hatred in his heart which had to be eased. Damned Woodrowe family. The old man costing him his herd, and now the son costing him his girls.

He went into the dining room and looked for them. They were not there. He waited on the street and saw them drive up in a handsome surrey and go into the hotel, the bitch hanging onto the Indian's arm. His lips did not move, but the words were a low mutter in his throat.

"All right, bitch," he said, "you tricked me out of my girls and you're going to replace them."

He had plans to make. He went back into the hotel and talked with the desk clerk. A small gold coin changed hands in payment for the information that Grand Woodrowe had told the clerk he would be checking out early the next morning. He had plenty of time. He wanted that girl. First he wanted her for himself, wanted to make her forget that she'd ever thought a damned Indian could be a man, than he wanted her in a money-making bed, taking all comers. She'd repay him for the loss of the girls.

He knew where to go, knew most of the hard cases who followed the rails, earning beans and booze by gambling, stealing, sometimes working as guards for the rails. More gold changed hands.

He waited on the outskirts of town, four men with him, horses hidden in a copse of trees from which there was a good view of the road leading south. They came out of the town just after sunup, Woodrowe driving the surrey, the girl seated beside him, a sunbonnet on her head. He told the men, once again, what he wanted, showed them the gold which would be theirs, in addition to what he'd already paid, when the job was done. They watched the surrey pass, then made their way down to the road, riding slowly well back out of sight until the town was some miles back.

"Good place in that next little hollow," he told them. "Remember, I don't want the girl harmed."

Grand heard the horses, coming hard from behind them, turned to see four men riding fast. He did not want to show his concern to Mindy, who hadn't noticed yet. But then she, too heard the hoofbeats and turned. For the first time in his life, Grand wished for a gun. But maybe they were just going somewhere in a hurry. He touched Mindy's hand and said, "It's all right."

When the riders were almost on them he pulled

the surrey as far to the right as he could to give them room to pass, but that, of course, was not their intention. One man pulled his horse up even with the heads of the team pulling the surrey and grabbed the bridle of the haw horse, pulling the surrey to a stop, the other three surrounded the surrey.

Grand knew the type well. They wore guns and there were carbines in each of the saddle holders. Men like them had long taken advantage of the loose conditions of law in the Indian Nations. He knew that it would be futile to resist them.

"All right, gents," he said, "I'm not armed." He held up his hands. "Problem is, I have only a little money."

"Listen to that, would you?" asked the self-styled leader of the four. "The injun talks jest like a man."

"Fancy injun," another said. "Dressed up real pretty."

Grand was reaching slowly for his wallet, in the inside pocket of his coat. He took it out, held it toward the nearest horseman. The man leaned forward and knocked it from his hand violently.

"All right, injun, get your ass down," said the leader. "You too, pretty gal."

Grand took Mindy's arm and assisted her from the surrey.

"All right," the leader said, "walk." He pointed a way into the scrubby woodland which bordered the road. "You," he said, pointing to another man. "Get the buggy off the road."

Grand was beginning to feel serious alarm, not for himself, but for Mindy. But he had no

choice. He led Mindy off the road and into the
trees. Three horsemen hemmed them in. Behind
him he heard a man yelling the team into motion
and the surrey creaked off the road and down a
small slope on the far side. If the men did not
want his money, then there was only one thing
they could be after. Miranda.

"When I say go," he whispered, as trees separated them from the horsemen momentarily, "run
like the devil deeper into the woods."

"What you talking about, injun?" the leader
yelled. "Keep your mouth shut."

Grand knew that he'd have to make his move
quickly. Already they were out of sight of the
road. On either side of them the small, wooded
hills rose. He could see large rocks on one slope,
and ahead there was a small creek, the trees and
brush thick around it. If he could get into the
brush with Mindy they would have to abandon
their horses and pursue them on foot. It was the
only chance. He waited until the horses, wending
their way among the trees, were separated from
them for a moment and yelled, "Go," grabbing
Mindy's arm.

Low-hanging branches slashed at them. Mindy
gathered her skirt in one hand and ran as fast as
she could, Grand pulling her along. A pistol shot
cracked out and the slug broke branches near
them.

"Hold your fire, you fool," he heard a man
yell. "You might hit the girl."

Now he was sure. It was Miranda they were
after. The thought gave him strength. He was
almost dragging her as she struggled to stay on
her feet. The creek was near.

"Into the brush," he panted. "Keep going. Get to the other side and into the rocks and keep climbing."

"No," Mindy sobbed, as she realized what he was going to do.

He pushed her on, turned. As one horseman, cursing and dodging low limbs, came abreast of him he threw himself at the man in the saddle, got his arms around his waist and tumbled him off the horse. He was a strong man and he was doing well until a second rider threw himself off his horse and, picking his moment, rapped Grand across the skull with the barrel of his gun.

Mindy, meanwhile, was clawing her way through the brush alongside the small creek, sobbing in fear, afraid to look back and afraid not too. She saw, with a quick glance over her shoulder, that Grand was fighting on the ground with one of the men and she saw the third horseman leaving his animal to plunge into the thick brush after her. She fell heavily at the edge of the stream, when her feet hit the slippery bank, and the water which wetted her was chill. And then the man was on her, seizing her and jerking her to her feet.

Her skirts sodden, the travel suit she'd chosen for the trip home torn by the brush, she was half-dragged back to the point among the trees where the three men, soon joined by the man who had moved the surrey, were busily tying Grand's hands and feet.

"Damned injun got me a good one," grumbled the man whom Grand had pulled from the saddle. He rubbed his cheek and looked at his fingertips to see if there was blood.

"What have you done to him?" Mindy asked. "What do you want?"

The leader pulled a rawhide strip from his pocket and lashed Mindy's hands together in front of her, then attached a lead from the bindings of her hands to a small tree, snugging her up close, the rough bark of the tree hurting her hands. She could look around the small tree, no larger than her leg at the height of her face, and see Grand lying on the ground, blood in his dark hair.

"Let's get on with it," growled the leader.

"Hey," one of the men said, "that's not a bad looking suit the injun is wearing."

"You want it, you take it off," the leader said.

The man began to strip Grand, having to untie his hands and feet to remove the coat, waistcoat and trousers, leaving Grand in his shirt and long underwear.

"Take off the long johns," the leader said.

The man who had taken Grand's clothing was trying on the coat. One of the others whistled and laughed. The leader repeated, "Take off the long johns." He pointed at the man who was trying on the coat.

"I ain't no pekker inspector," the man said.

The leader muttered a curse and bent over Grand. He used a knife to slash and cut at the long johns, cutting and ripping until he was able to pull off the lower portion, leaving Grand naked. Grand moaned and began to stir. The leader quickly lashed his feet and hands, hands behind his back, lying on them, his nakedness exposed.

"Luke," the leader said to the fourth man, the one who had moved the surrey, "you're the knife man. You do it."

"Please," Mindy cried, "please don't hurt him. What has he done to you?"

"Luke, you gonna do it?" the leader asked.

Luke nodded. "First time for everything," he said. He pulled out a knife and opened it, stood over Grand.

The leader came to stand by Mindy. "Now you watch real close, little lady. You're supposed to see it all."

"See what?" she asked. "Please let us go. We've done nothing to you."

"You ready, Luke?" the leader asked.

Luke was squatted over Grand, who was regaining consciousness. He groaned and opened his eyes, looking dazed, then began to struggle against his bonds. Unable to free himself, dizzy, he fell back.

"Come to, has he?" the leader asked. He walked to look down at Grand. "Gonna show you, injun, what happens to savages bed down a white woman."

"Guess you do this jest like he was a bull calf," the man called Luke said, extending a finger tentatively to push aside Grand's phallus. "Old boy's got a set on him."

"Hold on," the leader said, coming back to stand beside Mindy. He put his hands on either side of Mindy's head and held it, her face directed toward Grand and Luke. "Don't you close your eyes now, for that would be cheating, and you're supposed to see it all."

Then she realized what was going to happen and she screamed, and, mercifully, fainted dead away.

Miranda awoke with pain in her wrists. Tied to the tree, she slumped, her weight on her arms. She looked quickly toward Grand. Nature had been kind to him, bringing a merciful blackness. Blood still oozed from his groin. The four men were engaged in some sort of discussion, heated, vehement. Gradually the words came through to her. They were talking about her.

"You know damned well he said he wouldn't pay if the girl had been harmed."

"What the hell, it's only another twenty dollars. Twenty dollars wouldn't buy a piece like that in a Kansas City whore house."

"I don't know about you, but I can use that twenty dollars," the leader said. He stepped back suddenly, his gun appearing in his hand as if by magic. "Now that's the end of it, boys, we take the girl to him and get our money."

Luke, the knife man, grinned, holding his hands out from his side. "O.K., that's the best argument yet," he said. "Damned if you ain't done convinced me."

"Cut her loose," the leader said.

One of the men came and slashed the rawhide which held Mindy to the tree. She tried to run to Grand, but he grabbed her, his hands closing over her breasts. She fought, but the cruel fingers dug into her soft breasts.

"Man, she's a lot of woman," the man said, with a chuckle, kneading her breasts.

"Cut that out," the leader said.

"Little feel ain't gonna hurt her," the man said.

"Least we could do is take a little look," Luke said, stepping toward Miranda and thrusting his hand out to lift her skirt. "Man, look at them fancy underwears."

The leader, gun still in his hand, moved toward them. "Next man does something to her is dead," he said.

Unnoticed, the fourth man had fallen behind the leader. The man holding Miranda, his hands over her breasts and constantly kneading, feeling, nodded. She could feel his body against hers, could feel that he was erect, pushing the hardness into her back.

The leader didn't know what hit him. The fourth man hit him with his gun barrel. The sound was like a ripe watermelon being dropped on hard rock and the leader collapsed like a rag doll. "I don't know 'bout you fellers, but a man waving a gun makes me nervous," the fourth man said.

"How do you two fellers feel about it?" Luke asked. "Worth twenty dollars?" He lifted Miranda's skirt, ripped at her underwear, tearing, tugging, as Miranda's frantic kicking served only to help him strip her under the skirts. Then, one man holding her, Luke holding up the skirts, she was exposed, dark bush, long, smooth thighs.

"Gawd a'mighty," Luke breathed. He grabbed Miranda's legs and they threw her onto the ground, a mossy spot covered with fallen leaves. His hand went between her legs, a finger thrusting into dry, unreadied flesh. She screamed.

"I say it's worth twenty dollars," Luke said.

"Depends on who's first," said the man holding Miranda's arms.

"Well, we can draw for it," the third man said. He pulled a ratty deck of cards from his jacket pocket and gave them a quick shuffle. Luke drew first, a nine of clubs. The man behind Miranda's head drew a queen of hearts. The man who owned the deck shuffled again, stuck out his tongue in one corner of his mouth, took a deep breath and drew an ace.

"Too bad, gents," he said, beginning to take off his gun belt.

"Now you hold on," Luke said. "That ace is jest too much of a good thing."

"You saying I'd cheat?" the man asked, backing off a little, going into a crouch, the gun belt still in place but held loosely, one buckle already open.

"Hey, they's enough here for all of us," the man at Miranda's head said.

"Well, all right," Luke grumbled.

"Yawl hold her," the winner said, stripping off his pants, leaving on a pair of grimy, once white long johns. "I don't want to get my eyes scratched out." He knelt at Mindy's feet, put out a hand. Luke and the other had her spread-eagled, legs wide. His hand felt of her, ran roughly over her thighs. "Yeah," he said, crawling toward her.

And from the side there came a series of animal sounds, startling them. The man about to rape Miranda leaped to his feet, started to make a dive for his gun. Grand, having regained consciousness, seeing what was about to happen, was inching himself frantically across the ground, pain and outrage causing the sounds from his open mouth.

"Hell, it's jest the injun," Luke laughed. "You gonna take your turn or do I?"

"I think I can manage it," the lucky winner said, taking out a large and firm member, holding it in one hand as he knelt and positioned himself.

Miranda could do nothing, try as she might. The strength of the two men was too much for her. She closed her eyes and tried to pray, but could not, could not keep her eyes closed, watched, making a small, whining, mewling sound of shock and fear as the thing came closer, as the man put one hand on the ground at her side and lowered himself. She screamed once, shrilly, as sound exploded and, before her eyes, the man's head jerked sidewise and he fell, blood pumping from his temple to fall, warm and sticky, on her exposed thighs.

Luke and the other man, shocked into momentary stillness, saw him standing there, on the edge of the clearing, tall and calm, a smoking gun in his hand, dived for cover but too late, a slug catching Luke in the back and the other one in the forehead.

Miranda could not take it all in. She rolled onto her side, raised herself, looked up to see Rupert Glendower standing there.

"Oh, thank god," she said, crawling like an animal to throw herself onto Grand, moaning, touching his pale face with her hand.

"Mindy, oh, Mindy," he said, as darkness came, once more.

"Help him," Miranda said, looking up at

Glendower. "We've got to get him to a doctor." She looked down. Blood was still flowing. There had been a great deal of it, covering the ground. She sobbed, ripped a remaining portion of her undergarments, thrust the wadded material against the wound to try to stop the blood.

"Leave him alone," Glendower said.

"What?" she looked up, not understanding.

"Get away from him," Glendower said, his gun pointed at them. "We've got to get out of here."

"You?" she gasped. "You hired these men to do this?"

"Stand back," he said. "Let's get the injun out of his misery."

She threw herself across Grand. "You'll have to kill me too," she said.

"I've got other plans for you, missy," he said, stalking toward her. "You cost me my girls. After I get through with you myself you're gonna do their work." He seized her roughly and pulled her away from Grand. She tumbled and fell across the body of one of the dead men, hitting the ground with a force which pushed the air from her lungs. And with horror piling atop horror she saw Glendower standing, legs wide, looking down at Grand, the gun pointed at Grand's head.

"Too bad you're not awake to see it," Glendower said.

There was a gun. It protruded from a holster, hilt in the air. She seized it. Glendower, intent on the pleasure of revenge, did not notice. She held it with both hands, aiming at his chest, as he stood slightly sidewise to her, had to squeeze very hard, the heavy gun wobbling in her hands, and then it exploded and Glendower was falling, gun dropping from his hand. And it was over. There was an unearthly quiet in the woods. It was broken by a low moan from Grand and she ran to him, glancing at Glendower to see that he, too, was bleeding, from the head. It was the first time she'd ever fired a gun and she'd aimed at his body and hit him in the head and, as she tried to stop Grand's bleeding, she was grateful, was glad that Glendower was dead.

There was death all around her, horror, blood, and the utmost horror was in what had been done to Grand. She tried to think, to make plans. She couldn't possibly carry him out of the woods. She thought of the surrey. It could not come through the trees. But there were the horses. She could hear them, still snorting, frightened by the gunshots, but at least one of them still nearby. However, there was no way she could lift Grand to place him across the saddle.

"Grand, Grand, oh, please," she begged, patting his pale face. "Please, you must help me."

His eyes fluttered open. "Mindy?"

"Grand, it's over. They're all dead. Can you walk?"

"I can try." She tried to help him, but he fell back weakly. "Weak," he said. "So weak."

"Grand, could you possibly get onto a horse? If I help and lift can you make it?"

"I think so," he said.

She caught one of the animals with surprising ease. He was a well trained mount, followed her almost gratefully, it seemed, as she led him through the woods by the reins. And then began the terrible effort to get Grand into the saddle. By letting him put his arm around her neck he was able to stand and grasp the saddle horn, and then she put her arms around his legs and lifted and he managed to get one foot into the stirrup and then she was crying with effort and straining and with one last gallant effort Grand swung his leg over and fell into the saddle only to scream out in agony and fall forward, narrowly escaping toppling off.

Slowly, carefully, she led the horse out of the woods, Grand clinging to the saddle with both hands, his face white with pain. At last they reached the road and there he waited while she found the surrey, drove it back to him, helped him, as he screamed out once in agony, to fall into the seat. He half-lay in the seat, his head on her lap, as she urged the horses back toward Chouteau, where there would be a doctor.

"Mindy, my God," he said. "What have they done to me?"

9

There was a freight train running through his head and each truck struck a nerve which threatened to cause his brain to jump right out of his skull. He forced his eyes open and saw trees with double trucks, a patch of sky. It was a long, long time before he could send his hand in the right direction, it kept wanting to go its own way, but finally he felt the raw meat exposed in a groove along the right side of his head. After about a century he pushed himself up on one elbow.

At first he could not remember what had happened. He thought maybe he was back at Shiloh, but the dead men on the ground were not in uniform, and when it came to him he scrabbled for his gun and sat there, breathing hard, still seeing

167

two of everything, looking around and ready. But there was only silence.

An urgency grew in him. The girl and the Indian were gone. That meant trouble. He crawled on his hands and knees to inspect the damages. They were all dead except the back-shot man, and he was just barely breathing. He wouldn't last long. He had to get the hell out of there.

Standing up was one of the hardest things he'd ever done, but when he finally made it to the little creek and splashed cold water in his face and washed away the blood, he began to feel as if he just might live and then he began to get angry at himself for taking his eyes off the girl. She had to be the one who'd shot him. What he felt for her was beyond anger.

Well, at least the Indian, Woodrowe, had got what was coming to him. If he could get away before the Indian law or the soldiers came he'd have a long life to think of what he was going to do to the girl. He made his way carefully, walking as if he were very, very old, very fragile, back to where he'd left his horse. The animal tried to nuzzle him in a friendly way and almost knocked him down. He pulled himself into the saddle and sat there, breathing hard, thinking it over. Not the road. He had no idea how long he'd been out. They could be almost on him by now. He'd have to make it cross country.

He let the horse pick the way through the woodlands, up a steep hill where the going was rough, traveling toward the west. Once again he was on the run. Last time, however, he'd had company. He thought of her, back there in

Chouteau. She was just a little nigger gal, but she
was loyal. Of all of the six she was the only one
who had come back to him. He considered ways
of getting word to her, but that would be dangerous. The Lee girl had seen him kill three men
and start to kill her Indian lover. That was
enough to bring in the white law and even the
soldiers. Well, Wynema was a tough little nut.
She'd hold out. He'd get word to her somehow,
but first he had to get himself out of Cherokee
country and into Kansas and lay low for a while.

And then? Weak from the loss of blood, his
head full of devils, he sunk into a deep depression. What was it with the damned Indians? They
sat on some of the finest land in the country and
did nothing much with it and everytime he had
something going they came at him and took it
away. Well, it had happened for the last time.

Late in the day he managed to shoot a rabbit,
almost blowing its head off. He cooked it over
an open fire and ate it without salt. When he left
Chouteau he hadn't planned on having to rough
it. But the hot meat helped him. Next morning he
came upon an isolated farm house. He watched
it for a while, saw a Cherokee working in a field,
approached the house quietly and surprised an
Indian woman in the kitchen. He didn't have
time to talk or fool around, so he just grabbed
her, laid his gun barrel alongside her ear, not
too hard, and then helped himself to bacon,
beans, coffee, salt, and a couple of cooking uten-
sils. He took a couple of blankets from the bedroom, rolled all the stuff up into a neat bundle,
and was away.

With some food on hand, he halted at a safe

distance from the farm and rested for a day or two. The wound was scabbed over and his head didn't hurt so much when he started traveling again. Fortunately, he always carried a sizeable amount of money with him. He would not be destitute when he got to Kansas. He could always find more young girls, Indians, niggers, the deserted, the unwanted. But, somehow, that did not appeal to him. He was a long way from having his fine establishment with expensive white girls. No, it was time to think of another way, a better way to accumulate money fast.

He stayed a few miles to the west of the rails, made his way slowly northward. He had a good start on a beard when he crossed the Kansas line and rode cautiously into Chetopa. He didn't look like the same man, with his fine clothing trailworn and dusty, his auburn beard covering his face, his hair growing long and unkempt. He decided to risk it and went into a saloon and listened to the talk, got into conversations with railroad men and asked questions about how things were going. He asked leading questions about trouble along the rails and heard a lot of stories, but did not hear any mention of the killings outside of Chouteau. Later, a stroll past the sheriff's office and a quick look in at the window told him that, at least, his face was not posted on the wanted board, at least not yet.

He kept thinking of Wynema. He wrote a letter. He didn't give her credit for enough intelligence to check at the post office for mail, but there was a chance that someone in the post office had heard of her and would send word.

He didn't sign it, just wrote, "Get on the train and look for me in Chetopa."

After a couple of days when he'd gone so far as to speak to the local law while walking the streets, he felt certain that the Indian authorities hadn't put out a wanted on him. It was time to start making plans. The money he'd had in his purse wouldn't last forever. He hadn't done a real day's work since losing his herd in Choctaw country, and he didn't fancy the idea of going back to cowboying for a few dollars a month plus beans and board.

But to look at him, one would not guess that he was next to being down and out. He'd used some of his money to buy a new suit, and had had his beard trimmed. With the beard he looked older than his years, and rather distinguished. When he went into the railroad hotel bar he was greeted with courtesy. He looked the gentleman, but the gun belt under his frock coat told the world that he was a gentleman who knew how to take care of himself.

To Edward J. Smith, vice-president of the M.K. & T., Glendower was the epitome of the westerner. Smith was a city man, and he was finding Chetopa to be quite different from St. Louis. He saw Glendower belly up to the bar, prop a booted foot, push back a fine, white hat from the bush of red hair and survey the room and he nodded. Glendower returned the nod in a friendly way. They stood not three feet apart.

Smith raised his glass. "To your health, sir," he said.

"Your health," Rupert said. He really wasn't

in the mood to talk with some city dude. He had thinking to do. But when, after finishing the drink, the dude offered to buy, he thought, well, what the hell. But that bought talk and Smith moved closer.

"Nice weather," Smith said. Rupert grunted. But what the hell, the dude was buying.

"Not to be nosy," he said, "but I can tell you're not from these parts."

"No, indeed," Smith said, lifting his glass with a smile. "I'm out of St. Louis, on an inspection trip."

"Railroad?"

"Indeed, sir," Smith said. "I find that I must go into the Cherokee Nation and, quite frankly, sir, being a city man, I want to find out a little bit of what to expect. You, sir, have the look of a man who knows his way around."

"I've been there," Rupert said.

"I am not a coward, sir," Smith said. "Far from it. I did my bit in the war, you know. But, quite frankly, this trip has me worried. Is it truly as lawless as I've heard?"

"Well," Rupert said, "it can get pretty rough, but they've got soldiers along the rails now. You shouldn't have any trouble."

"That's good news," Smith said. "I had thought that it might be a good idea to have a, how shall I say, a bodyguard? Sounds so pretentious. A man who knows the territory, shall we say, a man who knows how to handle himself."

"Not a bad idea," Rupert said.

"Oh? You think I should have such a man, then?"

"Wouldn't hurt," Rupert said.

"Ah, you, sir, look as if you know how to handle that gun you're wearing."

"I do."

"Perhaps you, knowing the area, could suggest the right man for me," Smith said, looking at him with one raised eyebrow.

"Might," Rupert said. "How much does it pay?"

"Oh, I'd make it right," Smith said.

Rupert was thinking quickly. Under the protection of the railroad he might be able to get back into Chouteau and find Wynema. At least he'd have a start toward a new business. And being paid by the railroad at the same time wouldn't hurt his feelings.

"How long will you be in the Nations?" he asked.

"Oh, not more than a week, two at the most."

"I might be interested."

"You, sir?" Smith smiled. "I must say that even though I don't know you, I like your looks. Would one hundred dollars interest you?"

"If the trip lasts only a week," Rupert said, holding his breath. A hundred was too much. The man could hire three or four guns for a week at that price, but what the hell, wouldn't hurt to try for more.

"Say a hundred a week, then," Smith said. "By the way, I don't know your name."

Rupert told him. A hundred easy dollars and a chance to find Wynema. Maybe, at last, luck was running his way. He didn't know just how lucky he was until he found that Smith was traveling in his own private railroad car, a luxurious car with a cook and a bar and a private com-

partment for Rupert. And Smith was one trusting
fellow. He talked railroad business right in front
of Rupert and didn't hesitate to answer questions.
One of the things which was bothering Smith
was the unsettled question of the grants of land
alongside the tracks.

"Way I understand it," Rupert said, "the railroad won't get that land as long as it belongs to
the Indians."

"You're perfectly right, Rupe," Smith said.
"That's why the railroad, along with others,
spends thousands of dollars lobbying in Washington."

"Lobbying for what?" Rupert asked.

"For the best interests of the poor Indians,"
Smith said, with a chuckle. "It's unfair for them
to be cut off from the mainstream of American
life. We have their best interests at heart when
we say that it would be best if the government
would give them individual land grants and
throw the rest open to settlement."

"Sure you do," Rupert chuckled. "How much
do you pay to those Indians who openly advocate
becoming a part of the United States?"

Smith chuckled. "Some we don't have to pay.
They sincerely feel that the Indian will never be
equal until he competes on an equal basis.
Others?" He spread his hands.

"There's some fine land out there," Rupert
said. "I wouldn't mind having some of it for
myself."

"You've traveled a lot in the Nations?"

"Pretty much."

"How about the Unassigned Lands?"

"Rode through once," Rupert said. "Some of

the finest land. And of no use to anyone the way it is."

"This is where the Indians are most vulnerable," Smith said. "We put quite a bit of pressure on about the Unassigned Lands. We see it as being of great strategic importance. If we could, somehow, convince the Congress that there is no reason not to open the Unassigned Lands to white settlement we'd have a white outpost right in the heart of the Indian country."

"There are a lot of people want to get into that area," Rupert said. "All over Kansas you hear talk about it, about good land sitting down there not even being used."

"Yes, I know," Smith said.

"Ah, you've got a hand in that, too?" Rupert asked.

"Let us say we don't discourage such talk," the railroad man said.

Rupert was silent for a long time. He kept remembering how he'd heard men say they should just load up and move in and take the Unassigned Lands. "Mr. Smith," he said, "what would it be worth to you to have white settlers start moving into the Unassigned Lands?"

"I would have to think about that," Smith said.

"Now you and I both know that if settlers moved in, the government would send troops to make them move out, but meantime there'd be articles in the papers. You could show Congress that there is a great demand for homestead land."

"Yes, I don't deny that such activity would be valuable," Smith said.

"The feeling is there," Rupert said. "A good

man could round up a hundred, two hundred
wagons and sneak in, crossing the Cherokee
Strip at night, hiding out in the daytime. Be
there and be cutting timbers for houses before
anyone knew about it."

"Yes," Smith said. "And I suppose you happen to have a good man in mind?"

"I do," Rupert said. "If the price is right."

"All right, let's see if we can put a dollar value
on it," Smith said. "Suppose I offered you five
dollars a family for any settlers you move into
the Unassigned Lands?"

"I'd say it would take ten to make me work
real hard at it," Rupert said. "One hundred
families moved in, one thousand in silver or
gold."

"I will have to think about it," Smith said.

"Whether or not the federal troops come in
and move them out," Rupert stipulated.

"Give me a few days to think it over. We have
time."

The trip down the rails was, for Rupert, a
pleasant one. They stopped at various sites and,
on the day they reached the railhead settlement
at Chouteau, it was raining. Smith said he would
just stay in the car. Rupert, his lush, red beard
a banner which was soon dampened by the driving rain, put on slicker and boots and walked
along the tracks to the tent area. His heart quick-
ened when he saw that his tent was still in place.
The flap was closed, but there was the glow of
light from inside. He opened the flap and stuck
his head in, expecting to see Wynema. Instead,
he saw three railroad workers playing cards on a
blanket.

"Howdy," one of the players said. "Looking for some action?"

"No," Rupert said, "as a matter of fact I was looking for the fellow who used to live in this tent, month or so ago. Fellow named Glendower."

"Never heard of him," the man said. "Close the flap, rain's blowing in."

"Had some girls," Rupert said.

"Yeah, I heard about that," another player said. "There was some trouble. Heard that the Indians took the girls. Don't know what happened to the man."

"You ain't seen a little Indian gal named Wynema around town?" Glendower asked.

"Naw, but if you're looking for that kind of action, the Red Barn's the place," he was told.

He closed the flap. By rights, the tent was his, but he wasn't in the mood to try to prove it to the three tough looking men who had apparently taken it over. He had other things going for him now, anyhow. Things were looking good. He was making good money. He was sure that Smith would give him a good job with the railroad if his proposition were not accepted. He hoped Smith would go for his offer. It appealed to him. It would serve the damned Indians right. They'd cost him enough, now it was going to be his turn. He'd do everything in his power to show them how it felt to be down and out, to have one's last possessions taken.

They were on the way back to Chetopa when Smith announced his decision. "Rupe," he said, "I'll be going back to St. Louis. You can go with me, if you like. There's a job for you if you want it. Security guard type of thing. Good money."

"Well, Ed," Rupert said, "I appreciate the offer and I might take you up on it, but I'm really an outdoors type of fellow. You thought about that idea I had about the Unassigned Lands?"

"I've been thinking very seriously about it," Smith said. "Just being selfish. Hate to see a good man get out from under my personal thumb, if you know what I mean. You don't want the job with the railroad, we'll pay you ten dollars per family for any settler you move into the Unassigned Lands."

"Ed, you just spent several thousand dollars of the railroad's money."

"You deliver, and it will be worth it," Smith said. "Just one thing. There's a man in Arkansas City I want you to see and talk with. Course, our arrangement is strictly on the Q.T. You ever tell anyone the railroad's on your side and we'll call you a liar in public and sue you for slander, but this man will get the picture when you tell him you're going to do your personal best to open up the Unassigned Lands. Get what I mean? He's a newspaper man. You get some action going and it'll be spread all over the United States."

"By damn," Rupe said, with a grin. "All I wanted to do was get rich, not get famous, but if that's the case, I'll have to live with it."

10

When Rupert Glendower made his cursory
attempt to locate Wynema, she had been gone
from Chouteau for over three weeks. She left in
a manner which was quite unexpected to her.
She had returned to the town after escaping from
the marshal and his deputy tired, bruised, her
clothing torn, to find Rupert angry, angrier than
she'd ever seen him, and when he left her alone
the morning after she'd come back in the dead of
night she waited for him with mixed emotions,
half-hoping he'd get the other girls back, a part
of her hoping that he wouldn't. If he didn't get
the girls back then it would be as it was in the
beginning, just her and Rupert.

She didn't know what Rupert was going to

do, but he was mean enough to do almost anything, the way he was feeling, and she hoped he wouldn't do anything foolish and get into trouble. While she waited she put a salve on her bruises and washed and put on a nice dress. When he came back she'd make it real nice for him, have a good meal and then she'd show him that he had something left. The way he'd carried on it was as if she were nothing. He acted as if he'd lost everything.

He didn't show up that night. She had three customers and hid the money, burying it in a jar in the dirt of the tent's floor. The next morning she didn't see Rupert, either. And then it was noon and then afternoon and still no Rupert and she decided to go walking and look for him.

She was coming out of the general store, after treating herself to some candy, when the marshal's men came into town with a wagon. People started crowding around. She was curious enough to want to know what was going on, so she joined the crowd around the wagon and the marshal started asking if anyone knew the dead men. She got close enough to see, her heart almost stopping. She recognized two of the men. Rupert was not one of them and she breathed again. But men were talking around her and gradually the words began to come through to her. Her Rupert had killed those men. And he'd done other bad things and the marshal was looking for him and he'd been shot. When she heard that she almost passed out. But then the marshal was saying that he must not have been shot bad, because he was gone.

She went back to the tent, more than a little

bit worried. She didn't understand it. The dead
men had had nothing to do with the girls being
taken by the Cherokees, hadn't even been around.
Why had Rupe killed them? If he were going to
kill anyone it would have been the marshal or
the men with him.

He would, she knew, be back. He wouldn't
just leave her. She packed her things, to be ready
when he came or sent word. She had food and
a little money. He'd have to be careful, since the
Indian law wanted him, but he'd manage. Her
Rupe could do anything. And he wouldn't just
desert her. Never.

A complication entered her life that evening,
just after dark. She had lit the lantern and was
fixing herself a bit of food when the flap was
thrown open and a man who had been a customer before came in without invitation. Well, she
thought, she could always use the money. If it
took Rupe much longer to come for her she'd
be broke, so she smiled and asked the man if he
were there to do business. He was. They did the
business and she said, "Thank you. Two dollars."

He laughed. "Two dollars, is it?" He pulled her
to him roughly. "I ain't got two dollars, now how
about that?"

"Rupe no like that," she said.

He laughed. "Well, ain't that too bad, seeing
as how ole Rupe ain't here to tell me that his-
self."

"He be back," she said. "You pay. You go."

"I kinda like it here," he said, beginning to do
business with her again. "Think I'll jest move in
for a while."

"Rupe kill you," she said.

He hit her in the face with the flat of his hand. "You ain't Rupe's no more," he said. "Now you're mine."

He stayed in the tent all the weekend, doing business and eating her food and hitting her now and then, and then he had to go down the line to go to work and he told her to be there when he got back.

"Oh, Rupe," she said, alone, sore from her beatings. "Oh, Rupe, you come."

With the food gone, she had to do something. She went out and tried to get some business. A man came with her, but he, too, had heard about Rupert and when it came time to pay he laughed. She'd been hungry before in her life, but not since Rupert had bought her and taken her out of the Chickasaw Nation. She didn't like the feeling. She went out after dark and found a man who'd done business with her before. He'd been drinking. She caught up with him as he walked back toward his tent.

"Hey, Mr. Jake, you like do business?" she asked.

He went with her to the tent, so drunk she had to help support him. He had a lot of trouble doing business, but then it was finally done and she told him to give her two dollars. He was asleep. She went into his purse and took out two silver dollars and hid them. Then she got a cloth and wet it and wiped his face with it until he was awake.

"Jake, you go now. We do business again, O.K.?"

He mumbled something. She tried to lift him to his feet and couldn't manage it. She tugged and pulled until he was into his trousers and then put on his boots and tried again to get him to leave.

"I sleep now, Jake," she said. "Time for you go."

" 'Kay," he mumbled, struggling to his feet. "Long as it's free."

"Not free, Jake. Two dollars."

"Ha," he said. "Try and get it."

"Already got it," she said, before she realized her mistake. He swayed, not really understanding. Then he pulled out his purse and slowly counted the few dollars he had in it.

"You thievin' little wench," he said. "Gimme my two dollars."

"Jake, you always pay before. What's the matter you?"

"Different now," he said. "Gimme."

"No give," she said. "Do business."

She dodged his first blow and in doing so stumbled over the bed, falling. He was on her before she could recover, his huge fists hitting, hurting, making the world go dim. He kept telling her to give him his money and she would have done it, would have done anything to get him to stop, but his fist connected with her rib-cage and she felt something crack and a terrible pain made it impossible for her to speak and then he hit her in the face and all was darkness.

She was hurting. She was hurting so badly that she knew only that she was crying and that she wanted water. She tried to move and a lance of pain in her chest was like fire. She lay back, sobbing. He would come. Rupe would come.

In the heat of the day, feverish, in severe pain,

every movement a torture, she made it to the water bucket to find it empty. She wanted to die, then, for she wanted a drink of water more than she'd ever wanted anything in her life. She looked around the tent in desperation, through one eye which was almost swollen shut. Her very teeth hurt, and some of them were loose. And the pain in her chest was terrible. But she had to have water. Forcing herself to move, thinking that if she didn't she might simply die there in the tent on the packed earth floor, she crawled to the flap and put her head out. It was day. The sun was hot, bright.

"Help me," she called, but her voice was merely a faint croak. There was no one to help. There were water barrels over by the tracks. She crawled toward them, inching her way through the dry dust of the interminable distance which seemed to grow, rather than decrease. Water. She had to have water. Even if the movement killed her, she had to have water.

She could see the barrels. They seemed to swim in her limited vision. Only another eternity of effort and pain and then there'd be water. She could hear things, a roar, and then she looked up, lifting her head with great effort, and a carriage was bearing down on her.

"Help me," she croaked, and the effort, the sight of the carriage coming toward her, horses hooves pounding, stirring dust, were the last things she remembered.

11

It was a near thing with Grand. By the time Mindy got him back into Chouteau and the doctor had been located he'd lost so much blood that his normally dark complexion had the look of bread dough. Mindy, staying on her feet through nervous energy, insisted on staying with him.

The doctor was a young man. When not treating human patients on retainer from the railroad, he made an extra dollar curing the ills of various farm animals. Luckily, he was not out in the countryside when Mindy arrived with Grand unconscious in the surrey. The doctor hailed a couple of stout fellows, helped carry Grand into his makeshift office in a slab building through

185

whose walls one could see daylight. He looked at Grand doubtfully.

"Where's he shot?" he asked Mindy.

When she told him he looked at her unbelievingly. She had helped Grand into his pants back there in the woods, before the terrible ride out of the trees astride the horse. The doctor pulled off Grand's trousers and let out a gasp.

"By Gawd," he said. He leaned close. "Amazing he's alive. Big problem is how much blood he's lost."

He chatted as he went about cauterizing the wound with hot antiphlogistine, the tarry liquid first heated to boiling, filling the room with a coal tar smell, then, with Grand, fortunately, unconscious and unfeeling, poured into the open wound.

"Never had to do this to a man before," the doctor said cheerily. "Lot easier than trying to do it to a steer."

The smell of burning flesh was the final blow, the one tiny bit which took her beyond her ability to endure. She fainted. "Well, durn," the doctor said. But he could not leave his patient at the moment. He figured she'd landed without breaking any bones, so he went about his business, whistling cheerily. He cleared away the cooling antiphlogistine, trimmed up the skin flaps a bit, sewed industriously for a few minutes, bandaged the area, covered Grand up with a couple of blankets, for he was cold to the touch in spite of the heat of the day, and then he looked at Miranda, who had begun to stir.

"Back with us, are you?" he asked. He knelt beside her. "Feeling all right?"

She shook her head, ran a hand over her face. "I'll be all right," she said, and then the memories flooded back. "Grand—"

"Nothing more we can do right now, little lady," the doctor said, " 'less you believe in praying."

She staggered and almost fell as she got to her feet quickly. "You take it easy now," the doctor said. "I don't need another patient."

"Will he be all right?" she asked, moving to look down at Grand's pale face.

"He looks strong. Depends on how much blood he lost, I'd say. We'll know soon enough, I reckon."

She stayed with him. His breathing was shallow. His color was bad. Toward evening, the wind came up and she could hear it whistling through the cracks in the wall.

She slept in a chair beside the bed, sometimes leaning her head on the bed itself. In the cold light of dawn his color was somewhat better, but he did not move until late afternoon. The doctor had come and gone, had brought Mindy a meal from the dining room of the hotel. She had eaten little.

He moved one hand. She didn't notice at first, but the second time he moved it she saw and her heart leaped. She took it. It was no longer cold and lifeless, but seemed to burn with a fever. She thought of infection, always a danger.

"No," the doctor said, "too early for infection to cause a fever."

She had to leave him for a few minutes to talk with the marshal, who informed her that there'd been only four dead men, not five, as she had thought out there in the woods.

"But I saw him fall," she said. "I saw blood on his head."

"Some of these yahoos got thick skulls," the marshal said. "I got the word out on him, though. Doubt if it'll do any good. He's probably hell for leather for Kansas by now. Good riddance, I guess."

It was illogical, she knew, but she was glad. Although her main concern was for Grand, and she had spent little thought on having killed Glendower, she was relieved, in spite of her wish to see something terrible happen to the man, the man who had paid to have this horror committed on Grand. And yet, and yet, she could not see herself as a killer, and although she might wish him dead, she had to admit that she was secretly glad she had not done the deed.

But, in general, during the first days when Grand was so weak from loss of blood, when there was danger of infection, she was too tired to think of much of anything. She spent most of her hours beside his bed and it was not until it seemed that he was becoming much stronger that she had even half a night's sleep.

While the issue was life itself, no one talked about the cause of Grand's sickness. The doctor changed the bandages and nodded in satisfaction with the way the wound was healing. It was Grand himself, about three days after the bloody scene in the scrub oak woodlands, who brought up the subject.

"I didn't dream it, did I Doc?" he asked. "They gelded me, didn't they? Cut off my testicles?"

"Clean as a whistle," the doctor admitted.

"Don't think about it now," Miranda said. "We'll talk about it when you have your strength."

"I don't think *we* will talk about it at all, Miranda," he said stiffly. Miranda started to protest, but the doctor shushed her. He led her from the room when he had finished with his examination of Grand.

"You must understand, young lady, that he's had quite a blow, not only physical but mental. There's a word for it, you know. It's called emasculation. The very word is based on the Latin for male. Rightly or wrongly, the term takes into it a weakening, a lessening of his masculinity, a complete loss of virility. Now that can hit a man hard, much harder than the mere physical pain and weakness. I've seen you with him, and I guess I know when a woman's in love with a man, but if you truly love him, you're going to have to understand what he's feeling. He probably feels like the world has come to an end."

"I'll do my best," she said. "It would help if I know what to expect."

He shook his head uncomprehendingly.

"You don't know how it will affect him physically?" Mindy asked.

"What I'll do is write east and get some information. There's plenty of time."

"Speaking of time," she said, "when can I take him home?"

"Hard to say. I wouldn't want to move him for a while, for sure. Aside from the pain there's still the danger the wound will canker. We want to be sure he's pretty well healed."

She resigned herself to being in Chouteau for days longer, perhaps weeks. The building which the doctor used for his office had two small bedrooms, one for the doctor, one which he allowed her to use. The doctor was a busy man. He accepted her nursing of Grand as a matter of course. It was she who, in the early days, spooned soup and broth into Grand's mouth and, as he gradually grew stronger, stayed by his side, talking about everything under the sun except his mutilation.

His moods alternated between silent depression and a state so near normality that she grew hopeful. She told him that the doctor thought he was healing just fine, that they'd be able to go home soon.

"Home?" he asked, with a snort.

"To Crossroads," she said. "You'll need rest, a lot of time. Then we can do what you want, go back to San Francisco if that's what you want."

"I don't know what I want," he said. "I don't think it really matters."

"Darling, it does matter," she said. "It matters a great deal to me."

"I think it's time for you to consider your own position," he said. "I think it's time for you to go home. See your family, make your peace with your mother. You have no place out here."

"My place is with you," she said simply.

"Ah, the noble martyr," he said. "Well, Mindy, I appreciate it, but I won't accept your pity."

"You don't understand," she said.

"You're too young to saddle yourself to a half-man," he said.

"I am saddled, as you say, with the man I love," she said.

Well, he thought, that will change. He knew a little bit about it. He decided to shock her.

"Well," he said, "too bad it didn't happen when I was a kid, I'd be a fine soprano."

"Don't talk that way," she said.

"They're still singing in Europe," he said, "the *castrati*. In churches. Hundreds of them. Young boys gathered up by the music-loving Christians and de-balled so that their voices never change. They can sing higher than women. I can see myself now, singing a fine aria from Mozart or Gluck."

"Grand, please. It's different with you, and you know it," she said.

"Oh, sure," he said. "I don't have the advantage of a fine soprano voice, because my voice box is already formed. I won't even have the dubious pleasure of being a harem guard in Arabia, with all those voluptuous young virgins running around in scanty costumes. I could become a saint, you know. Saints are big on abstinence. I won't have any trouble there. You, on the other hand, would have to do something drastic, like Saint Francesca. She poured boiling bacon fat over her pudenda to quench the flames of evil desire."

Miranda was weeping silently, for each word came from his mouth as if it were a separate spasm of pain.

"If you'd like to join me in my holy state," he continued, "I'll help you apply hot oil to your breasts and then bind them tightly. It takes only a few weeks to dry them up, empty them out, leave nothing but a pair of baggy flesh sacks."

"You're being horrible," she said.

"Mindy, I feel quite horrible. I don't know and the doctor doesn't know fully what to expect, but it can't be good. I've read where powerful Roman ladies had men castrated so that they could enjoy the pleasures of the flesh without the risk of getting pregnant. The accounts are rather incomplete, dealing more with the sensational aspects rather than with the effects of the lucky lovers who were chosen to be castrated, but I do remember where one writer said the safe lovers ceased to be of any use, except to other men, after a few months."

"You don't know," she said. "You admit it yourself. You don't know. The doctor is sending for some material on the subject." She went to his side, took his hand. "And even if the worst happens," she said, "that won't make any difference in the way I feel about you. I love you. I want you to marry me."

He laughed wryly. "That would be like trying to cook a steak with a single match. No, Mindy. I won't do that to you. You're young. You'll find a life for yourself. I want you to go back to San Francisco."

"And you?"

"I don't know. I just don't know."

As he grew stronger she occasionally went out into the town, to walk, to purchase food, just to have some fresh air. Already the tent city was smaller, the boom moving down the line, some of the hangers-on already having moved ahead to establish the next boom town at Gibson Station.

It was on one of her walks that she found herself near the tracks. The weather was warm, there having been no rain in several days, and the streets were dusty. She was deep in thought, wondering what was going to be the outcome of Grand's mutilation, walking with her head down. She heard the sound of a vehicle coming, looked up just in time to see Wynema crawling in the middle of the road. She recognized the girl immediately. Funny how the little dark-skinned girl was always coming into her life. The red dress the girl wore was torn and dirty. She seemed to be in great pain, crawling slowly, then falling onto her face.

It seemed for a moment as if the carriage were going to run her down, but Mindy gathered up her skirts and ran forward, yelling to the driver to stop. He stopped the horses a few feet from the fallen figure. Mindy fell to her knees and picked the girl's head up out of the dust.

Wynema, feeling hands on her, opened her eyes, saw the face before her, took a few moments for it to register.

"You," Wynema said. "You get away from me."

"You're hurt," Mindy said, as Wynema fainted.

With the help of the driver of the carriage she took the girl to the doctor's office. The doctor was away, taking a look at an Indian child out on a farm. She directed the man to put the girl on her bed.

"You'll have to delouse the place," the man said, his nose curled up at Wynema's smell.

"I'll take care of it," Mindy said. "Thank you for your help."

"Just one of the little whores," the man said. "Don't get too involved with her, lady."

She stripped the filthy garments from Wynema's frail body, washed her. Wynema roused at the touch of the cool cloth and said, "Water." Mindy gave it to her and she grasped the glass and emptied it. "More, more," she said.

"Not now," Mindy said. "In a few minutes. Let's get you cleaned up. The doctor will be back soon to take a look at you."

As Miranda started to wash an area of bruised, discolored skin under the girl's left breast the girl screamed in pain and fainted again. Mindy finished the job carefully, then warmed some broth. When Wynema awakened again she drank the broth eagerly. She looked up at Mindy through her swollen eyes. "Why you help me?"

"Because you're hurt," Mindy said.

"Why you have marshal take girls?" Wynema demanded.

"Because they were only children."

"They happy with Rupe."

"Not the one you were beating," Mindy said.

Wynema made a face with her swollen lips. "She get to like."

"It wasn't right," Mindy said.

"Right for me. Rupe my man."

"But he's gone now."

" 'Cause of you."

"Maybe. He did some horrible things."

"You see him?"

"Yes."

"He hurt bad?"

"I don't know," Mindy said. "It looked bad. He was shot in the head, but when the marshal got there he was gone. They didn't find his horse, but they found tracks leading away from the place where he killed some men."

Wynema was silent for a moment, and then she drifted off into a sleep which was on the verge of swoon. When the doctor came he examined her, announced that aside from some severe bruises she was fine except that two ribs were broken. And then Mindy had two invalids on her hand, insisting that the doctor let the girl stay. She would pay.

"What happens me?" Wynema asked her, lying, her chest bandaged heavily, feeling much better, the pain in her chest eased by the tight bandages.

"We'll find a nice place for you."

"Well, what do you expect to do with her?" Grand asked. He had gathered enough strength to walk a bit, and had had many questions when he walked into the other room and found Mindy tending the girl.

"The other girls went to the mission," Mindy said.

They were in Grand's room. "The mission won't take her," he said. "They'll make all kinds of excuses, but they won't take her."

"Whyever not?"

"Because she's black."

"But she's a human being," Mindy protested.

"I can't change the world," Grand said.

"Then we'll take her with us, to Crossroads."

"Those at Crossroads won't thank you," he said.

"Chota would help," Mindy said. "I know she would."

"Yes, she's an idealist, like you."

"Just until she's recovered."

"And then?"

"I don't know. There must be someplace for her. She's only a child."

"Thirteen going on thirty," Grand said. "A hardened little whore, Mindy." But he smiled. "Oh, I know. We must help her. That's the problem with being a decent person, I guess. You get into positions which go against common sense and you have to bull your way through."

"Wynema," Miranda said, a couple of days later, "we're going to take you with us."

"Where?" Wynema asked. She'd been doing some thinking. Rupe hadn't come. He'd find her someday, if he were alive, but it was obvious that it might be a long time. Meantime, she couldn't do business without a protector. Her battered face and broken ribs told her that. The doctor had told her it would take a long time for her to heal, and she didn't like the idea of being hungry, at the mercy of the men along the tracks. She hated this beautiful white woman. There had been nothing but trouble from the first day she'd seen her, up in Chetopa, when Rupe hit her in the dining room. It was because of this woman that the other girls were gone, that Rupe was in trouble. But what choice did she have?

"In just a few days we'll be going south, into the Choctaw Nation," Mindy told her. "You'll go with us, and you'll have a place to stay until you're well. Then we'll have to decide what to do with you."

"Take care of myself," Wynema said.

"Well, we'll see."

To all outward appearances, short of a rather gingerly walk, Grand looked normal when the three of them boarded a stage. The journey made Wynema's chest ache, but her young bones were healing rapidly.

Word of the trouble had spread. Chota met them with tears in her eyes, hugged Mindy first, then put her arms around her son. "Are you all right?"

Grand laughed. "What's left of me is fine."

When the situation was explained to her, Chota took the black girl in with willingness, doing her best to make her feel at home. Wynema was weakened by the trip, and spent the first few days at Crossroads in bed. Grand secluded himself in his room, coming out at mealtimes, withdrawing into himself. The days passed, summer growing hotter, drier. The girl, Wynema, was up and about. She worked willingly. The question of her ultimate disposition was still unsolved, and it had ceased to be a concern. Something more immediate and more intensely personal took all of Miranda's attention. Suspicious for some time, she was now certain that she was pregnant.

Chota had noticed it, but she was not speaking about it. She had, however, noted the morning sickness which struck Miranda hard, often made her leave the breakfast table to retire to the privacy of her room, there to vomit into the chamber pot, to empty it when no one was looking. She was waiting for the proper time to tell Grand, but he was so withdrawn, so intent on her going back to San Francisco, that she did not know how to go about it.

She welcomed it when Chota, knowing that something had to be done, brought it up. They were shelling fresh peas in the kitchen. Wynema was watching the store. She had fallen in love with the place, spent all her spare time there, cleaning, dusting, looking at the heaps of yard goods, the gleaming knives, all the hundreds of items of merchandise which, to her, represented luxuries she'd never known. She was able, because of the similarities between the Chickasaw and Choctaw languages, to talk with the Choctaws who came in, and gradually, under careful supervision, Chota allowed her to tend customers. A few seemed to resent the black, but Chota told one of them, in heated terms, that the girl was not the only one in the Choctaw Nation with black blood in her veins. "So, we're not Seminoles," she told the old woman who said nasty things to Wynema. "We didn't take the blacks into the tribe as they did, but we had our slaves, both in the South and here before the war and some of our people bred with them. Just look around you. You'll see many faces which are not purely Choctaw."

As she sat hulling peas, looking at Miranda Lee's delicate hands, the quick, small fingers, the dusky white skin, she knew it was time. The girl was becoming more and more agitated.

"Something troubles you," she began.

"No, not really. Well, Grand. He's so withdrawn."

"My dear young friend, Miranda," Chota said. "It is time for us to speak frankly. Let me begin by saying that I knew from the beginning that there was more between you and my son than you said."

Mindy flushed, and looked away.

"It is true," Chota said. "And don't forget that I am a woman who bore two children, one of which died. I know when a woman has life in her stomach."

"Oh, Chota," Mindy said, tears forming.

The older woman put down her peas, put the pan into which she had been shelling them on the table, stood to place her hands on Mindy's shoulders.

"How long?" she asked. "From the morning sickness, I'd judge at least two months."

"Yes," Mindy said, "I have missed two moon periods."

"And you have not told him."

"No."

"You must. As soon as possible. He is my son. He has been done a great wrong, but he is a man. He will do the right thing."

"But that's just it, Chota," Mindy sobbed. "I don't want to force him into it. Once he asked me to marry him, and I told him no. I don't know why. I felt, I suppose, that I'd pushed myself onto him, that I had no right to expect him to marry me."

"I see my son in your eyes," Chota said. "Once I had that light." She laughed. "It is still there, but it grows dim with age, although none the less strong." For a moment she was silent, thinking of her husband, Caleb. For a while it had seemed that he would rally, would overcome the wounds. The news of Grand's tragedy had hit him hard.

Now he was only half alive, his legs becoming
more and more useless as the days passed, spending his days in his bed, another reason why
Chota was pleased with Wynema's interest in
the store.

"You love him, don't you?" Chota asked.

"Very much," Mindy said.

"And he loves you. So there is only one solution." She bent and kissed Mindy on the cheek,
took her seat, looked into Mindy's face. "Unless
you do not want to be tied to half a man."

"He will never be half a man," Miranda said.
"What's happened to him makes no difference in
the way I feel."

Chota smiled. "Yes, I would be disappointed
in you if you felt any other way. Go then. Go to
him now, this minute. Perhaps the knowledge
that at least a small portion of his manhood is
left, in the form of the seed which he planted in
you, will give him hope."

He was in his room, seated, a drawing pad
across his knee, but he was not working. He was
staring out at the hot sun on the garden plot, his
face blank. He didn't look at her when she came
into the room. She sat near him on a chair.

"Grand, we must talk."

"Yes, I agree. It is time to make some deci-
sions."

He was healed. He looked very much the man,
a whole man, handsome, just a bit thinner in the
face than he had been, the result of weight loss
during his illness.

"I've been thinking, Mindy. It's time for you
to leave, to go home."

"My home is where you are," she said. He started to speak. "No, hear me out. I have told you, Grand Woodrowe, that I love you. I have loved you from the beginning, and now I have even more reason to love you."

"I told you," he said hotly, "that I don't want your pity."

"To hell with pity," she said. "There are more important things. What I carry here is more important, vastly more important." She stood, placed her hand on her stomach.

He looked at her, his eyes narrowing.

"My child will have a father, his own father, you."

He did not speak, but there was a softening in his eyes. A smile formed. He rose, touched her as if she were something very dear and very fragile. "Is it true? How long have you known?"

"Not long," she said. "At first I thought it was merely the result of newness, of change."

"But is it true?"

"He will be kicking soon," she said. "Then you can feel him."

"A child," he said. "By God, a child." He whirled her around gaily. "Oh, by God, what a gift you have given me, what a wonderful gift."

He halted. "I didn't hurt you?"

She laughed. "No, silly."

"Oh, Mindy, Mindy, you can't imagine what this means to me. I had thought—"

"Yes, darling, I know," she said. "And I should have told you sooner, but I wanted to be sure."

"We'll have to get married, directly."

"Chota thinks we should."

"She knows?" He frowned in mock severity. "So everyone has been in on the secret but me, eh?"

He started to kiss her, pulled back. "Oh, damn," he said. "No. It wouldn't be fair to you, Mindy."

"Grand," she said, "you know I don't use profanity. But listen to this. I will not hear any more of this self-pitying *holani*, this shit, from you. You've made my belly swell, as the old saying goes, and, by God, you're going to be a father to your son."

"Or daughter," he said. "Yes, you're right. It does change things, doesn't it? There's someone else now. We cannot think only of ourselves."

The wedding was a simple one, performed by an Indian Baptist minister. At the feast which followed it, the entire community celebrated. Grand seemed to be himself, proud, handsome, gay. Wynema, helping Chota with food and service, had never seen anything so grand and gay. And she had never seen a more beautiful woman than Miranda. In the weeks she'd been at Crossroads an entire new life had opened for her. Once she'd been one of many children in a hovel, with never enough to eat. Then the time with Rupe, plenty of food, but with blows, often, with smelly old men. It had been a long, long time since a man had "done business" with her, and she found that she didn't miss it at all. She took great pride in her appearance, even if it was a little drab by her former standards, her dresses long, lacking the pretty feathers and the low-cut neckline. She was always clean and neat and she had come to adore Chota.

Wynema had heard whisperings about what had been done to Grand by her man, Rupert, but aside from Grand's liking for privacy and his melancholy, he looked very much the man. And Miranda. Never had she seen a woman so beautiful, so kind, so considerate. For Miranda and Chota she worked hard, never complaining, often taking on tasks which had not been asked of her. And the world of the store was a magical one of which she never tired.

She wondered, as the wedding feast came to a close, what effect the new status of Mindy and Grand would have on her. There had been no talk for weeks about finding a good place for her. The thought of leaving Crossroads made her want to weep.

Mindy, glowing, happy, saw the last guests out the door and sat down with a pleasant tiredness. "I get you something, Miss Miranda?" Wynema asked. "Food, drink?"

"No thank you, Wynema," Mindy said. "Oh, it's been such a lovely evening."

"You so pretty," Wynema said. Then, because Chota had been working with her, trying to teach her better English, she said, carefully, "You are very pretty, Miss Miranda."

"What a lovely thing to say. Thank you, Wynema."

"You—are you happy?" Wynema asked.

"Very. And you?" She looked at Wynema with a smile. "Are you happy, Wynema?"

Wynema thought out her answer carefully and

said, in impeccable English, "If I should become
any happier—" and then she blew it totally "—I
bust gut."

They were alone for the moment. Mindy
laughed. "So you like it here?"

"Very much."

"Think you'd like to stay for a while?"

Wynema felt a chill. Was this the time, with
the marriage and all, that she'd be told she was
going to have to leave?

"I like—I would like very much to stay, Miss
Miranda. I work hard." It wasn't always possible
to remember how to speak properly. "I do everything. I clean, I cook. I take care of baby for
you."

"Ah, you know about that, do you?"

"See you sick ever' morning."

"You're terrible," Miranda said, with a fond
smile, "spying on me." There'd been such a
change in the girl. It was hard to believe, from
looking at her cheerful face, that she'd been
crawling in the dirt, beaten, a child whore. "But,
yes, Wynema, you will stay with us. I'm sure
Chota feels the same way. You're a big help to
all of us, in the store, with the work. You may
stay as long as you like."

Impulsively, Wynema bent, threw her arms
around Miranda. "Thank you. Thank you so very
much."

Chota had suggested a honeymoon trip, but
neither Grand nor Mindy would hear of it. Caleb
was a total invalid. And it seemed that the paral-
ysis had affected his mind, so that he was often
vague, always disinterested in life.

Grand came in from helping the last guests

hitch up their horses, Chota behind him. He took Mindy's hand and led her into Caleb's room.

"Well, dad," Grand said, "it's done. We're all legally hitched."

The old man opened his eyes and looked at them disinterestedly.

"We're married," Grand said. "Miranda and I. And there's something else, dad. Something which I think you'll be happy to learn. Miranda's going to have a baby."

For a moment there was a spark of life in the old man's eyes. Then he opened his mouth and the words were a blow to Miranda. "By who?" he said. "Not by a gelding."

Sick as he was, she could have hit him, not for the insult to her, but for what the words did to Grand. "It happened before the—" She could not find a word.

"Before the gelding," Grand said bitterly.

"Well," Caleb said, speaking clearly, seeming to be very much alert, "I hope it's a man child, so that he can grow up quick and do what neither you nor me is man enough to do, go get that bastard."

"Yes, you always have a nice way of putting things," Grand said, but Caleb had sunk, once again, into his usual state of near unconsciousness. Miranda put her hand on Grand's arm and led him out.

"He's right, you know," Grand said. "Glendower shot him in the back and then he cut off my balls. And I'm not man enough to go after him."

"It doesn't matter," Miranda said, hurting with

him. "It's all over. Someday he will be punished. I won't have you talking like this. I won't have you thinking of going after him. You're needed here."

He prepared for bed in another room, entering the room which had been his, and would be theirs, in a long nightshirt. He blew out the lamp and crawled into the bed. She was lying on her back, in a pretty little nightgown. He did not touch her. She did not break the silence for a long time. And then, fearful, but determined, she said, "Doesn't the bride get a kiss?" She rolled over, leaned on one elbow over him. The light of the moon coming in the open window was on his face. His eyes were open, staring. She bent and put her lips on his, held the kiss, put her weight on him. Gradually she could feel the change in him. When his arms came up to clasp her she sighed, and let her body sink against his.

"Oh, Grand, Grand, I do love you."

He did not speak. She didn't know what to expect, but her pulse pounded wildly when his breathing changed, and his hands began to know her, as they'd known her before, clasping the smooth buttock under her gown, lifting it, running his hands up and down her legs, her thighs, her rump, into the heated softness there, between her legs. And, wonder of wonder, as she extended a tentative hand, he was there, man, rigid, hot to the touch.

"Oh, my," she gasped, as her fingers closed over the rigidity. "Oh, my."

He laughed. "I don't know about the future, but right now let's get rid of this." He meant her nightgown. She sat up, lifted it over her head, then tenderly denuded him, placed her woman's softness atop him, feeling his staff hard and firm between her legs. His mouth took her in total surrender, she felt melty, all softness and want. His hot, wet mouth covered her breasts, traced fire down her stomach, onto her neck, and then he was turning her, positioning her.

And just before he entered, he halted, hardness there, just touching. "The baby?"

"It won't hurt, darling. It won't hurt the baby."

Ah, ah. "Oh, God," she moaned, having him, taking him, seating him deeper with an upward motion, legs going high to clamp themselves around his body, wanting him to keep on going in forever and ever to fill her, to make her his so totally that he could never, never again go away from her into his shell of melancholy. "So long," she whispered, "it's been so long, and you're so very, very good."

Skyrockets. Thunder and lightning. Fulfillment. The squeezings and spasms seeming to go on forever and then, into it, into the midst of the most paroxymal experience of her young life, came his jerkings and he clung to her, and it was as it had always been.

"Oh, my dear love," she said, clinging, kissing, weeping in joy.

He groaned happily, holding her close. And before the dawn came, after a long, long siege of talking, he took her again, all the old fever there, all completeness. For over a week she was steeped in passion, luxuriated in being loved, gave of herself totally. It was so sweet, so total with them that when, in curiosity, she ran her hand under his rigid staff to feel the emptiness there, to let her fingertips caress the weals of the scar tissue, he merely laughed.

"Ask any man what's the best part of him," he said, "and nine times out of ten he'll jokingly say his balls. Only thing is, he's not joking. But I can't say I miss them too much."

He had already used her, hard and long, completely and with great energy, and, as he came to her again she felt, at first, a bit of soreness. "If you were any more a man," she said, "I couldn't stand it."

But then the stage came with mail and there was a package of books. She found him bent over a thick medical tome. He had not mentioned ordering the books, and she asked him what he was reading.

"Getting educated," he said in a noninformative way. Seeing that he was bemused by the book, she left him. When he came out for dinner his eyes were red from his reading under the dim light, for he had been at it all day and into the evening.

"All educated?" she asked.

"More than I'd like to be," he said moodily.

She brought up the subject again when they were in bed. He broke the pattern of the past few nights by lying on his back, hands under his head, his eyes staring at the ceiling.

"Grand, what is it? Something in the books?"

He turned his head. "Nothing. Nothing, really."

"Hey," she said, "this is Mindy. Your wife. The mother of your child. Remember me?"

He laughed, rolled to take her in his arms. But, as he came to her, after their mutual passion had reached a point near explosion, he said, "Better make the best of it. Get it while we can."

She didn't push him. Instead, while he was out, she went to his books. He had left book marks at selected places. She had trouble with the large words and medical terms, but, after an hour of reading, she had the idea. She knew why, suddenly, his happiness, his optimism, had turned into moodiness.

"Grand," she said, when they were alone, in bed, her head on his shoulder. "I read your books."

"Ummm," he said.

"What it amounts to, Grand, is that no one really knows. Isn't that right?"

"There were two or three excellent case histories," he said.

"Yes, and they were inconclusive," she said. "One man had a normal life."

"And others didn't," he said.

"But you'll be like the one who had a normal life," she said. "I know you will."

"Will I?"

She used her hand, seized his limpness and, with her newborn expertise, began to manipulate him. There was an immediate response. "Any doubts?" she murmured, as he grew within her clasp. And then, with a quick movement, she threw off the sheet, kissed his chest, his muscular stomach, and, with a gasp of desire, closed her full-lipped mouth over the soft-hard tip of his manhood. He groaned in pleasure.

"All we have to do is work at it," she said. "See how long it takes? Hours." He laughed, for her attentions had put iron into his manhood.

"You'll always have me. If you have problems I'll apply some of the old magic," she said, using her tongue to send him into spasms of delight.

For long months, as her stomach grew and they had to find alternate positions, it being uncomfortable for him to be atop her, it seemed that she was right. The baby grew with its mother in a haze of sensuality, with the father never able to get enough of her body. And then it was time, the baby being quite large, to abstain. Grand complained good-naturedly, saying that the little brat was being selfish, taking up so much room.

Caleb Woodrowe died two days before the baby was born. It was not unexpected, for he had apparently lost his will to live. He was buried in the nearby Choctaw cemetery under an icy clear winter sky while old Indian women chanted the ancient words and Chota's Baptist minister added the words of the Bible. Mindy's first hint of a contraction occurred while she stood by the graveside, and she didn't mention it. The discomfort continued as friends and relatives came, bearing food, to comfort the survivors in the age-old manner.

Grand, unaware that her time was near, spent as much time as he could alone, secluded in their room. She found him there, thinking that he was in private mourning for his father.

"I wish I could have known him before the shooting," she said. "From what you and Chota say, he was a wonderful man."

"More man than his son," Grand said.

"Grand, don't," she said, going to him, her stomach huge, feeling the beginnings of another contraction. "Don't blame yourself."

"The man who shot him is still alive," Grand said. "All my Choctaw ancestors are spinning in their graves."

"That's long past," Miranda said. "It's been over a century since the Choctaw engaged in bloody revenge killings."

"He's still alive," Grand said. "And I'm only half alive."

The contraction hit in full force, her face went white, and she had to sit down, clasping her bulk. He did not notice at first, then he saw and leaped to kneel in front of her.

Births and deaths come together, nature replacing the dead with a new person, red of face from the forced entry into strangeness, wailing weakly in protest against the new world into which he has been jerked from the safety and warmth of the womb. Swiftly, after mourning, there is rejoicing at a new life.

She saw him fresh from her womb, the wetness of the birth still on him, hanging from Chota's hand by his heels as Chota slapped his bottom and the protesting wail carried through the house to relieve a worried Grand, pacing the parlor, exiled by the women.

"A boy," Chota said. "A fine one."

"He is grand," Miranda Woodrowe said.

It was a fairly easy birth. Like most first-time mothers, her labor was long, but when, at last, the contractions came close together the baby was not long in coming. And she had been fully aware, with no mind-numbing drugs. Long talks with Chota had prepared her for it. On the removal journey, pregnant women merely fell out of the line of march, squatted beside the trail, gave birth and rejoined the cavalcade, perhaps being allowed to ride for three or four days after giving birth.

"There is only enough pain," Chota had told her, "to show you what to do. It will hurt, but it is a sweet hurt."

And so it was and she was there, alive, feeling, fully aware, to be told when the baby's head was first showing, when the head came out, grunting with effort, then feeling the huge, tearing, spreading delivery and going black for only seconds.

"Grand," she said.

"Yes," Chota said, "he is a fine little boy."

"Healthy looking little bugger," Wynema, who had assisted, said with a laugh.

"Grand," Mindy said weakly. "That is his name. Grand Caleb Woodrowe, Jr."

"That is your decision?" Chota asked.

"Yes."

"Then the grandmother approves," Chota said, placing the newly cleaned baby at Mindy's breast.

And so the new year began in death and in new life as the always undecided weather alternated between clear, almost warm days and days and nights of howling wind as the huge, cold masses of air moved down from the great plains to the north and west bringing snow and sleet. Mother and son had been installed in a room of their own, a room which Wynema took as her responsibility.

"I do declare," Chota complained, "that girl does love you, my daughter, so much so that I find it difficult to be a grandmother." And, to Wynema. "Now here, child, give me that baby. Grandmothers have some rights around here.

You can't be playing with him every minute he's awake."

Later, in the light of events, Miranda blamed herself. When there is a new baby in the house, the father becomes superfluous. In the bustle of midnight feedings, croup, baby's bowel problems, the joys of seeing the early development when baby first moves his eyes to follow a finger, for example, the father is there to be an observer, and to gingerly lift the small bundle, fearful of breaking it, and made funny sounds. Mindy knew that she wasn't seeing much of Grand, but she was so busy with the baby. She knew he had some construction project underway, had, indeed, started it before the birth of the child, but she didn't see it until one day in late February.

She began to realize that she was seeing Grand only at mealtimes, that he had, once again, withdrawn into himself. Little Grand was now a month old. She was back on her feet in good style and had only some loose stomach muscles to show for her child-bearing. She dressed warmly and went in search of him.

The building was not a work of art. It was barnlike. Of boards, with a split cedar roof, it was almost thirty feet long and not quite as wide. From a tin smokepipe there emerged heavy smoke which, on that day with a new norther just beginning to threaten, poured down over the cedar shakes and clung to the chill ground. She felt the chill on her cheeks as she crossed from the living quarters at the back of the store to the new building and when she stepped in it was as if a blast of warmth hit her. The building was tight and it was warmed to the sultry heat of a

July day by a roaring fire in a Franklin stove
which glowed red on the sides.

Grand was painting. He appeared not to hear
her come in. She unwrapped a bit and walked to
stand behind him. The canvas on the easel was
not a composition, but a group of heads, full face
and in profile, the faces of the Choctaws.

"Ummm, nice," she said.

Grand merely said, "Ummm."

"You told me once that you'd never painted
anything from your Indian background," she
said. "I'm so glad you're working."

"Yes," he said, looking up at her to give her
a fleeting smile. "Just doodling, really."

"Do you know," she said, "I've scarcely seen
you in weeks. The baby has just demanded all
my attention. Poor Grand, neglected and lonely."
She put her arm on his shoulder and squeezed.
"Have you missed me?"

"Yes, of course," he said, but he was reaching
for a brushload of paint.

"All right, since you're involved, I'll go back
into the house."

"All right," he said.

He looked at her again. There was something
in his face. She examined him as if seeing him
for the first time. Yes, a heaviness. His face was
not as lean, more rounded.

"See you at dinner," she said, kissing him on
the cheek.

As the days passed, Grand's habits became
established. Breakfast, a look at the baby, a few
minutes of play, holding the boy who was learning all sorts of interesting things like how to hold
onto father's finger, and then he would seclude

himself in his new studio, coming out only to eat lunch, often going back after dinner to paint by lantern light or to read, sitting in front of the glowing stove. At times the sound of his ax could be heard from the house as he split wood for the fire.

Mindy made it a point to visit him in the studio at least twice a day, taking hot coffee, a snack. He had become a voracious eater and, indeed, he was putting on weight. His lean frame filled, but aside from a new roundness in the face he carried the weight well. He was always considerate and polite, but Mindy began to realize that unless she initiated conversation her time with him was spent in silence.

She went back to his bed without being asked. It was, she felt, time. She had glowing memories of those few months before the baby was born when neither of them could get enough of love, and now that her time of waiting was past, birth damage completely healed, she approached his bed with some misgivings and with much anticipation.

He was already abed when she came in in a newly made nightgown. He was reading by the dim light of a lamp.

"Ruin your eyes," she said.

"Ummm," he said.

"Sir, at the risk of being forward and brazen," she said, seating herself on the side of the bed, "I must remind you that it is time for you to resume the swift and eager completion of your conjugal duties."

He looked at her. A faint smile crossed his lips. "Has it been that long already?" he asked.

"It may not seem long to you," she said, throwing herself into his arms. "But, oh, darling, it's been a long time for me."

His kiss seemed to be somewhat reserved. "You haven't missed me," she said playfully.

"Oh, but I have," he said. "I have missed you, more than you'll ever know."

And she let herself sink into his arms, into the warmth and strength of him. Her young and healthy body was crying out for him, loving his caresses, his lips at her breasts. She was not thinking, really, only feeling, knowing that sweet desire to be possessed by the man she loved. She sat up, threw off her gown, and pressed her hot nakedness to him, began to work at removing his nightshirt.

"No, wait," he said, holding her hands, then beginning to make love to her so totally that she sank into a sweet and furry bliss, taking his kisses on neck, breast, stomach, knowing the tenderness of his hands. His skilled fingers sought and found a lovely spot, that bunched little rod of pure nerves which extended to the very core of her, manipulated, pressed, rubbed, fingers wetted by the glow of her passions, and, with a gasp, she pushed his hand away. It had been so long, so long, and she wanted more than that, wanted to know him and to have his entire body, to be penetrated.

"Oh, come to me, my darling," she whispered, reaching for him, trying once again to pull up his nightshirt. He held her hands, positioned himself, was atop her with his torso, his kisses so deep, so manly, his mouth so demanding. She sank into her bliss again and felt his sweet, warm kisses on

the sensitive skin of her stomach, his tongue
making circles around her naval, then his face
lowering, the heat of his breath, the feel of soft,
warm, wet lips on the most intimate portions of
her inner thighs and then, with a gasp, she
heaved up involuntarily as his mouth closed over
her womanhood and an eager tongue touched,
whipped back and forth and then probed.

"Oh, oh, please," she begged, but lost in it, so
deep into it that not even the crying out of her
entire being for all of him could give her enough
strength to make him stop. Heaving, not even
thinking that her wildness pressed so hard, so
hard against his soft mouth and then it was on
her and she cried out and it went on for an eternity with his soft lips and tongue and then she
was laughing.

"My God," she said. "But you're a beast, you
know."

"Yes," he said. He came to her and held her
in his arms.

"Well, as an appetizer," she said, and she extended her hand quickly, before he could stop
her.

To find only limpness.

"Grand?"

He put his hand on her wrist, and the clasp
was hard, painful, pulling her hand away from
him.

She felt a great surge of guilt. She had not
thought of him at all, had assumed that he felt as
she did. "Oh, darling," she whispered, raining
kisses on his face. "It's all right. What you did
was so lovely. I wasn't thinking. It's all right."

He pulled away from her and leaped from the

bed. She had to find her nightgown to follow
him. He had gone out of the room into the cold,
was standing on the porch. The wind whipped
her gown. She shivered, went to him, stood
behind him, close, arms around him, and his
chest was heaving and over the sigh of a cold
north wind she heard it, the heartrending, tearing,
painful sound of his sobs.

"Come," she said. "It's cold." And, like a
child, he let her lead him back to the bed. He
huddled, knees up. She cradled his head to her
breast and, gradually, his weeping ceased.

He had eaten an early breakfast and was in
the studio when she awoke, reaching out for him
to find him gone. When she had fed the baby
and finished her own meal she went to the studio,
trudging through new sleet, the skies above her
low, dark, threatening more weather.

"Mindy," he said, when she came to stand beside him to see, on the easel, a swirl of dark,
frightful colors. He had thrown paint, smeared
it, daubed it, and the result was a winter storm
over the sad, grey, barren trees of the hillside
outside his window. "I'm sorry."

"Grand Woodrowe," she said with mock severity. "I won't have such talk."

He was silent. He looked at the wet canvas
and, with a snarl, ripped it away from the easel,
tossing it to the unpainted plank flooring.

"It was quite powerful, the painting," she said.

"How the hell would you know?" He was
sorry immediately, looking at her pleadingly. "I
didn't mean that."

"I know you didn't."

He dropped his eyes. "Something's happening

to me, Mindy. It's happening and there's not one damned thing I can do about it."

"There is," she said. "And I'll help. Will you let me help?"

"Yes," he said.

"Do you want to work now?"

"I think so."

"Work then. I have little Grand's bath to do."

Inside, the house warmed by generous wood fires, it was cozy and the gaiety of Chota and Wynema was contagious. She could not, being so happy with her child, loving her mother-in-law so much, be unhappy for too long. She was sure that her love, her help, would bring Grand back from the dismal, melancholy place where he was. She had full confidence, planned what she would do, cheeks flushing as the spirit of her sensual thoughts filled her. She'd always been able to inflame him with a mere kiss. Surely, remembering how he'd loved her so thoroughly during the early months of pregnancy, it could not be impossible to arouse those feelings in him again.

Her thoughts were broken by the arrival of two Choctaw men, members of the Council, looking for Grand. She directed them to the studio. At lunch she was unable to contain her curiosity, asking him what they wanted.

"Just to talk," Grand said.

He ate quickly and heavily and went back to his studio. The days passed in pleasant talk with Chota, with caring for the growing little boy, with an impromptu English lesson, delivered by both of them to a willing Wynema, who had, it seemed, become a part of the family.

Miranda went to his bed. His apparently disinterested kisses made her have a moment of doubt, but she would not give up easily. Naked, having coaxed him into the same state, she lay in his arms and whispered of her love and slowly, slowly, let her kisses cover his face, his lips. He seemed relaxed. He seemed to enjoy the feel of her. And, although she was thinking only of giving, the contact, the kisses, served to arouse her quickly so that it was sheer pleasure to make love to him. She did not hurry it. So nice to press her firm, full, milky breasts against him, so pleasant to open her legs and take his thigh between them, to feel his body pressed against her hot wetness. He'd always liked that. Once, when their relationship was new, he'd teased her into pressing that intimate portion of her anatomy against every surface of his body she could touch with it, and the scene had ended in an explosive togetherness.

They did not talk. She didn't know what to say, for the first time fearful of saying the wrong thing. Instead, she acted, a warm, passionate woman doing her utmost, using every weapon she could muster. She postponed touching his staff for a long, long time and then, hopefully, fearfully, she teased her way toward it, using her fingertips to tickle, to touch. She knew her first hint of fear when, upon reaching her destination, she found no sign of response.

When, her own passions a fire within her, she knelt over him, her hair loose, falling to tickle his stomach, his thigh, she used the ultimate weapon, soft lips and a hot tongue and, after long, long minutes of it found only smallness, limpness, there in her hot mouth, she did not know what to do. She persisted until he put his hands on her shoulders, half-lifted her, placed her on her back and gave a long sigh of, was it tiredness? Desire? Defeat? He lowered his face to her and quickly, almost brutally, brought her to swift completion with his mouth.

Three nights later the results were the same and, in desperation, she went to his books, reading them while he was in the studio. Nothing was explained fully. She resolved to find more books, books which would answer her questions. But in the meantime she could only try.

"Stop," he told her, that night. "I won't have you belittling yourself further."

"It isn't belittlement," she said.

"It's useless."

"Grand, we must try."

He pulled her away, forced her to lie beside him. "I have thought it all out," he said. "It's over for me, Mindy. We have to face it. That which made me a man is gone. The juices which once made fire in my veins at the sight of you have dried up."

"We don't know that. No one knows for sure. The book cites one case where a man continued a full sexual life for years."

"I've read the books," he said harshly. "The usual thing is total impotence after a few months."

"The book said that in some cases the impotence seemed to be mental, rather than physical," she said.

"I told you I've read the damned books," he said. "Now you have to face it, Mindy. I know you're a young woman, full of life. I'll do my best for you. There are ways. I have asked myself if it's all in my mind. Have you read the book by Sir Richard Burton?"

"No," she said.

"He gained the confidence of the wife of a eunuch. He was told that the husband practiced, and I quote, the manifold *plaisirs de la petite oie*."

"And what is that?" she asked.

He placed his hand on her, used his fingers to bring immediate feeling to that small core of bunched nerves. "This," he said. "And this." He thrust a finger carefully into the soft folds of her. "And," he said, "above all, this." And he fell down to use his lips and tongue and she tried to push him away, wanting to protest, to tell him that he must try, that she wanted him, all of him, but his sweet kisses weakened her, left her to fall into it, to lift, to heave and know completion. Then it was she who wept.

The next night, she kissed him sweetly. "Good night, my love," she said.

"Good night." He turned his back to her and she lay awake, wanting him, quiet tears wetting her pillow. He did not come into the house for lunch, and she, feeling guilty but not wanting to spoil her day by his gloom, did not go to him. And thus a pattern was established.

When she did go into the studio she would find him hard at work, immersed in it. Faces. Indian faces. And, gradually, he seemed to gain direction. He prepared a large canvas and, as the winter days became longer, the sun in the sky ever more strong, he sketched out a scene,

mounted Spanish soldiers in gleaming breast-
plates, Choctaws in the ancient garb of the tribe.

"I think it's going to be very powerful," she
said.

"It's just a preliminary thing," he said, almost
grudgingly.

"Preliminary to what?" she asked.

"For that, you'll have to wait and see," he said.
"I must tell you, Mindy, that pleasant as your
presence is, it distracts me."

Hurt, she was silent for a moment. "Sorry,"
she said. "I'll go."

"Yes," he said.

12

While Miranda's young son grew fat and sassy and while Grand secluded himself more and more in his studio, the Choctaw Republic was entering one of its most troubled periods. The railroad had pushed south from Chouteau and Muskogee. The problems began immediately after the rail construction crossed the Choctaw border. The railroad refused to make payments for right of way, claimed an exemption from taxation by the nation, disrupted the ordered business dealings of the Nation by purchasing wood, stone, supplies from individual citizens in complete indifference to the law which placed such dealing under the control of the Nation. Minor problems, too, added to the burden of the new Principal Chief, the sad-eyed William Bryant.

Choctaw hogs ran wild in the woods under common ownership, and they were the main source of meat. Stupid animals, they quite often fell victim to passing trains and railroad claims agents arrogantly refused to pay, saying that it was up to the Choctaws to protect their hogs. Other livestock were killed, since the railroad failed to fence the right of way.

Great bitterness was aroused by freight and passenger charges, which, for reasons unexplained, were excessive. It was cheaper to buy a ticket anywhere outside of Indian Territory, for the railroad charged double fare to points within the Nations, and freight charges were so high that one of the main benefits, the shipment of farm produce out of the territory, was not realized.

Former Chief Coleman Cole had protested all those things to the Secretary of the Interior, without satisfaction, and Chief Bryant was doing his best to get the ear of Washington, also without satisfaction.

When he came to the home of the Woodrowes, he had all those things and more on his mind and he became quite angry when Grand refused to come from his studio to talk with him. Chota did her best to smooth things over, telling the Chief that her son had not been the same since his tragedy.

Bryant, who, to Miranda, looked as if he had considerable white blood, had been a close friend of Caleb Woodrowe. He knew that Chota had a good mind, and, in fact, he needed someone to talk with. He swallowed his anger with the good, hot coffee she served.

"I will speak with him," Chota said. "It is my guess that you want something of him."

"We have others who can speak for us," Bryant said. "But young Grand has an Eastern education. He has lived among the white men and he knows their mind."

"Mr. Bryant, if I may speak," Mindy said. "I am sorry to say that in his present condition I don't think my husband will be interested in helping."

"Well, that is a sadness," Bryant said. "In the time of troubles the Nation needs all of her sons. But we will have to cope."

He settled back and found himself telling the two women about the problems with the railroad. And then he surprised himself by telling them the most serious worry. "There is a bill presently before Congress which concerns us very much," he said. "It is, of course, backed by the railroad. If it is passed I fear that it will be the beginning of the end."

"What is this bill?" Chota asked.

"There are many in Washington and elsewhere who laugh when we call ourselves a Nation," Bryant said. "They say it is a fiction to say that the Indian tribes are sovereign, that we have the right to make treaties with the United States, the right to bargain with the railroad. If the law is passed, the congress will dictate to us the terms with which we deal not only with this railroad but with all others in the future. We had, in fact, wanted your son to go to Washington to speak for us, to tell the Congress of our thoughts."

"I wish that he would," Chota said, "but he is not himself."

"May I speak?" Mindy asked.

Bryant nodded. How things had changed. Now the Principal Chief of what was once the largest tribe of the East was being counciled by women.

"You will think I am forward and foolish," Mindy said uncertainly. "But perhaps, if you'd allow me, I might be able to help in a small way."

"In what way, my child?" Bryant asked.

"The Senator from California has visited my mother's house quite often," Mindy said. "I know him well. I know he is only one Senator, but he is a respected and powerful man. If I could speak with him, explain to him the entire situation here—"

"And do you know the entire situation?" Bryant asked, with a smile.

"I've had a good teacher," Mindy said, smiling at Chota. "And I've heard my husband talk. I was with him in Chouteau when he was in conference with the other tribes. I'm sure I don't know everything, but you could help me, tell me what to say. If we could get the Senator from California on our side—"

"Yes, we need all the help we can get," Bryant said. "But to send a woman as a representative." He shrugged. "And a white woman at that."

"Perhaps white listens to white better than white to Indian," Chota said.

"I would not be an official representative," Mindy said. "But the Senator is a good friend of my mother's. He will remember me. He will, at least, listen to me."

"It is a novel idea, and not without merit," Bryant said. "In such times we must grasp at all straws. Yes, Mrs. Woodrowe, if you will do this thing for my people—"

"For our people," Mindy said. "Forgive me, for that is the way I feel, in spite of being white."

"Yes," Bryant said. "Well, time is of the essence."

He spent the rest of the afternoon talking with them, telling Mindy the problems, instructing her, advising her, and all the while feeling quite strange. It was such a departure from tradition, but then the old traditions had been dying one by one from the arrival of de Soto in Mississippi, so what was one more tradition to break? He would not however, tell his Council, his fellow members of the government, that he was entrusting a mission of great importance to a young white woman not quite past her childhood.

When she told Grand that she would be leaving, told him the nature of her journey, he did not turn from his canvas. "If you feel that's the thing you must do, then do it," he said, in that distant and disinterested voice which had been his for weeks, months. Her eyes misted, but she had no time for weeping. She did weep, and quite openly, as she kissed her son goodbye and boarded a surrey for the ride to the railhead. Wynema was overjoyed, for it had been decided that she would accompany Mindy as friend and servant, to look after Mindy's clothing and her needs.

"I am going with Mrs. Woodrowe to see the Great White Fathers in Washington City," she said to the Choctaw boy who was driving the surrey.

"Perhaps they will scalp you," the boy joked.

"My mistress would never allow such a thing." Wynema was quite proud of her newly learned English, and always thought before speaking, rarely breaking into her old broken ways of speaking. And while the train was still in Indian Territory, she began to ask, "When will we arrive in Washington City?" Until, wearied by trying to explain, Miranda told her simply to shut up and go to sleep.

At the first layover, when she rested from the long trip by spending a night in a Kansas City hotel, Miranda did something she'd been putting off for a long time. She labored over the wire for hours before arriving at the final version:

MOTHER, AM FINE, MARRIED GRAND WOODROWE. PLEASE WIRE SENATOR AM ON WAY TO WASHINGTON SEEKING MEETING. EXPLANATION BY LETTER. YOU GRANDMOTHER BABY BOY.

And then there was the letter to write and she found that even more difficult. In the end, she decided to be absolutely frank, filled page after page, ended with a plea for forgiveness. As she reread it, she could hardly remember the shock and unhappiness she'd known, and was amazed to find that she had not thought about the original purpose of her trip east, the idea of finding her natural mother. It no longer seemed important, for, having opened her heart on paper, she realized how much she had missed Liberty Lee, her mother.

The rest of the trip seemed long and wearing and even the improved sleeping cars could not make rail travel totally comfortable. Wynema's wide-eyed amazement at the cities, at the hugeness of the country, were a continued source of amusement to her, and she spent much of her time, a child herself in years, telling another child in years all she knew about the huge country which surrounded and threatened the Choctaw Nation.

Just how different the outside world was Wynema was to discover when she was refused a room in the hotel which Miranda had selected in Washington. The capital of the Union, which had fought to free the slaves, had its share of white-only philosophy. However, a place was found, not quite as desirable, and Miranda sent a messenger to the Senator's office announcing her arrival and her request for an early meeting with the Senator. In return, she received an invitation to tea at the Senator's house that very evening. She was pleased that things were moving so swiftly, for she missed her son very much.

She made the journey from the hotel to the fine, large house of the Senator in a hansom cab, arriving a few minutes early to be announced into a pleasant drawing room where the Senator was seated with his wife. He bounced up.

"This is young Miranda Lee?" he asked, beaming, taking her hands in his. "It can't be. Why you're all grown up and as beautiful as your mother."

"Sir," she smiled, "now I know why you are so successful in politics. You have a silver tongue."

His wife came, embraced Miranda, seated her after taking her wrap, served tea and asked if she'd had a pleasant trip from California.

"Oh, I haven't come all the way from California," Mindy said, "Only from Indian Territory."

"What on earth are you doing in Indian Territory?" the Senator asked.

"I live there," Mindy said, "with my husband and my son."

"It sounds quite exciting," the Senator's wife said. "Do tell me about it. Aren't you afraid, living among savages?"

"Madam, they are not savages," Mindy said.

"Well, I suppose your husband takes care of you, keeps you safe," the white haired lady said. "What is he, an Indian Agent?"

"Lots of rail activity there now," the Senator said. "Perhaps he's a railroad man."

"He is a Choctaw," Mindy said.

The lady gasped and covered her mouth with her hand. The Senator looked at her blankly.

"Actually, only part Choctaw," Mindy said. "He is an artist."

"Perhaps," the Senator said, "you'd best state your purpose." There was a noticeable chill in the atmosphere of the drawing room. The Senator's wife was still looking at her in shock.

"You actually live with the Indians?" she asked, reaching nervously for her teacup. "In a teepee or whatever?"

"We live with my husband's mother," she said.

"It's quite a comfortable house, not as grand as in the city, of course, but neat, clean, with plenty of room."

"Yes, well," the Senator said. "And to what do we owe the pleasure of this visit? I had assumed, from your mother's telegram, that it was social. In fact," he cleared his throat. "I had planned a social occasion in your honor." His wife looked at him, raising her eyebrows.

"There's no need for that, Senator," she said. "I'm quite eager to get back. I merely wanted to speak with you about the bill presently before the congress which would, in effect, take away the sovereignty of the Indian Nations."

He cleared his throat. "We have heard the views of the Indians," he said.

"Senator, my husband is an educated man. He holds two degrees from a fine eastern college. He is an excellent artist. When he was living in San Francisco he painted portraits of the best known people in society. He is a thoughtful man, and feels that eventually the Indian must become an integral part of the nation. He feels, however, that it is too soon. The Indians must have time to educate their children, to grow more accustomed to the white man's way. You know and I know that this bill is merely the first step. Next there'll be more attempts to give individual allotments of land to the Indians and then open the remaining land for white settlement and the Indian is simply not ready for that. I agree with my husband. I beg of you to consider what I have to say. Help to do away with the unfairness with which the railroad is treating the Indian. Give him more time."

"Your Choctaws have had hundreds of years," the Senator said. "I'm sympathetic. I don't think the Indian is ready to become a part of society, either. But I disagree with your husband on one matter. I don't think he ever will be ready to live as a white man lives."

"Oh, sir," she said, "I know I'm being presumptuous, but if you could only know them as I've come to know them you'd see how wrong you are. They are a gentle and intelligent people. They've worked hard, thinking that their Nation is their country forever. They've built schools and churches. They have a democratic form of government, a true Republic. They've had so many promises broken. Please try to convince the government that it should keep its last promise to them. Please help to defeat this bill. If the Nations are deprived of their right to negotiate with railroads, they'll simply be ignored and their land will be given to the railroads and the railroads will bring swarms of white men into the Nations to eventually overwhelm them."

"When I cast my vote," the senator said, "I will be voting the way I think best serves my own constituents in California and, secondly, what best serves the nation as a whole."

"I understand," she said.

"And I can understand your concern. You state your case very well, for one so young. I told your mother I would do everything I could for you in Washington, not knowing at the time the reason for your visit, and I will keep my word. I must warn you, however, that the Congress is in a mood of expansion. The whole country is feeling growing pains, and we're all intensely proud of what this young country has done in a few short years. From restricted areas on the eastern coast of this continent we've expanded from the Atlantic to the Pacific. There will come a time, my child, when the United States of America will be a force to be reckoned with in this world. We've fought two wars with one of the world's most powerful nations, and we've won. We're respected in every capital of the world. To continue to hold the position we've made for ourselves and to become even more respected, we need people, producing farms, industry, and we need expansion. You're not going to find very much sympathy for obstructionist talk. There are many who feel that we cannot long endure a totally dead and non-producing spot, a rather large spot I might add, right in the nation's heartland."

"But, Senator, it is not a dead spot. The Indians are producing. Do you know that they can't ship the farm surplus they have out of the territory because the railroad charges them prohibitive prices? If they paid the shipping costs the railroad is asking, then their goods would not be competitive outside of Indian Territory."

He mused for a moment. "Yes, that seems rather strange, doesn't it? As I say, my dear Miranda, you are quite convincing, in spite of your youth. I will arrange for you to speak, to state your case."

"I can ask for nothing more, sir," she said, "and I am grateful."

"I had planned, with my wife, a sort of gala for you," he said, "a purely social event. However, in view of our seriousness, I think we'll forego the dancing and music. If you're free, say Friday night, I'll arrange to have a few important people here and I'll see that you get an opportunity to give your full views."

She was more than ready when Friday night came around. She had spent the intervening time in seeing the sights of Washington City and in buying a simple little black dress for the occasion. The affair was a semi-formal dinner, with some sixteen people at table. Before the dinner she was introduced. There were three senators present, four of the more influential members of the House of Representatives and a man who caught her attention immediately. He was slim, tall, dressed in evening wear which fit him as if it had been designed for him, which, of course, it was.

"Miranda," the Senator said, "I want you to meet Mr. James Allen. Of all the men here he's the most knowledgable on Indian Affairs, with good reason."

"My question is this," Allen said, with a charming smile. "Why should such a lovely lady concern herself with anything other than staggering the senses of us helpless males, which she is doing?"

He was a young man, mid-thirties, she guessed. He had an air of assurance which spoke of education, background, wealth. When he smiled his face looked younger and there was a virility about him which caused Mindy to look at him in no less admiration than that which he was bestowing on her.

"James has been working closely with the

congressional committees involved in Indian Affairs," the Senator said. "Moreover, confirmation of his appointment to head the Bureau of Indian Affairs under the Secretary of the Interior is assured. I'm sure he'll be interested in your views."

"I'll be interested in anything you have to say, dear lady," Allen said.

They were joined by a congressman, the gentleman from Vermont, whom Mindy had met previously. "I don't know whether the Senator told you, but I'm vitally interested in helping to maintain the sovereignty of the Indian Nations," Mindy said.

The Congressman snorted. "My dear, that is a fiction which is out of date. A Nation? My word, how can a rational man look upon a few thousand Indians, who have steadfastly refused to accept the benefits of our American civilization, and equate them with a country such as, for example, France, or Great Britain? I assure you that the House of Representatives is sick and tired of this pretense, and sick and tired of the never-ending demands by these people. Every time I turn around the President is coming to us for more money for some reason or the other to give to the Indians, and it must stop."

"It will stop, Congressman," Allen said, with a mild smile, "if the Senate comes to the point of agreeing with the House."

"They will," the Congressman said. "Why, since Andrew Jackson, men of reason have thought that treaties with the Indians are an absurdity. Once this bill is passed no so-called Indian nation will be recognized as an entity with whom the United States government has to deal as if they had the power of a huge and powerful country."

"But that's exactly the wrong way to go about it," Mindy said. "The Choctaw Nation, with which I am very familiar, is a nation, in fact. It has a governing body, it has laws, a system of taxation—"

"Poppycock," the Congressman snorted. He smiled an oily smile and his harsh, Yankee voice filled the room. "You've been led astray, little lady, by the bleeding hearts. I hear of the valuable culture of these Indians. But let me tell you, I have studied the matter, and we are not trying to destroy anything valuable, anything rich and worth preserving. We are merely intent on bringing civilization to a people whose history is superstition, savagry and ignorance."

Mindy looked helplessly at James Allen, who shrugged. The Congressman, having preached his sermon, excused himself.

"Oh, dear," Mindy said.

"I fear that he is expressive of the majority opinion," James Allen said. "I'm sorry."

"And you?" Mindy asked. "How do you feel about it?"

Before he could answer, a servant announced that dinner was served. Mindy went into the dining room on Allen's arm. "I'd like to answer your question in detail," he said, "since you are so vitally interested, but I fear this isn't the place. Would it be too improper if I asked you to take dinner with me tomorrow night?"

She thought for a moment. If the bill passed,

as it seemed it would, James Allen, as head of the Bureau of Indian Affairs, would be a man whose slightest whim could have devastating effects in the Nations. He seemed to like her. It would not hurt at all to be nice to him, to, at least, try to convince him that not all Indians were savages and ne'er-do-wells. "I will be delighted," she said.

She had her chance at table, upon the Senator's cue, to talk about the achievements of the Choctaws and of their problems. The important men at the table listened politely, and one senator agreed that the Indians had not always been treated fairly. She could not assess how much impact she made before the topic of conversation went on to the recurrent scandals in the Grant administration and then fragmented into small groupings.

James Allen picked her up the next evening in a handsome carriage drawn by two beautiful white horses. The restaurant which he selected was quiet, luxurious, and the food delicious. He talked charmingly about the city, about his love for it, and revealed bits of information about himself along the way. The eldest son of an old New York family, he was, apparently, quite wealthy. His family had been among the original settlers, had fought in the French and Indian Wars and in the Revolution. To prepare himself for his important job, he had traveled to the far west, there to see some of the campaigns against the wild tribes. He readily admitted that he knew little about the so-called Five Civilized Tribes of Oklahoma country.

"If you should ever decide to take a tour of inspection," Mindy said, "we'll give you our best hospitality."

"The idea is interesting," he said. "Especially if you are the hostess."

"Our home is yours. It's not as grand as this, but it's comfortable. I'd like you to meet my mother-in-law. I think she'd give you a new insight into what Indians can be."

"I haven't dared ask how on earth you came to be married to an Indian," he said.

"Actually, I take more credit than I deserve. He's not full-blooded. His mother is three-quarters and his father white."

"To win you, he must be a wonderful man."

"He is." And she felt a wave of sadness, thinking of Grand as he was after the terrible mutilation at the hands of Rupert Glendower's thugs. "He's quite a fine artist."

She accepted his compliments as politeness, thinking nothing of it. When the meal was concluded, he suggested a view of Washington by night and drove past the Capitol, down the quad. It was a city of contrasts, beautiful in places and squalid in areas where displaced southern Negroes had built shanty towns. There was more serious talk about the problems of the Choctaws.

"I can only promise, as I assume my new position," he said, "to do my utmost to be fair, as fair as possible within the framework of laws passed by congress."

"We can hope for no more, I suppose," she sighed.

"And now I think we've had enough seriousness," he said. "A young and beautiful lady can't spend all her time fighting for others. I shall not let you leave Washington without seeing some gaiety. It happens that there is a ball to-morrow night. There you'll see the cream of Washington society, and I'll warrant you that you'll outshine them all."

"Heavens," she laughed. "I haven't danced since I was a young girl."

He laughed heartily. "And now you're an old lady? Well, we'll see. I'll come for you at eight-thirty." He gave her no opportunity to say no.

She knew that she should not accept the invitation. It was strictly social, had nothing to do with her mission, and yet he had said that important people would be there and perhaps she might have an opportunity to speak of her cause. Secretly, she knew that she was being selfish. Bright lights, gay laughter, music, people. It was all so different from life in Crossroads. A little self-indulgence would not be too sinful.

It was a huge and sprawling affair in a stately, rich mansion in an outlying area. The weather, unseasonably warm for early spring, allowed a spilling of people into lantern-lit gardens and patios. The main ballroom was crowded with ladies in their finest and gentlemen in frock coats. She danced with James and felt a lifting of her heart so that she was laughing happily. All the problems seemed to be so far away. She was a wife and a mother and yet she felt as if she were sixteen again, free to accept the compliments of the gentlemen who flocked to fill her dance card, although James reserved several dances for him-self.

Tables of fine foods tempted her, cold wine

cooled her from the heated dances. At times there would be half a dozen young men gathered around her. James was quite attentive and her dances with him were heady, exciting. He was an excellent dancer, making it easy for her to regain the skill which had been neglected. And his compliments, the look in his eyes, made her feel lovely and adored. When her conscience rose up she squelched it. She had earned a moment of ease. She deserved to be able to forget, for one night, that she was married to a man who had been mutilated, to forget his somber depression, to put aside all the problems and the day to day life in the Nation which had nothing to rank with the excitement and gaiety of Washington.

Throughout the evening and during the ride back to her hotel, James was the perfect gentleman. He took her hand to help her from the carriage, smiling up at her. And for a brief moment she was lost in the feeling of it, for his touch created a jolt of excitement in her so that she was reluctant to let go of his hand, standing there on the sidewalk looking up into his handsome face.

"It's been lovely, and I thank you for it," she said.

"My pleasure. I hope that it will not be our last evening together."

"I must be going home soon," she said. "I think I've done all I can. I have a little son and I miss him very much."

His face went serious. "Can't I keep you here for a few days longer?" He brightened. "If I should arrange for you to speak to a House committee working on differences between the House and the Senate would you think that worthwhile?"

"Of course," she said.

"It may take a few days."

"I'll be very grateful."

"Then show your gratitude by having dinner with me every night."

She withdrew her hand from his. "Sir," she asked, with a little smile, "are you trying to turn the head of a respectable married lady?"

"Alas," he said, with mock pain, "I know that it is hopeless, and I'm asking only for the pleasure of looking at you." He smiled gravely. "I shall, of course, respect your marital status."

"Then I shall be selfish and accept your invitation," she said.

She was a bit disturbed when he announced that she wouldn't be able to speak before the committee for five days, but she soon forgot, for now he took her on a whirl, sight-seeing by day, rides into the countryside, dinner and gay gatherings in various houses at night. As the day of her appearance before the committee approached, she looked forward to it with mixed emotions. She knew that she should quickly plan to return home as soon as the appearance had been made, and she felt a sense of great loss to think that it would all be over, that she would be on an uncomfortable train and that she would soon be back in Crossroads with Grand gloomily seeking the privacy of his studio each day.

She was aware of her atraction to James Allen and, in her bed alone at night she castigated herself for indulging her childish whims. She had a man who loved her, a man whom she loved.

But she had done nothing wrong, nothing of

which to be ashamed. It was friendship, and nothing more, and James was sweet to want to show her the gay life of the city before she returned to the slow pace of life in the Choctaw Nation.

And so, torn by conflicting desires, she was prepared and yet not prepared for what happened. She made her appearance before the house committee, was questioned rather rudely by the Congressman from Vermont, a member, and received courteously by the others. Again she did not know if she'd done any good, but at least she had tried.

James was waiting for her outside the committee room when she finished.

"Well done," he said. "Frankly, I don't think you can change any minds, but you may very well have eased the hard attitudes of some of them."

"You've been so kind," she said. "You have my thanks, and the thanks of everyone in the Choctaw Nation."

"That sounds like a farewell speech," he said.

"I'm afraid so. I must go home."

"Yes, I suspected it." He took her arm and led her from the building, installed her in the carriage. "I've taken the liberty of arranging a farewell luncheon."

He drove into a fine area of stately houses, gave the team and carriage over to a black retainer and guided her into a house which left her breathless. It was more luxurious than anything she'd seen in California. In the golden spring weather a light but delicious lunch was served by polite servants in a little spring house beside a fish pool containing giant, long-tailed goldfish who ate hungrily of crumbs from the table.

They sat there, moving from the small table, which was quickly cleared away, and had a glass of an excellent after lunch wine. He was moodily silent, his eyes riveted to her face. When he spoke his voice was intense.

"So now you're going."

"Yes, I must."

"You come into my life like a burning new star in the heavens and then you leave, without a backward glance. The skies will be black."

"Oh, James," she said. "Please don't."

"I know I shouldn't," he said, "but I can't help myself. When I think what might have been, Miranda—"

And it flashed through her, too. What might have been. A vital and handsome man, the excitement of the city, witty and sophisticated people. At the moment the charms of the Indian country looked dull and forlorn in comparison. But that was, she knew, a dangerous state of mind.

"Look, the fish are begging again," she said. She took crackers from a snack tray left behind by the servants and walked to the edge of the pool, arranged her skirts and sat on a rock to crumble the crackers into the pool. He came and sat by her side. A huge goldfish made gulping sounds as his snout extended out of the water in search of crumbs.

"I call him Ulysses, because he's the biggest fish in the pond," he said.

"Ulysses," she said, "you simply must learn not to eat with your mouth open, you gluttonous little monster."

He laughed and she turned her face to look at him. A charged current seemed to flow through her, for he was quite near. Her lips parted slightly in shock. She was unable to move as he leaned closer, closer, and then his lips touched her. The thrill almost caused her to swoon. Her eyes seemed to roll upward as they closed involuntarily, and her limbs felt filled with a leaden but golden inertia.

She made no resistance as he pulled her to her feet and, with a gusty sigh, took her into his arms. She accepted his kiss, her arms moving irresolutely, wanting to go around him, knowing that they should not. When, in the end, she was unable to resist, she clasped him, feeling his manly body against hers, his lips becoming more demanding.

"Oh, my Miranda," he breathed, and then resumed the kiss.

Weak, feeling her body fill with it, the sweet song of a spring bird, the buzzing of bees on nearby blossoms, the smell of the garden, a roaring in her ears, she melted into him and as he took her hand walked with him, her face upturned, accepting little, soft, pecking kisses as he led her toward the house, entered, went into a huge room with various chairs and sofas, one of which was quite huge and accepted them, she allowing him to seat her with his lips on hers all the while.

She was aware only of his hunger for her, of the sweet and sudden thrills which chased themselves up and down her spine, and the warm and buttery feeling of her stomach as he pressed hard against her, his tongue beginning to know the sweet insides of her mouth.

Her mind whispered "No, no," as he positioned her, lowered her, his arms strong and reassuring, to lie on the sofa and feel the weight of his body on hers, to know that he was trembling in need of her, to accept the cupping of his hand over one breast and to wiggle, position herself, offer no resistance when that seeking hand went under her clothing and pressed the bare breast under its bindings.

She was a woman of naturally passionate nature, and she had discovered it early in her life, at the age of sixteen, in Grand's arms. And for months she had been ignoring the natural desires, unable to satisfy them in her husband's bed because of his disability. She was caught quite by surprise by the almost paralysing force of it when he kissed her and it was as if her mind had blanked out all reality, knew only the delight of his fingers upon her breast.

Had he moved quickly it would have happened, but he, himself, was agonizingly conscious stricken. Captivated by her as he'd never been by any woman, he wanted her with all his body, all his mind save that part which told him he was doing wrong, wrong to her, wrong to himself. She was much more than a mere vessel for the release of his passions. She was a dear and lovely creature with the natural innocence of youth and he, a man of experience, was taking advantage of her.

And yet he could not stop, had to know more,

felt her breast burning in his hand and, fumbling, the clothing tugging uncomfortably in her soft skin, pushed and pulled until he had one sweet mound partially bared, lowered his lips to it. A molten and flowing passion grew under his lips and caused her loins to lift upward, to feel his manhood pressing through so many layers of clothing, her entire body crying out to be freed of the encumbrances, to be with him. And then he teasingly nipped the warm and swollen nipple and a picture of burning clarity burned into her mind. Little Grand, her son, her baby, at that same breast for other reasons, for his sustenance, not for passion.

And Grand, big Grand. Oh, God, she thought. How could she betray him when he'd gone through what he had, when his very life was ruined and she and the baby and his art were all he had?

Mind cleared, desire still burning but being overcome, she pushed at his chest. "No, James," she said. "No." And so firmly, so convincingly did she speak that he recognized the lost moment.

He removed his weight from her, sat on the sofa with his head in his hands. "I'm sorry, Miranda."

"It was as much my fault as yours," she said, sitting up, arranging her clothing.

"I beg your forgiveness," he said.

"There is nothing to forgive." She leaned and kissed him gently on the cheek. "It could have been, you and I, but it is too late. I must go now."

She was on board a train in the early morning,

with Wynema eager to get back home, telling her mistress that although the city was exciting it couldn't offer what Crossroads did, nice people who loved them, the beautiful openness of the big sky.

She did not try to look back. Soon she was into the trip, trying to block from her mind the memories of the past few days. She had her place. She had chosen it of her own free will, and had Grand not been reduced to the depths of despair by his tragedy, she would have been happy with it. The trip to Washington had taught her several things. First, she now knew that the Indians had few friends there, that they must recognize the inevitable need of becoming more like the white man. She had also learned something about herself. She was not the mature and self-sufficient adult she had thought herself to be, but had fallen victim all too quickly to the strain of passion which ran through her. She could not trust herself ever again. Never again would she allow herself to be put into a position where that natural sensuousness would betray her.

The days continued to warm as the train traveled westward and it was early summer heat, in spite of the earliness of the season, when they reached Chetopa and, wearied by the trip, she decided to rest one night there so that she would be fairly fresh on arriving home. Only two or three more days and she would see her child. She went to sleep thinking of him, of her little Grand. She awoke next morning to Wynema's insistent voice.

"Miss Miranda, wake up. It's getting late, almost six." She moaned, rolled over, opened one eye. "Message for you already," Wynema said. "The desk clerk sent it up."

She took the envelope and opened it and read the words which would bring back one of the unpleasant aspects of her life, a fact that she chose, most often, to forget.

13

The message which would change Miranda's life came as the result of a coincidence which had happened, without Miranda's knowledge, some months previously. It had its roots in her past and in the mind of Rupert Glendower. Since leaving Indian Territory for the second time with the law on his heels, much had happened to Glendower. At first, he had gone about his attempts to organize an expedition of settlement into the Unassigned Lands, and had quickly become discouraged. Although there was much talk about the unfairness of the land not being used, no one was interested enough to actually try to take the land by going in without government permission to settle on it.

Another event drew Glendower's attention and sent him on a different path which would, surprisingly, have a direct effect on Miranda. He came out of the Territory with gold in his pocket and so he was not reduced to hunger or work for the moment, and with gold in his pocket, after weeks without a woman, he made a visit to the place which still enjoyed the protection of the Arkansas City sheriff.

After an exchange of coins, he was escorted into a bedroom and told to wait. He took off his coat and boots, poured a drink, and sat down with his feet thrust out.

The woman who entered the room was not as young as he would have liked. She was dressed in a flowing lounging outfit which featured many feathers and much lace and showed off the creamy curve of breasts. She smiled at him.

"Would you like to fix me a drink?" she asked, with a smile which showed rather nice teeth.

"Sure," he said.

She sat on the edge of the bed, the dressing gown falling open to reveal one well-formed leg crossed over the other. He handed her the drink. "I hope you're not in a hurry," she said. She had a hint of what he knew was a Texas drawl.

"What part of Texas?" he asked.

"Ah, you're quite perceptive, eh? The gulf coast, originally. I was born in New Orleans."

"Little French?" he asked.

"My father was French," she said.

He examined her a bit closer. She had full lips, broad cheeks, dark eyes and hair which had been no telling what original color but was now blond. There was just a touch of swarthiness to her skin.

"And a little Indian," he said.

"Ah, but we don't talk about that, do we?" she asked.

"Why not? Some of the best women I've ever known were Indian." He sat beside her and let his hands get a little familiar. She accepted his attentions with a smile. Up close one could see a few tiny wrinkles around the eyes and mouth. He guessed her, however, to be no more than late thirties.

"I will make you forget them," she promised, kissing him. "Once you have loved Madame Girondin you will always want to come back to her."

"Well," he said, his blood becoming more and more heated, "we'll see about that."

"Was I right?" she asked later, eyes hooded, smiling up at him as he grinned down at her, relaxed, the initial rush over.

"What's this Madame stuff? Don't you have a name?"

"It is," she said, "Lilah. Do you like it?"

"Sure," he said.

He liked other things better and there was little talk for a while. Then they drank and he just looked as she lay in a seductive pose on the bed, clothing nowhere in evidence.

"And do you have a name?" she asked.

"Rupert."

"Not Rupert Glendower?"

"Why do you ask?"

"I've heard of you. Ran a string of young bangtails, right?"

"Right."

"So why do you come to Lilah?"

"Lost 'em. All of 'em."

She was curious, and he found himself telling her all. And in the course of it, as he spoke of his out and out hatred for Grand Woodrowe and his San Francisco slut, Miranda Lee, she began to question him more closely. She laughed when he told of how he'd fixed the Indian by cutting off his balls, and said, "Ohhh," when he told of Miranda's lucky shot which almost killed him.

"Someday," he said, "I'll get that little bitch where I want her."

"Her name, you say, is Lee?"

"Yes. She came east looking for some kid, some woods colt dropped by her father by a woman named—" He paused, looked at her closely. "By God," he said.

She was not looking at him. There was a pensive look on her face. "How old are you?" he asked.

"Old enough."

"Old enough to have had a kid by one Danny O'Lee about seventeen or so years ago?"

"That is my business," she said.

"You're Lilah. You're from Texas. You're what, about thirty-five, thirty-eight?"

"Close enough," she said. "Tell me about the girl."

"Ah," he said. "By God, it is you. Now you tell me, damnit, you're her mother, aren't you?

She wasn't looking for some kid, she was looking for her mother."

"Did she say that?"

"She gave me cock-and-bull stories," he said. "But you shacked up with this Danny O'Lee and you had his kid, right?"

"Yes," she said. "Is she pretty?"

"She's a beauty," he said. "She'd be worth a million dollars in a house."

"But she's with an Indian?"

"Part Indian. Married to him now, I hear. Oh, God, do I owe that wench."

"I'd like to see her," Lilah said. "Not speak to her, just look at her."

He was thinking a mile a minute. "She's very pretty. Dark hair and dark eyes. Same lips."

"My hair is naturally dark," Lilah said.

"Lilah, listen. If you want to see her, she'd come to you if you sent a message."

"I don't know," she said. "I've never seen her, you know. I didn't even look at her when she was born. They took her away and an Indian woman wet-nursed her. Then he took her, I understand. Did she say?"

"I don't know. I just know she's from San Francisco. Wears nice clothes, talks educated. Has the instincts of a whore."

"You can't know that," Lilah said.

"I know that I owe her," he said. "Listen, I've got a proposition for you. How much money are you making here? I know how much I pay, but how much of it do you get? Hell, you don't even have to answer that. I'd guess you get maybe half. You're a fine looking woman, Lilah. And

I'm a man with ideas. I'm gonna have me a house which will make these places look like the dumps they are. And you can run it."

"All of a sudden you're a big man," she said.

"Now you take Chetopa. It's wide open. I've got a little nest egg there. We'll build a place and you'll run it and it'll have the finest bar and the best furnishing in any house in the west. We'll get some young gals—"

"I don't like that," she said.

"Well, the customers do. Indians, what have you. We'll have the regular girls, they're a dime a dozen if you have a nice house, but we'll specialize in the young ones. You run it. You'll be my partner."

"Do you really have money?" she asked.

"Enough," he said. "You interested?"

"I like one word you used. Partner."

"All right, fine. We'll leave in the morning."

"Not so fast, buster," she said. "First I see the money."

"All right," he said. "I'll go ahead. I'll get things started. I've been planning this in my head for a long time. I know just what I want. You know any girls who might like to come along with you?"

"I can think of maybe two."

"That's a start. I know how to get the young ones."

It was true that he had money. The way he got it was his own business. He'd come out of the territory with some in his pocket and there was some stashed in the bank in Chetopa, money he'd saved during the heyday of his traveling show with the six young bangtails. And there was

more. When, on getting back to civilization, he'd
realized that he didn't have enough money in his
savings and his pockets to do the thing he'd decided to do, he did just the one job. He rode
miles away from Arkansas City and luck was
with him. He shot the guard from ambush, winged
the driver, chased down the runaway horses and
told the two passengers in the stage that all he
had to see was one face and they were both dead.
The strongbox had over a thousand dollars in it.

It was so very easy it was tempting to continue,
but he was smart enough to know that it's the
repeaters who finally get caught, the people who
are so stupid they're not content with one good
haul, but keep going out with a gun time and
time again. In his case, dead men told no tales.
Neither the driver nor the shotgun was alive to
describe him and he'd been masked, on a stolen
horse which he ditched quickly. One good haul,
that was all he wanted, and he'd been lucky to
have so much in the strongbox.

He hired workmen and made drawings and began to order the furnishing from Kansas City.
Things were going damned well and he'd sent
word to Lilah in Arkansas City to join him with
the girls she'd hired. And then he saw the little
Indian girl. She wasn't more than fourteen and
she reminded him a lot of Wynema. It was easy,
because she was peddling it already. She was
laying it down for fifty cents in the freight yard
of the railroad and he took a look at her. Scrawny,
dirty. But she'd clean up. Trouble was his liking
for the young ones. He had to sample the merchandise.

Six days later he went to the outhouse and almost screamed as the flow of his fluid was accompanied by a pain which hit him in the most intimate portion of his body and lanced upward. The discharge started that night. Infuriated, he beat the little Indian girl, kicked her bodily out of the shack he'd rented for her, and made his way quickly to the local quack.

Treatments with mercury seemed, at first, to have it under control. He went about his business. The house was rising, the walls up.

"Looks like you're one of the lucky ones," the doctor told him. "Sometimes it can be bad, but I think we've got it whipped."

He was almost ready to laugh about it. Not as bad as he'd thought. So he'd had his dose and he'd learned his lesson. No more strays. He'd be sure when he began to gather his young ones that they were clean. He began to look forward to the arrival of Lilah and the girls. Try them out. Hell, the owner had to audition talent, didn't he?

But the day they were to arrive the pain hit him like a burning arrow in the soft regions far up inside him, back there where, although he didn't know much about anatomy, his prostate gland had become abscessed. He thought he'd die before he could get to the doctor. The mercury treatments were doubled.

It was left to Lilah to watch the rest of the building, for he was so damned sick he couldn't walk. The slightest movement gave him terrible pain. If he could have put his hands on the little bangtail who gave him his dose he'd have killed her. But then, finally, it got better and the doctor told him, sure, he was safe.

To celebrate, both his recovery and the completion of the house, he threw a party. It was just him and Lilah and the three girls they'd found so far and a few influential men, railroad men and a couple of townsmen. It was a grand party and Rupert kept putting off the finale, because it had been a long time and he wanted it to be good and uninterrupted. He looked over the three new girls and decided he'd wait to try them out, for Lilah was by far the best-looking. So when it was late and the men from the town had gone, well pleased with the new business, he took Lilah to bed.

And nothing would happen. He'd be steaming. He'd wanted it so badly he'd be shaking and nothing would happen. In the end he had to tell her. "Now don't worry, I'm safe. It's not catching, but I had a dose and it settled up inside."

"Oh, honey," Lilah said, "that's bad news. I knew a man once had that happen. He never got a hard on again." Sometimes she could use crude language with a sweet little accent and a sophistication which made it sound almost normal.

"I don't detect any physical damage," the doctor told him, having donned a rubber glove, anointed his finger with petroleum jelly and gone aprobing into Rupert's innards. "Maybe it's in your mind, Mr. Glendower. The fear of it happening again."

"Well, if that's it, we'll soon fix that," he told Lilah. And again nothing happened.

Well, it was bad, but the world hadn't come to an end. The doctor kept assuring him that it would pass, and meantime he had business to

attend to. He had his grand opening. It was a
roaring success. His bar was the longest, shiniest,
prettiest in the west. His carpets were the red-
dest, his girls the wildest. And he went a-scouting
and bought himself two little orphan Indian girls,
age fifteen and thirteen, and installed them and
got the word around that young stuff was damned
good—and at a premium. He, himself, tried
more than once to cure his affliction by sampling,
and nothing happened except the frustration
which sometimes made him think he'd go crazy.

He gradually came to accept it. Life was exciting. Lilah was doing a great job running the
place and the way it looked he'd have his initial
investment back in months and then start coining
money. But, God, how he hated that little Indian
wench. What the hell was it with him and Indians? Everytime he got around them something
bad happened. Now and then he'd get so mad
he'd go and beat the tar out of one of the little
Indian girls, until Lilah told him that he was
damaging the merchandise and should stop it.
They were bringing in a lot of money, those two.
He raised the price for them, higher than anyone
in the house except Lilah, who took only selected customers. Word got around and they had
more applications than they wanted until Lilah
had a staff of ten white girls and the two
little redskins.

All was right in his world until by accident
he saw the Woodrowe bitch get off the train and
go to the railroad hotel, and then all his hate
came back to him. He remembered how the Indians had cost him his herd, how they had taken
Wynema and the girls away from him because of

the trickery of that bitch who looked so smug. He'd had part of his revenge, by gelding the Indian. He went a little black, thinking of that. He wondered if Woodrowe had the same problem as he. And then it was just a step toward blaming them for his present condition. If they hadn't stole his girls he wouldn't have been in Chetopa at the same time the little Indian with gonorrhea was there and he'd still be a whole man.

And another thought came to him. If it were in his mind, maybe that Miranda girl was just the ticket to cure it, for, although he hated her guts, he had always wanted her. Just the thought of it made him squirm.

He didn't tell Lilah. He sent the note himself. He had one of the girls write it in a feminine hand, threatened to kick her ass if she said anything about it, and sent it over to the hotel by a messenger. The note read:

Mrs. Miranda Lee Woodrowe,

Through John Warren, I have heard of your search for a woman who knew your father, Danny O'Lee, in a manner which you and I alone know. I am very curious. After all these years, I long to see you. I must ask you to be secretive, for I have a position to uphold, and I'm sure you would not want to expose me to shame after so many years. If you are curious, as I am, please take a carriage and meet me, alone, on the road leading eastward out of town at ten o'clock in the morning.

Mme. Lilah Girondin

14

Miranda felt almost as if the letter and the necessity she felt to obey its instructions were an intrusion into her life. Now that she was so near home, only the train ride to the railhead and the stage ride the rest of the way between her and her son, she was eager. The exciting city seemed to be not only miles behind her but years behind her in time. She thought often of James Allen, but only with a sort of nostalgic regret.

She could wish, as she prepared for the meeting, that she'd never overheard the secret about herself, but she had. She knew of the existence of the woman who called herself Lilah and her curiosity was too much for her. Wynema wanted to go. She had come to fancy herself as Miranda's protector. Miranda told her to wait in the room, that she'd be back shortly, in plenty of time to catch the midday train into the Nations. A surrey was brought around by the hotel's liveryman and she dismissed the driver, taking the reins herself.

She had driven about a mile in the green countryside when she saw, under a spreading tree beside the road, a carriage with curtains drawn. The driver's seat was empty. She felt a moment of disease, and then, because the sun was bright and the day beautiful and she had things to do, she clucked to the horses and moved them toward the stationary vehicle. She drew up alongside.

"Hello," she called. "Is anybody there?"

A veiled female head peered around a curtain. "Will you please join me here?"

Well, Miranda thought, she's certainly being mysterious enough about this. Was she the wife of some prominent citizen?

In fact, the woman inside the carriage had never heard of Miranda, knew only that she'd been ordered by the boss to do certain things and to keep her mouth shut about it. With her, seated at the ready on the forward seat, were two men who had been recruited for the job by Glendower. He had laid his plans carefully.

The door opened and Miranda looked inside, seeing a woman in a red dress and then, just as rough hands seized her and started to jerk her into the carriage, she saw the two men. She screamed out, but her cries were quickly silenced by a large hand over her mouth and she was suddenly yanked bodily from a state of normality into terror. She could not fight successfully against the three of them and she was soon trussed, her eyes covered by a black bandana which cut off all light. Another bandana was drawn tightly over a silken handkerchief which had been thrust into her mouth, so that the sounds which escaped were merely muffled groans.

One man got out and the other climbed into the driver's seat and the carriage jerked into motion. The man who remained went into the bushes and brought out a jar filled with a red substance. He went to Miranda's surrey and poured the liquid over the seat. It ran down and puddled in the floorboards, the rich, coppery smell of fresh pig's blood in the air. The man then went back into the thicket, mounted his horse, and soon overtook the carriage.

Miranda was being bounced around on the seat onto which she had been thrown, unable to see, her hands and feet securely tied, her mind in a turmoil. She could not imagine what was happening. Although she was frightened, she was calm enough to listen to the whispered instructions when the horseman caught up with the carriage and, on the move, swung into the door. She felt hands on her, felt her gag being removed.

"We're not going to hurt you, honey," a feminine voice said. "All we want you to do is take a couple of swallows of this stuff."

Miranda kept her mouth resolutely closed. Male hands tried to pry her mouth open and she bit a finger, which brought rough curses. Then she felt a hand thrusting under her dress, burrowing into her underclothes roughly, thrusting up the legs of her pantalets until, with a gasp, she felt the man seize her pubic hair in his hand.

"Now you open your mouth, missy," he said, "or you're going to be bald." He pulled painfully and Mindy stifled a scream.

"What is it?" she asked. "What is it you want me to drink?"

"Just some wine, honey," the woman said, "to calm you down."

The man yanked and it was painful. She reasoned that if they wanted to do her harm she could do nothing to stop them. She opened her mouth and drank. It was wine, but there was a strange taste about it. It was only minutes before she felt drowsy. A pleasant and debilitating lassitude came over her and she felt her bonds being loosed, moved an arm lazily.

"Just another swallow, honey," the woman said, and she obediently swallowed.

In a dreamy state of comfort and ease, she could hear sounds, the sound of hammers, the passing of wheeled vehicles, voices, and from a far distance she knew that she was in a town. The carriage made a couple of turns and then came to a halt. Mindy obeyed meekly and was led from the carriage, which was halted in a sort of alley at the back door of a wooden structure, into the dimness of a kitchen. She was scarcely aware of her surroundings, feeling very, very drowsy, seeing the world in a sort of swimming haze in which reality mingled with fancy so that a chair took on a stark beauty which held her attention, her head turning to stare at it, entranced, as she was led back and up a flight of stairs.

The bed onto which she was placed was so soft, so soft, and the female hands which undressed her were so gentle. She lay there, eyes half closed, in a dream world of peace and beauty. Her eyes closed and she dreamed and the dream was sultry, building a warm glow in her body.

It had gone off without a hitch. Rupert saw them bring her in. Ah, the bitch had a surprise coming to her. She was obviously under the influence of the laudanum which he'd instructed them to give her. She moved slowly. Her eyes were half closed. He waited until she was in the room upstairs and then he went to her. She lay with her lower body covered, her breasts, beautiful firm mounds, exposed. He felt his breath catch in his teeth and he tiptoed to her bedside. She seemed to be asleep.

He had not told the doctor who treated him for his disease why he wanted such a large amount of laudanum, and, when the proper amount of money was exchanged, the doctor had shown no curiosity. The idea had come to Rupert when, ill, finding it painful to move, at the worst of his illness, he had been given a little book published in England to help pass the time of day. The doctor had explained that he might be interested, since the pain-killing medication he, himself, was receiving was the same tincture of opium which the writer, Thomas De Quincey, had become addicted to and about which he wrote in the book called *The Confession of an English Opium Eater*.

"Rupe," the doctor said, when he asked for a large amount, in a tincture a bit stronger than usual, "You're not going to follow in De Quincey's footsteps, are you?"

"Hell, no," Rupe said. "I don't want to drowse my life away. Little booze suits me. The girls like to have it, after a busy night. Helps them sleep."

"Just watch it, Rupe," the doctor said. "That's potent stuff. Now I've written down the amount of the proper dosage for relaxation. Someone takes too much of that stuff and it can be serious. Some gal takes too much and she'll get sleepy and from sleep she'll go into a coma, then she'll get clammy and her lips and the tips of her ears will get red and the pupils of her eyes will contract. If you don't do something quick, like get her to vomit by making her drink lots of hot salted water, then she'll just stop breathing."

"I'll see to it that there won't be an overdose," he said. "I'm gonna confess, doc. What I plan to do is use this stuff to train my young girls. I understand that just enough of it will make a gal sort of dreamy and unable to resist anything and let her get het up at the same time."

"Rupe, you're an unregenerate scoundrel," the doctor growled. "Just be careful." And he made notes on the dosage.

But as Rupert stood beside Miranda's bed he was afraid she might have had too much. He checked for signs of redness in the tips of her ears, pulling back her hair to see that the creamy skin there held its natural tone. She was breathing evenly and deeply. He threw back the sheets and looked at her. She had a beautiful body. He felt the beginnings of desire. He let his hands begin to explore her body as he bared his teeth and let his breath hiss in and out. Yes, yes, it was going to do it. He knew he was going to do it. There was such a delicious heat in that warm and intimate spot between her legs and she obligingly opened for him so his hand had access.

Everything seemed to be working just as he'd planned. Even in her drugged state her body responded to his caresses. And he, himself, wanting her for so long, was shivering in his eagerness.

So clean, so sweet. Not like even Lilah, who was a fastidious woman, but a whore, nonetheless. He looked at that full and nude body and wondered how many other men had seen it naked and he would have bet his hat that he was one of a very few. The idea sent fire into his veins.

With a growing impatience he walked quickly to lock the door, stripped his clothing away, climbed into the bed. He lay close to her. She seemed to be in a state of sleep, but she knew, by God, she knew, even with her eyes closed, that nice things were being done to her. Her body seemed to follow his pressures, and her breathing increased, and when he put the flat of his hand over her mons and pressed, she answered the pressure.

He knew in his heart that he was going to do it, that his long inability to know the pleasures of the flesh was going to end right then and there and to increase his passion he began to kiss that creamy, clean, sweet-smelling body, covering every inch of it with his lips, moving to that hot and moistened, sweetly flowing secret area and his heated ministrations there set up a soft little heaving in her loins and he could feel himself getting more and more into it. It would happen soon, he knew it would.

And as for her, she was sighing and moving her hips and dreaming lovely, lovely things. In her mind it was James Allen who was making her body burn with desire, and it seemed as if it were happening to her and yet to someone else at the same time.

Panting, trembling, he looked down at himself and uttered a curse. The damned thing was not even wiggling. Limp, useless. All in his mind, he told himself. He willed that part of himself to engorge itself, to grow, and he coaxed it on by straddling her, by pressing that useless limpness into the oiled and heated petals of her, and still nothing happened. After a long long time, when he was almost beside himself, he cursed, pulled away, and got off the bed.

But there was time. When her surrey was found, bloody, deserted, she'd be assumed dead, killed by outlaws. No one except his one girl knew she was in the house, for the two drifters would have taken their money and lit out.

Several times that day he returned to her room, each time instructing his girl to give her a draft of laudanum beforehand. He was not ready for her to see him. When he was ready to take her he wanted her awake and aware.

"Miss High and Mighty," he told her, she unhearing, after still another attempt had failed, "I will have you, and when I'm through with you you're going to be the leading attraction around here. Once the word gets around you'll service six men a night, maybe a dozen. We'll see how high and mighty you are then."

But nothing happened.

At times, when the effects of the drug wore

off, she would be awake and would be fed. Food tasted delicious. She had no idea where she was, but she was comfortable and safe, so far. There was a strangeness in her, a seemingly inspired hunger which was with her at all times, a need for love, a desire which expressed itself in dreams which were so real that she was in a constant state of need while she was awake. She tried to ask the girl who tended her questions, but the girl was silent, speaking only to give her orders.

"Get up and use the chamberpot. Walk around a little, honey. Get into the tub and wash yourself, honey." She always obeyed without questions.

And without her knowledge another factor was to enter the tangled situation. In the middle of a warm afternoon, business quite light, Rupert and Lilah were in the parlor talking about the way business continued to grow, making plans to hire at least one other girl. The door opened and a tall, well built young man with unruly black hair came into the room, paused and looked around.

Lilah's reaction was surprising to Rupert. She went white and one hand swiftly came to her breast before she leaped to her feet and ran to the man, crying out, "Tony, Tony." He took her in his arms and lifted her off her feet, kissing her on the cheek.

"Oh, Tony," Lilah cried, as he put her back onto her feet. "It's so damned good to see you."

"It's good to see you, too, Mother," the man said. "You're looking well."

His interest aroused, Rupert stood. "Oh, Rupe," Lilah said, looking prettier than he'd ever seen her look, "this is my son, my big, handsome son. Isn't he gorgeous?"

"Well, I wouldn't pick that word myself," Rupert said, with a grin. "I'm Rupert Glendower," he said, extending his hand. "Your mother is a fine woman."

"Tony Girondin," he said, taking the hand and shaking it with a firm grip. "Yes, she's always been quite a woman."

"Oh, Tony," Lilah said, holding onto his other hand. "I'm so glad. I thought you were in California."

"Was," Tony said. "Got tired of it. Felt a hankering to see the wide open spaces and your face. What's this setup? Looks fancy."

And, with Rupert opening a bottle of champagne to celebrate the occasion, Lilah and Tony talked, bringing each other up to date. "Glad to hear you're doing well," he told her. "Well enough to give up active work and just run the place, eh?"

"Well, I still have a very select clientele," she said. She smiled at Rupert. "He never approved, you know. As a boy he was ashamed of me. I told him that I had no other way of supporting us."

"That's long past, Mother," Tony said. "I think I understand now."

"Listen," Rupert said. "You can be proud of your mother. She'd damned good at what she does."

"Oh, I know, I know," Tony said, with a trace of bitterness.

"All right," Lilah said, "let's stop talking about

me and talk about you. I want to hear everything you've done since I saw you last."

Rupert left them. Alone, he felt the bitterness, the beginnings of his long frustrated desire, and he went back to Miranda's room to repeat the fruitless process, the main result of which was to leave him in helpless rage and need and to lift Miranda into a drugged state of desire. And as he looked at her, looked down at his useless member, he decided, at last, that it was hopeless. That part of his life was over. Not totally rational, he looked at the beauty on the bed and blamed her for it. She had tricked him out of his girls. If she hadn't done that he'd be down at the railhead with his little harem and he'd never have seen the little Indian bitch who gave im his dose and ruined his life.

Yes, she was responsible, and she would not escape. And she'd replace the little whores in his house, just as he'd promised her long ago. But first she'd be tamed, shamed, reduced to such a state that she'd be happy to service his customers. Inspiration came to him. He and he alone knew the secret, that not only did Lilah have a son in the house, she had a daughter, too. And the method of her ultimate shame came to him.

"Tony," he said, as they stood at the bar having a drink that evening, "you've given Lilah great joy. I do hope you plan to stay with us for awhile."

"Well, I'd planned to ride on south, down into Texas," Tony said.

"No hurry, is there?"

"No."

"Well, stay. This house is yours. Plenty of food, plenty of booze." He grinned. "Plenty of another vital commodity if you're of the mood."

Tony laughed. "I'll have to admit I've been casting a look or two at that Frannie girl of yours."

"Yeah, Frannie's all right. Clean, good at her work." He snapped his fingers. "But I've got a better idea. I've got a new girl, just in. She's pretty green and she needs some practice before I turn her loose on my favorite customers. She's the most beautiful girl you're ever going to see. You'd be doing yourself a favor and me, too, if you'd sort of break her in for me."

Tony Girondin stood an even six feet, and he was possessed of a muscular lankiness. His eyes were dark and laugh-crinkled at the corners. He thought it was a strange world. And yet, over the years, he'd adjusted to it, well, mostly. As a boy he'd had to learn to be tough, because when the other kids said things about his mother he had to fight, even if the kid were twice his size, and over the years necessity made him a small tiger. The biggest bully in the New Orleans neighborhood where he spent his young years had only to say, "Your mother does it for money," and he was up and fighting. He took a lot of lumps and he began to give out more as he grew into a sturdy young teenager.

He wouldn't believe it at first. He knew, as a child, that he had a lot of uncles. He also had colored "aunts" who looked after him while his mother was away, which was often. At times she took long trips and he had heard talk about her going all the way to Texas once when he was just about a year and a few months old. So later, when she took him into Texas and up into the mid-continent to follow the progress of the inter-continental railroad, he would ask questions and she'd always be vague.

By the time they left New Orleans for good, he knew her for what she was and he was shamed. There was no longer any excuse about the men being "uncles." They were men who paid her money for the use of her body. He, Tony Girondin, was the son of a whore. But a whore who loved him with a warmth which he could not deny. And so he alternated between shame, hate, and intense love for her. He had dozens of different tutors in various boom towns all across the west. He learned to read and write and cipher and he spoke excellent French.

And as soon as he was fifteen he left her. He hired on as a rider in a cattle drive, then tried his luck as a gandy dancer on the railroad. He had no desire to be rich. If he had food and a place to sleep, even a blanket roll under the stars, he was content. He wanted to see as much of the country as he could, and he saw a lot. He knew that when he wanted to see his mother all he had to do was find the railroad and there she'd be. He was pleased when she stopped freelancing and went into an organized house. At least there she had a man to protect her in case a customer got rough. It always broke his heart to see her with bruises on her where some man had hit her.

He liked this man Glendower. He seemed to be a decent enough fellow and genuinely fond of his mother. She was a full partner and making more money than she'd ever made, although he didn't know what she'd do with it when she had all the clothing and jewelry she wanted. But then, could a woman like Lilah ever have enough clothing and jewelry?

"Rupe," he said, "I want to thank you for taking my mother on as a partner. I think you're good for her."

"Well, I couldn't do without her," Rupert said. "She runs the joint. She's the brains of the operation."

Tony was not without knowledge of the pleasures which can come from a woman's body. He was a healthy, normal man, and in the west when a man wanted a woman there was one place to go, the local brothel. In a country where men outnumbered women by vast numbers and the shortage was so severe that many men sent back east for women whom they'd never seen to come out and marry them, there was a definite need for the oldest profession. It was no disgrace for a man to go to a brothel.

So when Rupe offered him the chance to "break in" a new girl, the idea sort of appealed to him and he said he reckoned as how he couldn't refuse to do the man who'd made a great place for his mother a favor.

Rupe took him up to the room wherein Miranda Lee was locked, having sent the girl ahead with the dose of laudanum, and they stood there and looked down.

"Why's she drugged?" Tony asked.

"She's scared," Rupert said. "She wants to get into the business, but she's scared. Had a bad experience. Raped. Frightened of men. So I told

her she'd feel everything and get to know that
it didn't hurt her."

"Rupe, are you joshing me?" Tony asked suspiciously. "You ain't shanghaied this girl?"

"Hey, would I do a thing like that?"

"I don't know, would you?"

"Hell, no. I tell you she's willing. I'm giving
it to you straight."

"O.K."

"There's just one other thing," he said. "I
promised her one other thing. Just a whim of
hers, but I promised her I'd do it. I told her
I'd get some nice young fellow to do it to her
first. She said she didn't want to know who he
was."

"Rupe, there's something fishy here," Tony
said.

"No, no. She's just a little spooked by the
rape, that's all. She figures she's a ruined woman.
She says she'll get her revenge on all men by
selling them what one of them took by force and
by never giving them much of anything. She's
got the whore's mentality, Tony. You know most
of 'em hate men."

"I've known a few," Tony said. "All right. I'll
go along with it."

"So here's what we do," Rupert said. "You
don't say a word at any time. And you wear
this." He produced a hood fashioned of white
silk.

"I'll be damned," Tony said, putting it over
his head. There were eyeholes and a place for
his nose and the mask fit closely around his
mouth, exposing his nice lips.

"She's all yours," Rupert said. "Take your

time. This might even take a few days. Not bad duty, eh?"

Indeed, he'd been looking at her and even with Rupert present he could feel the growth of his manhood. He'd never seen anything quite so beautiful. She lay with the coverlet down exposing a part of her dark bush, breasts proud and firm.

Alone in the room, he hesitated only a moment, then he took off his clothes. He was well built, quite adequately manned, and he was in a state of excitement. His first impulse was to open those lily-sweet legs and take her quickly. But she deserved more than that. One man had hurt her. He would not. He began and he found her skin to be velvet sweet and her lips like honey and her body so warm, so soft. And it went on for a long, long time as he kissed, caressed, felt, probed, felt with fingers and then, with a gasp, with his mouth, the slightly aromatic secretions which oiled her and made the tender flesh so enticing.

Ah, she was dreaming again. So sweet, so sweet. She felt her body begin that delicious melting. She felt the desire building and it was as if a loving man, James Allen in her dreams, were ravishing her with lips and hands, skillfully playing on those very areas which were most sensitive. It was the most realistic dream she ever had. For now he was putting his weight on her. Now he was entering her, and her loins, feeling the penetration, lifted. So great was her need, so long had she been stimulated, that she reached the heights immediately and the strength of her sensation burned through the effects of the drug so that, even as she clung and gasped her completion, she opened her eyes. So strange. He had no face, only a soft whiteness with a hint of eyes, nose, mouth, a mouth which covered hers and was wet and wonderful as he ended his pleasure in delightful spasms.

Rupert Glendower had made one more preparation. From an adjoining room he peered through a hole punched through the wall and watched with hate, desire, frustration, all making him want to beat the wall with his fists. But she was getting what he had promised her, even if not from him. And he had one more surprise in store for her.

He timed it properly. Tony, with the appetites of a strong young man, kept Miranda busy for a while, into the night, and then, the day's work finished, he was following what had become a custom between himself and Lilah. They were in Lilah's room discussing the events of the night.

"Got a surprise for you," he said. And he spun the same tale he'd told Tony. Lilah was eager to see the girl, and he noted, with a hidden smile, that her eyes widened in surprise when she saw how truly beautiful the girl was. For he knew Lilah. She didn't hate men, but she had known too many of them. She had little use for them on a personal basis outside of the business. He knew that she took her pleasures in the beds of the two girls she had brought with her from Arkansas City. Rupert knew that, like many whores, she shared a taste for the pleasures of Sappho. He counted her that to accomplish the second phase of his inspired plan.

"She'll be coming out of it soon," he told her. "Why don't you stay and talk with her?"

"Sure, sure," Lilah said, musingly.

"She's a little nervous about joining us," he said. "Anything you can do to calm her down and make her feel at home will be good for her."

He went immediately to his spy hole through the wall and watched with interest. Lilah sat on the side of the bed, musing. At last she extended a hand and soothed it along the soft, exposed skin, and he saw a shiver of anticipation go through her.

But De Quincey had discovered for himself what all doctors who prescribed laudanum regularly already knew. To achieve the same effects, dosage must be continually increased. The body builds up a tolerance for the opiate, and when Miranda once again became aware of stimulation, she managed to open her eyes to see that the hands which were exploring her body were, shockingly, female hands, that a rather pretty older woman was looking at her intently with a strange expression on her face.

For the first time, she could speak. "What— what are you doing?"

"Ah, you're awake. Welcome to our little home," Lilah said. "I'm Lilah, and I'm sure we'll be good friends." Her hands continued to sooth, to explore.

"Please don't," Miranda said, her voice sounding strange from the drug and from disuse.

"Doesn't it feel good? Relaxing?"

"Please don't," she begged.

"Rupe tells me you've had a bad experience," Lilah said.

The name burned into her brain, made her ever more aware. Rupe. Rupert Glendower? Was he the one responsible for her strange existence? Faint memories. The drive into the country. The closed carriage. And the people who had tied her, who had made her drink what was obviously drugged wine.

"You're so pretty," Lilah said. "I could just eat you up." And she bent to plant a kiss on Miranda's lips.

"Leave me alone, please," Miranda begged, for, although she was aware, she was so weak. "Why am I here? What have you done to me?"

Lilah drew back, puzzled. Rupert, seeing the danger of having his little scheme foiled, rushed to send the girl in with a dose of laudanum. And so, for the moment, Miranda was spared still another degradation.

But she was becoming more and more aware of the continued attentions of the man in the strange white hood. There were times when her mind was almost clear. She managed to get out of bed alone one day and walked to the window. She was surprised to see that she was still in Chetopa. She tried to think of ways to escape, but she was strangely weak, almost without will. The window was impossibly high, the door was locked. And when the strong young man came to her, bared his fine body, made love to her, she was helpless. It was as if his love acted on her as the drug acted, making her want more and more of him, never satisfied, although she achieved thunderous pleasures.

Rupert wanted her to know what was happening to her. He cut the doses of laudanum and now when Tony, his face hidden, came into the room, she was dreamily aware of him, eager for his attentions, and only when she was alone and awake did the shame of it come through to her. Her growing tolerance for the drug, and the lessened doses, allowed her to think, to wonder. What was Glendower's scheme? Yes, yes, he had said to her once that since she had taken his young girls away from him he was going to have her fulfill the duties of the girls. But she was sure that the man who came to her, often in the afternoon, always at night, was the same man. Glendower? The thought sickened her. But when he came that night she could not conquer the lust for him which filled her.

It was about time, Glendower thought, to let her know what he had in mind for her, but he still wanted to put the icing on the cake, to play the final trick on the bitch, to let her know, when he finally stopped giving her the drug, that not only had she been making passionate love to her half-brother, she had also made love with her own mother. That, he felt, would take the last bit of fight out of her, and, having degraded herself so utterly, would be more than content to hide from the world in one of his rooms, making him money all the while.

And so he continued to send Lilah to her. And when Lilah went, he increased the laudanum, so that Mindy was, once again, dreamily drowsy and almost asleep.

When Lilah lost her control and ravished the young girl's semi-conscious body, he watched with excitement which made him hope, once again, that he could overcome his handicap. He went to her herself and it was as useless as ever.

Now, he felt, the time had come. He would allow Tony one more night with her, and then he'd cut out the laudanum and tell her what she'd been doing with her brother and her mother.

He was, however, a little concerned about the reactions of both Tony and Lilah when they found out Miranda's identity, so he delayed. While he was trying to figure out a way to accomplish his total revenge on Mindy without upsetting them, a skinny, gaunt, bearded man in homespun came into the parlor.

"Praise the Lord, brother, you're looking well," said the scarecrow figure.

"Well, Alphonse," he said, "how's the world treating you?"

"The world treats me ill," Alphonse said, "but our Kind Father looks out for me. I have come, my friend, to bring the blessed word to your children, who live in sin."

"Have a drink at the bar, Alphonse," he said. "I'll go get Lilah."

"Crazy Alphonse is here," he told her. She smote her forehead with her palm and laughed.

"How long are we going to run a charity for that old bum?" Lilah asked, but she was smiling fondly.

"He amuses me," Rupert said. "And the girls like him."

"A bit of God's Holy Word before he gets a bit of a woman's holy hole," Lilah said. "Oh, well. The girls don't mind and they get a kick out of him. I guess we'll let him make the rounds, eh?"

They went together to the parlor where Alphonse was having his drink and talking to Tony. Alphonse was telling Tony how many souls he'd saved on his last revival circuit. "And you, my boy? Are you saved?"

"Well," Tony said, "I'm not very religious."

That was enough to launch Alphonse into a sermon, from which Tony was delivered by the arrival of his mother and Rupert.

"Ah," Alphonse said, "are the evil children ready to be chastised with the Holy Word?"

"Go get 'em, Alphonse," Lilah said. "Mary's busy right now. That's the room just at the head of the stairs, so let her finish her job before you preach to her, O.K.?"

Gulping the last of his drink, Alphonse rushed up the stairs.

"Is he for real?" Tony asked with raised eyebrows.

"You wouldn't believe how real a lot of people think he is," Lilah said. "He goes all over Kansas and into the Indian Nations holding revival meetings in brush arbors. When he's in full flood the Bible rolls out of him in waves. He can make the darkest sinner weep, and he's brought more lost souls into the fold than any preacher in Kansas."

"He's going to preach to the girls?" Tony asked, unbelievingly.

"Only for a few minutes each," Lilah laughed, "until he makes up his mind which girl is to be honored with his holy rolling in a bed of lust."

"You're pulling my leg," Tony said.

"My fine lad," she said. "Even a holy man has natural desires."

"And you let him—"

"Call it our contribution to the church," Rupert laughed.

And then he had an inspiration. He went up stairs and caught Crazy Alphonse between rooms. "Got a new girl," he said. "Guess she could use some of the Holy Word."

"Always happy to oblige," Alphonse said, with a grin behind his beard. "New one, eh?"

"I think she needs a lot of the Holy Word, if you know what I mean."

He unlocked the door and let Alphonse in. He locked the door and went to his peephole.

Miranda was almost totally herself, with only a lingering feeling of unreality. When the strange man came into the room she sat up in bed and jerked the cover to her chin.

"The wrath of God is upon you, my daughter," Alphonse thundered, taking a pose, one hand high, the other in the lapel of his ratty coat. "For you have sinned in the eyes of the Lord and for this your soul will burn forever more in hell's fire."

"Who are you?" Mindy asked. "Have you come to help me?"

"I am who I am," Alphonse intoned. "I am the power and the light. I am the shepherd who has come to lead you safely into the fold of the master shepherd. Cry your shame, my daughter. Beg God's forgiveness."

And as he preached in that wondrous, deeply toned voice, he was opening buttons, shedding clothes, until, his bones showing through his skin making him look like a walking skeleton, he was naked, save for his socks, out of which both sets of his toes stuck through ragged holes. As he approached the bed Mindy cringed away. He reached out to touch her and she hit him.

"Daughter," he said, his voice reproving. "Don't fight the will of the Lord."

"Who are you?" Mindy repeated.

"I am Brother Alphonse. I carry the word of God all over this heathen territory. I have come to allow you to atone for your sins by washing them away in the arms of God's messenger."

"If you touch me, I'll scream," Mindy said.

Rupert, watching through his peekhole, was chuckling to himself. He was very interested in seeing what happened next, but at that moment there was a gunshot from downstairs. Trouble. He cursed and leaped for the door.

"Child, it is all right. I am a man of God," Alphonse said, reaching for her.

"If you're a man of God, you'll help me," she said. "I'm being held here against my will."

"Is that true?" he asked, pausing in the act of crawling onto the bed.

"Yes," she said desperately. "I've been kidnapped. I've been drugged. I've been forced to do evil. Please, please, if you love God, help me."

"And who did this evil thing to you?" he asked.

"Rupert Glendower."

"But he is my friend."

"He subjects me to shame regularly," she said. "I want to go home. I have a baby who needs me. I have a husband."

"But why would he do such a thing?"

"Will you help me?"

"If I can bring myself to believe your story.

I must help you," he said, reaching for his trousers and pulling them on.

She poured out the story to him, how Glendower hated her and her husband and why. "Young girls," he said, shaking his head. "I knew Rupe was a sinful man, but this. And if you're telling the truth that is even more sinful."

"I swear before God I'm telling the truth," she said. "Help me get away. You'll have to get me some clothing. I don't have any at all."

He was thinking with a frown on his face as he buttoned his shabby coat. "Yes," he said. "I will help you. When it is dark I'll come to your window with a ladder."

"Just go and tell the sheriff," she said. "Tell him to come for me."

"Oh, I couldn't do that," he said. "It would get my friends in trouble."

"All right," she said. "But you will come tonight?"

"I will be here. While they are quite busy with the night's business, I'll come. I'll throw pebbles against your window and you will open it. I'll bring something for you to wear. It might not be fancy, mind you."

He paused, frowned. "There is one thing you must promise me. What Rupert has done to you is wrong, but he is my friend, as are the others. You must promise me that you won't cause them trouble."

Trouble? She wanted to see him dead. "I promise," she said, willing to promise anything to get out of there.

"Good," he said. He looked at her, his head

cocked to one side. "Are you sure you wouldn't like to work your sins away in the arms of the true messenger of the Lord?"

"Oh, please," she said.

Naked, she walked the floor, praying, hoping that he would keep his word. She feared that the man in the white hood would come again and she vowed that before she submitted to him again, she would break the window and throw herself out of it. But, with a sob of shame, she realized that she had a twinge of need just thinking of him. And the women. Oh, God, she had even felt that feeling with her, had squirmed and fought with her loins against soft hands and hot lips. What had happened to her? What had she become?

She did not know that trouble with a drunken railroader downstairs was occupying the attention of both the man in the white hood and Rupert Glendower. Now did she know that upon leaving her room, having knocked on the door to have it opened by the girl who looked after Mindy, the Man of God had gone to the room at the head of the stairs, preached a brief sermon while disrobing, and was now working away Mary's sins, while she laughed delightedly at his eagerness.

15

If a surrey and a team of horses had not been involved Wynema would never have convinced anyone that there was trouble. When her mistress did not return by mid-afternoon she went down to the desk and asked the man there for information. He checked with the stable and told the girl without concern that Mrs. Woodrowe had not returned the vehicle. By evening Wynema was seriously worried. She had been badgering the man at the desk to do something for hours and he had become irritated with her, telling her to shut up and get back in her room or he'd throw her out of the hotel.

In desperation, she went to the sheriff's office. There, too, she met with indifference. When she

wept and pleaded the deputy on duty said he'd
have a look. She went back an hour or so later
and the deputy said he'd checked around town,
but there wasn't anything to worry about. "She's
probably visiting," he said.

"But she knows no one here," Wynema protested.

It was the morning of the next day before a
farmer, driving into town in a farm wagon, found
the surrey and the team of horses and brought
them in trailing behind his wagon. To the men
at the sheriff's office the blood on the seat and
floorboard of the vehicle seemed to be the end
of it. A man rode out to the spot where the
surrey had been found. He came back to tell a
sobbing Wynema that she might as well go on
home.

"She's a goner," the man said. "Probably never
know how. My bet would be outlaws. She probably resisted. Can't understand why a young
woman would be riding around alone anyhow."

So Wynema had no choice but to use the railroad ticket which had been left on the dresser
in the hotel room to make her way back, in sadness, to pass along news of the tragedy to Chota
and Grand. The news seemed to burn through the
indifference which had been possessing Grand
and he said that he would go to Chetopa immediately.

Chota, shocked and grieved, began to think
about it. Wynema had seen the blood. She felt
in her heart that Miranda was dead, and the idea
of her son, in his new state of hopelessness and
lassitude, facing the world alone did not seem
advisable to her.

"My son," she said, "I know your feelings, and it is a great blow, but what purpose will be served by your going there? If the law could find nothing what could you hope to accomplish?"

It took surprisingly little to convince him. He sought his solitude immediately and no one saw him weeping in the privacy of his studio. And so another tragedy had struck and Chota was left with the care of the infant. With the running of the store and the house she was more than pleased by Wynema's continued presence. The girl was invaluable. They had a good weep together and, as people will do, talked of the dead Miranda, remembering small incidents with tearful fondness.

"Now we must do what she would want us to do," Chota told Wynema. "We must do our best for the boy. We must continue our lives."

But there was a pall of gloom at Crossroads. As for Grand, he rarely came out of his studio and there, unseen, he had begun a project. He had had too much shock, too much tragedy. His mind seemed to rebel, to preserve itself by dulling the pain of Mindy's loss, pushing it behind an almost neurotic need to work. He labored over preparations for a massive work, the events of history boiling and simmering in his mind. When it was ready it was a series of connected canvases stretching for twenty feet in length and four feet in height. And on it, growing from the turmoil in his mind, driven to work to escape the hopelessness of his life, the grand design began to grow. He could see, in his mind, the beginning of the present day troubles, the day when the first Choctaw to see a white man came face to face with a Spanish soldier awesome in gleaming breastplate and helmet.

As far as he was concerned his life had ended, save for one aspect of it. His entire being was concentrated on the canvas, on the broad and violent history of his mother's people, on the tragedy and the perfidy and the sadness. Nothing else existed for him. He did not think of Mindy. He seemed to have forgotten that he had a son. He did not even halt his work when Wynema or Chota would bring him a plate of food. Sometimes he ate, sometimes he didn't.

To Chota, it was as if she'd lost everything, her husband, her lovely daughter-in-law, and now her son, who was like the dead, except that he moved when he was standing in front of the canvas on which images began to appear in powerful swirls of color.

16

The trouble in the downstairs parlor was not bad. The gunshot which had drawn Rupert away from his observation of Mindy and the preacher had not been fired in anger but in drunken good spirits. It took some time, however, for Rupert to explain to the happy railroad man that he had to pay for the mirror behind the bar, and more time for Rupert and Tony to escort the man back to his lodgings. He was a regular customer and it was good business to see to it that he got home, got into his bed, and didn't get into trouble.

When Alphonse came downstairs after his prayers and his stay in the bed of the affable Mary, he found Lilah Girondin alone. He had been thinking about what the lovely girl had told him and he had come to his conclusion. He had decided to face Rupert Glendower, ask if the girl's charges were true, and if so, to castigate Rupert for his sins and insist that the girl be freed. Luck was with him, however, for Rupert wasn't there.

"My dear Mme. Girondin," he said, "matters have come to my attention which bear discussing."

"I don't have time, Alphonse," she said impatiently. "You've had your contribution to the church and done your preaching to our poor sinners, now beat it."

"You must listen to me," he said imperiously. "There is a girl upstairs—"

"There are several," she said.

"This one says she's being held against her will," he said. "I speak of one Mrs. Miranda Lee Woodrowe, who has asked for my help, telling me—"

"Shut up a miniute," Lilah said. "What did you say her name was?" She hadn't even bothered to ask, simply referring to the girl, as Rupert did, as Mindy.

He repeated the name. "She says she has been kidnapped. Now I must insist—"

But the name was still ringing in her head and she was reminded that once Rupert had asked her about the child she'd borne to Danny O'Lee. And he'd mentioned a name, Woodrowe.

She felt her face flush with shock and fear. She told herself it could not be. "Go on about your business, Alphonse," she said, "and I'll see to it."

"Ah, I was sure you'd listen to reason," he said, but Lilah was already rushing up the stairs, skirts held high.

Mindy had removed a sheet from the bed. Wrapped in it, she was standing before the window. When she heard the door open she whirled. Her head was quite clear. She expected to see the man in the white hood and she was ready to defend herself with all her strength. Instead, she flushed as memories came to her on seeing the pretty woman.

"Who are you?" Lilah demanded.

"My name is Miranda Woodrowe."

"Where are you from?"

"I live with my husband, my son and my mother-in-law in a small community in the Choctaw Nation," Mindy said, sudden hope springing up. "I am being held here against my will."

"Oh, damn," Lilah said. "Stay here. I'll be right back." She was back in minutes with clothing. Mindy's hope grew as she dressed and, feeling almost decent for the first time in days, said, "Please help me. I want to go home."

"You will," Lilah said. "First I want to know something. Why are you here? What does Rupert have against you?"

She told her, and as she talked the older woman looked at her as if seeing her for the first time and Mindy did not know, then, the turmoil in Lilah's mind.

"So it is you," Lilah breathed. My God. Her own daughter. She'd known lust for her own daughter. That damnable Glendower! "You say you have a son?"

"Yes," Mindy said. "A little boy. Please help me return to him."

Strange, the way she felt. She had not thought about the child she'd never seen for years until Rupert had brought up the subject. And now she was standing before her and she'd been defiled by a man Lilah trusted. And, worst, she, herself, had been tricked by Rupert into making love to her own daughter. A cold fury grew in her, calm, hot, and she knew that only one thing would quench it. First, however, she had to get this girl out of here.

"Come," she said. She led the way down the stairs. She sent one of the girls for a surrey. She knew there'd be trouble, but that was only a part of it. When this girl, who was not much more than a child, told her story, there'd probably be no place for her in Chetopa. Especially not after she did what she had to do. "I'm going to take you to the hotel," she told Miranda. "You won't have to worry about Rupert Glendower again. This I promise you."

"Oh, thank you," Miranda said.

"I didn't know," Lilah said, feeling the hopelessness of it. She wanted to explain, to beg forgiveness. But her good sense told her that the girl had been through enough. No need to burden her with the knowledge that the woman who had come into bed was her mother.

She heard footsteps on the stoop. "There's the surrey," she said. "Let's go."

But the door opened and it was Rupert Glendower who came in. "What the hell's going on?" he demanded. "Get this bitch back upstairs."

She drew the small gun from the folds of her

gown, a little derringer, two barrels, a woman's gun. "No, Rupe," she said. "Get out of my way."

"Lilah, you're crazy," Rupert said. "I've got plans for this girl. She's going to make us a lot of money."

"No," she said. "You'll never make money again." Her finger whitened on the small trigger and the tiny weapon barked. Rupert, not believing it, saw her hand tense and threw himself to one side, the bullet whizzing past him, and he knew she had another barrel and he was on the floor tugging at his gun and the gun swung to look at him. Small, but at that range it would kill. His own .44 exploded once.

Lilah was thrown backward by the impact. She fell, not making a sound, and blood began to ooze from the white lace which covered her breast. She was very still.

At first Mindy was paralyzed. Then, as the action started, she moved quickly, having been slightly ahead and to one side of Lilah. She darted for the door even as Glendower started to get up off the floor. She caromed off a tall young man and ran, stumbling for a moment, down the steps into the street. The young man continued on the run into the house.

She did not look back.

When Tony burst into the room the first thing he saw was the crumpled form of his mother on the red carpet, her own blood redder than the floor covering. And Glendower was moving toward the door, a gun in his hand. When he saw Tony he froze, pointed the gun at Tony's middle.

"Rupe?" Tony asked, not being able to take it all in.

"Get out of the way, Tony," Rupert said. "The girl's escaping."

"You've killed my mother," Tony said. "You've killed her."

He was blocking the door. Rupert knew that he should kill him, too. He knew that it would be to his advantage to shoot him right then and there, but his judgment was impaired by his hate for Mindy. He wanted her back. He moved toward the door, gesturing with the gun. "I'm going after the girl, Tony. Then we'll talk. I can explain."

Tony, still stunned, moved to one side. Rupert started to move swiftly past him and, the gun barrel pointed away from him, Tony jumped him. They went down onto the floor in a tangle of struggling limbs. Both were strong men and for a few moments neither could gain an advantage. Girls, startled by the shots, were pouring down the stairs. One screamed when she saw Lilah's body on the floor.

Rupert managed to free the arm holding the gun. Girls were screaming and crying. Tony was trying to claw out his eyes. He laid the gun barrel across Tony's scalp, hard, and extracted himself from the suddenly lax hands of the man. He was thinking quickly and it was damned well clear. Once again the girl, that damned girl, had done him in. He'd had it in Chetopa. He'd killed a very popular woman. He couldn't shoot Tony now with all the girls there. There was only one thing for him to do.

"All right," he said. "One of you go for the doctor. The others take these two upstairs. Everything's going to be all right."

Like hell it was. The girl was probably right now in the sheriff's office and there was a dead woman on the floor. While the girls fluttered and wept, moving to do as he said, he ran up the stairs to his private quarters, opened the small safe there. He could carry his gold in one carpet bag. He didn't bother with anything else. He went down the back stairs and saddled his best horse. He made it out of town without trouble, riding west. This time, maybe he would make it all the way to California.

Mindy had run breathlessly toward the hotel. Her appearance there, her face flushed, her hair falling, startled the desk clerk, and he was even more startled when he recognized her. He gasped.

"My things," she said. "My railroad ticket."

"But they said you were dead," the clerk said.

"Where are they?" she half-screamed, for she had only one thought in mind. She wanted only to get away from the shame and horror of the past few—she didn't even know how many—days.

"Why the girl, your girl, she took them."

"Please help me,'" she said. "I need money for a ticket on the train."

"But it's about to pull out now," he said.

"Please, please," she begged. "It's only a few dollars. When I reach home I'll mail it to you."

Dazed, the clerk opened the cash register and gave her the money she asked for. "What else could I do?" he asked the hotel owner later. "If a dead woman asked you for train fare what would you do?"

She had to run. Fortunately the railroad hotel

was near the depot. She caught the train just as it started to move and fell into a seat. Then and only then did she have time to think. Glendower should be punished. She should have gone to the sheriff, but the very thought of staying longer within the reach of the monster who had killed her father-in-law, emasculated her husband shamed and defiled her was abhorrent. She could think only of escape, of getting back to the people she loved, of forgetting. She purchased her ticket from the conductor and then fell into a stunned and exhausted sleep, but not before asking the conductor to send a telegram at the next stop. She did not want Chota and Grand to have the same shock that the hotel clerk had felt. She told them she was alive, and coming home.

At Crossroads, Chota and Wynema wept happily. Grand seemed to be unmoved by the news. He merely nodded and went off to his studio. Chota thought he was quite mad, but not even continued concern for him could dampen her happiness. The day that Mindy arrived home was a happy, weeping, laughing, excited occasion. She hugged little Grand to her bosom and wet his face with tears so that he scruched up his eyes and tried to wipe away the tickle with his pudgy hands.

It was minutes after she was in the house that she asked, "But where's Grand?"

Chota and Wynema were asking her excited questions about what had happened to her. At her own question, Chota's face went grave. "He's changed, Mindy. He's not himself."

"Is he in the studio?" she asked.

He did not look up when she came in. She walked slowly to him, rounded the corner of his vast canvas which was suspended on a wooden framework.

"Hello, Grand, darling," she said.

He did not speak for moments, did not look at her. He attacked a portion of the canvas with a laden brush, driving the paint as if he intended to punch it through the canvas. She looked at the work he'd done so far.

It was vast. It was overwhelming. It was so powerful as to be almost painful.

"It's magnificent," she said.

"You should have gone back to California," he said.

"I know, but I didn't."

"I'm glad you're alive."

"Yes," she said.

At last he turned to her. "I couldn't even weep for you, Mindy. I've been dead for a long time."

She wanted to weep, to scream and wail out her sadness, but she controlled it. "You want to work. I'll leave."

"Yes, thank you," he said.

To see him beaten, so withdrawn, looking pudgy and overweight, his once-handsome face buried under folds of fat was a sadness she could not face.

"What did he say?" Chota asked, when she was back inside, holding her son in her arms.

"We've lost him, Chota," she said.

"I know."

"Oh, what can we do? What can we do?"

"The best we can," Chota said. "Take care of

him, pray for him, hope that someday he'll come
out of that place where he's gone."

In her own bed she told herself that it was
over. No more could happen. Word had arrived
that the Congress had passed the bill which, once
and for all, took away national sovereignty from
the Indian Nations. Her trip had been for nothing. All that had happened to her had been for
nothing. The way she nearly jumped into the
bed of the first handsome man who wooed her,
the degradation she had undergone at the hands
of Rupert Glendower and the woman who had
died trying to get her out of Rupert's house, all
had been for naught.

So now she would forget. She would not tell
Chota all of the truth about her captivity. No
need to let that kind and sweet woman know
that the nemesis of the Woodrowe family had
struck again. She would stay where she belonged,
with Chota, with Wynema, with her son. She
would teach him to grow strong and healthy and
to respect his father's heritage. She considered herself to be a ruined woman. She felt great hatred
for her body, for that body had responded to
Glendower's lovemaking, and to the sinful caresses of the woman. Well, that problem would
solve itself. Never again would she touch a man.
It was all over. All of it.

Except the telegram which arrived for her
days later, a vindictive gesture by a bitter man.
It was a long and expensive telegram and as she
read it she considered ways to end everything,
to take her own life. Only the fact that she was
holding little Grand in her arms as she read
stopped such thoughts.

WANT YOU TO KNOW MAN WAS NOT ME.
WAS TONY GIRONDIN, YOUR HALF-BROTHER.
WOMAN WAS YOUR MOTHER, LILAH GIRON-
DIN.

And he even had the gall to sign the wire with
his own name. Rupert Glendower.

Mad. He was mad. Nothing she had done to
him could have inspired him to go to such lengths
had he not been mad. And, oh God, she had
enjoyed her sinning. Her own brother. Her own
mother. She wept in self-hatred.

For days she, herself, thought she might be
going mad. And then her natural health, her
youth, her love for those around her came to
the fore and she was able to push those memories down and suppress them, except in dark
moments. Life was good and it went on. Her outlook improved gradually until she was, once
again, vitally interested in the life at Crossroads,
working the garden, cleaning house, helping
Chota and Wynema in the store, caring for the
baby. She even found time to write a barrage
of letters to congressmen and senators on behalf
of the Choctaws, pointing out continued injus-
tices.

So quickly and so thoroughly did she recover
that when she knew for certain that it was not
all over she took it with calmness. She was carrying a baby. She could no nothing about it, but
it was an intolerable thing. Unknowingly, she
had committed a cardinal sin, the sin of incest.
She knew that she could never raise a child which
was the result of such a union. Of such unions,
too, monsters were produced.

She made her plans quietly. She would not share her shame. She told Chota that she was going away for some time, that she would be back when she could resolve certain questions in her mind. She confided only in Wynema and swore to her that if she breathed a word, then or at any time in the future, she would flay her alive.

Once the subject was opened, Wynema was not satisfied until she knew all the story. "Rupe did that?" she asked. "It was Rupert Glendower?"

"Your old master," Mindy said.

"He should not have done that to you," Wynema said. But she could remember the pride she'd once known to be Rupert's woman. She asked questions. She heard of the fancy house, the beautiful woman whom Rupert had killed. And she felt just a bit of resentment, although she was very happy where she was. He could have made an effort to find her, however. She'd loved that man, and he had made no effort to find her. She had always known that Rupert was a mean man, and what he'd done to Miranda, a woman she'd come to love, made her blood boil.

But those problems were past. The present problem would begin to swell Mindy's stomach in a short time and she was determined to hide the ultimate shame. "Well, we go out of the Nation," young Wynema said.

"I don't want to be around people," Mindy said. "I'll think about it. I'll let you know."

But it was Wynema who came up with a solution. The time of good living, of good food and regular hours of sleep and of happiness had caused her to blossom. Her young body had filled out and in spite of her dark skin there were those among the young men who came into the Crossroads store who found her most interesting. One in particular had caught her eye in return, and there had been some aspects of the rituals of courtship between them. His name was Jimmy Bemo. He had come out of the small Seminole nation to work in the coal mines in Choctaw country.

The Seminoles, more than the other tribes, had mixed with the Negroes both in the south and in the new territory, and so Wynema's blackness was not an obstacle with Jimmy Bemo. He had worked in the mines for over two years and had saved his money and was ready to go back to his home country, but he wanted Wynema to go with him. In his efforts to persuade her he told her of his people, and talked endlessly of the beauty of the Seminole lands and, immediately to the west, the vast and almost empty area where, maybe someday, they could take up a homestead and have a place of their own.

Wynema, although not averse to his occasional kisses when opportunity arose, could not quite bring herself to put her life into the hands of another man, not when she was so content with Miranda and Chota. However, when Miranda's problem became known, she saw possibilities.

"There is a man," she told Miranda, "and I think you should speak with him."

"Why?" Mindy wanted to know.

"Come, and I will tell you," Wynema said, leading her outside where Jimmy Bemo was sitting on the porch swing.

"I want you to tell my mistress what you told me about the place in the Unassigned Lands where you used to go to hunt and to visit with the spirits."

Bemo, at first shy, told of a lovely valley, of broad and open grazing lands on which no cows grazed, of a small, crystal clear creek. There was a log cabin there, built by Bemo and his young friends. It was comfortable and tight. There was plenty of wood for the fireplace and the rude cookstove.

Miranda looked at Wynema and smiled. "It sounds such a lovely place," she said.

"I think you would like it," Wynema said. "But we would need a man to chop the wood and to give us protection."

"You want to go there?" Jimmy asked in puzzlement, wondering why this beautiful white woman would want to go to such isolated areas.

"We would," Mindy said. "And we would like to stay through the winter."

"Then you would, as Wynema says, need a man."

"Would you like to go there?" Mindy asked, having seen by the looks exchanged between Jimmy and Wynema that there was a bit of fire there.

"You are going?" he asked Wynema.

"I go with my mistress."

"Then I will go."

Miranda swore both of them to secrecy. She announced to Chota that she would be going to visit her family in California, asked her to keep the baby, since such a trip would be hard on little Grand. Chota wept to think of losing her for months, but she agreed. The mechanics were simple. It was natural for Mindy to take Wynema as a companion and a lady's maid. They sent the carriage back home from the railhead, bought horses. Jimmy Bemo had met them there. Mindy rode hard, for there was a chance that the horse riding, the roughness, the bouncing, would solve her problem through abortion, but they made their way northwest, across the South Canadian, into Seminole country without incident. She was beamingly healthy. In the Seminole country they laid in supplies. And then they traveled westward, three young people of different racial backgrounds, of differing shades of color, but all enjoying the feeling of exploration, of seeing new country every day.

"It is called Tandy Creek," Jimmy announced, as they sat horse at the top of a sloping rise and looked down onto the beautiful valley. The stream was small, but icy and crystal clear. Huge crayfish were to be had in it. It was the finest drinking water. Grass at times brushed the bellies of the horses as they rode down and to a grove of trees among which nestled the log cabin. And then there were a few days of frantic housecleaning. The soiled bedticking was emptied of old, moldy grass and washed, then restuffed with fresh dried grass. The cookstove produced meals of rabbit, squirrel, and deer.

Of that time Miranda would remember most the beauty of that little valley, the Tandy Creek valley. She spent long hours riding alone as her stomach grew and the seasons changed. She knew that a relationship had developed between Wynema and Jimmy Bemo, and she gave it her tacit blessing.

Strangely, she was at peace. She would not

have minded staying there forever in that lovely
little valley which belonged to no man, which
was a part of the territory which had been promised to the Indians, but which had been leased
from them by the government for future use in
settling, perhaps, the warring western tribes. It
seemed a shame for so much rich and beautiful
land to be so empty, but she reveled in her privacy, loved the clear, crisp autumn days, welcomed the onslaught of winter.

The baby was born in December, almost a
Christmas baby. While a worried Jimmy Bemo
stoked the fires in both fireplace and cookstove
and walked the floor, Wynema positioned Mindy
on the kitchen table. Mindy's labor was mercifully short. The baby, a girl, was born in the
early hours of a chill December morning with
sleet sizzling on the tin roof of the cabin. Wynema
lifted the infant by its feet and slapped the little
red bottom. The child did not respond.

She knew the feelings of her mistress. She
knew that Miranda hated the man who had
planted the seed in her, and, as a result, hated
the baby. She had seen her mistress do everything possible to try to abort the child. It was
a blessing, she knew, that the little girl would not
breathe. And yet the tiny thing she held in her
hand was so beautifully formed, so lovely, so
defenseless. She continued to slap the bottom
lightly. Mindy had passed into a swoon upon
the last effort. And then, in desperation, knowing only that the tiny bundle of flesh should live,
deserved a chance to live, Wynema dipped her
hand into a bucket of water, icy, fresh from the

creek with skim ice along the edges, and flicked the water into the baby's face.

The little face screwed up, lungs pumped, and there issued a faint cry which grew in strength as Wynema quickly cleaned away the residue of the birthing and wrapped the infant.

"It is a girl," she told Mindy, reviving her with a cool cloth dipped into the same water which had given life to the baby.

"I don't want to see it," Mindy said. "You know what I want you to do."

"Oh, Mindy, she's such a pretty little girl," Wynema said, tears forming.

"If you love me, Wynema, you will keep the promise you have made," Mindy said in a dull voice.

"I will," Wynema said.

She bundled into her clothing. She took the well wrapped infant and went into the sleet storm. Jimmy followed her, his face expressionless. They walked, the sleet stinging their exposed faces, to the creek. And, even though it was not logical to be concerned, Wynema carefully protected the baby's face by folding coverings over it.

She stood by the icy creek, tears streaming down her face.

"You will do this?" Jimmy asked.

"I promised."

"It is a great sin to stifle that small spirit."

"A great wrong was done my mistress. She could never love the baby."

"And so you will drown her in the ice water of the creek," Jimmy said.

"I have promised."

"There is, in the Bible, the story of Moses," Jimmy said. "He was to die, but his mother put him into a bundle of reeds and set him adrift on the Nile, so that he lived when he was taken in."

"Oh, I wish this were the Nile, then," Wynema said, kneeling.

"Don't," Jimmy said harshly, as she held the baby outward preparing to sink it into the water. "Give the child to me."

She could not have done it, anyhow. She handed him the child gladly. "Little girl," Jimmy said. "We will give your small spirit a chance at life."

"What will you do?"

"I will ride with her," Jimmy said. "I know of a couple, Seminoles, who have no children. They will, perhaps, take her in."

"Oh, yes," Wynema said. "Oh, do it, Jimmy, please."

And she told Mindy that the deed was done, that Jimmy had taken the small body into the hills for burial. She wept with relief, knowing that the small girl was nestled in Jimmy's arms, warmly wrapped, on the way to a life. Mindy's bitter tears were different.

Winter's gloom had settled down into the valley and into the log house. When Mindy was strong again, they closed up the cabin and rode outward, through the Seminole Nation, selling their horses and taking a stage back to Crossroads. There they were greeted with joy. Once again Mindy hold her son in her arms, and she could almost forget, but not quite ever, that she had caused the death of her own child.

Now, at last, she could settle down to rearing

her son, to the quiet life at Crossroads. She was pleased when Wynema announced that she would marry the Seminole, Jimmy Bemo, and he would continue to work in the mines, nearby, so that she would not have to leave those she loved for some time.

However, one final shock awaited her. It was some time before Chota remembered that a man had been twice looking for her. "He would not give his name," Chota said. "He asked for you and said that he would keep coming back until you returned from California."

He came in the early spring, a tall, handsome young man who rode into the community sitting straight and proud in the saddle, went directly to the store to find Mindy there. She was alone in the store at the moment.

She looked up as he came in. She did not recognize him, of course, since she'd never seen his face nor heard his voice during the times he came to her bed.

"Hello, Miranda," he said, looking at her with piercing dark eyes, a faint smile on his face.

"Hello. Do I know you?"

How beautiful she was, Tony Girondin was thinking. He had not been able to get her out of his mind. And he was apprehensive. After Rupert left and he'd buried Lilah, he'd pieced it all together. What Rupert Glendower had done to this lovely girl deserved death, and he'd spent months looking for Rupert to avenge the death of his mother and the wrongs which had been done to her daughter.

"Yes and no," he said.

"My, how mysterious," she said, but she did

not like the way she was feeling. There was something disturbingly familiar about the tall young man whose smile had faded and whose face was now serious.

"Miranda, I must talk with you, and I want you to promise me that you'll listen. Some of what I say will be a shock to you. Could we go somewhere where we will not be disturbed?"

What was it about him? He was handsome enough. He exuded a masculine virility. He seemed, from his speech, to be well educated. His clothing was not rich, not poor, but typical of the sort of man who was accustomed to traveling great distances alone on horseback.

"Yes," she said. "I suppose we can. Let me call my mother-in-law." She got Chota, who came in with little Grand in her arms. She did not ask questions. Mindy led the stranger to the house and offered coffee. He sat and waited as she served and then she seated herself opposite him.

Tony had long been thinking of what he would say. He sipped coffee, then looked at her. "For the past few months I have been traveling most of Kansas looking for a man called Rupert Glendower," he said.

She felt faint. A hand fluttered to her breast.

"If I had found him I would have killed him," Tony said. "I would have killed him for what he did to you and for what he did to Lilah Girondin."

"Oh, no," she said, the shock of it almost too much for her. She had done her best to put it all out of her mind, and now this stranger was bringing it back. "But how did you know?"

"My name is Tony Girondin," he said.

She felt her brain reel and the room seemed to dwindle. The telegram had said, the man was your brother, Tony Girondin. She managed to rise. "Get out of my house," she said.

"Miranda—Mindy—I didn't know. Please understand that I didn't know."

"Get out, or I will call men and have them kill you," she said. "How dare you come here? Haven't you and your kind done enough to me and my family?" She was running for the door.

"Mindy, listen," he begged, rising. "I knew nothing of Glendower's plan. He was mad."

"But you took advantage of it, didn't you?" she asked, rage in her voice. "You certainly took advantage of a helpless and drugged woman. Now will you get out?"

He stood and reached into the inside pocket of his coat. "Yes, I thought you might feel this way. I will leave this for you and perhaps you will read it at your leisure. We have much in common. Will you, please, see me again? I will, someday, find Glendower and kill him. He killed the woman I loved most in the world, and he did horrible things to you, to whom that woman gave birth."

Looking out the door, she saw Wynema and Jimmy Bemo driving up in front of the store. "Jimmy," she called, "bring a gun and help me."

Startled, Jimmy sat motionless for a moment, then pulled a Winchester from the boot installed on the surrey and came running.

"I'll go, Mindy. I don't want to cause trouble. But listen. He told you, didn't he, that I was your half-brother?"

"And you shamed me," she said. "You came

in that white hood and shamed me. You, who share common blood with me."

"He told me you were merely a new girl in the house. And, Mindy—"

But Jimmy was bursting into the door, rifle cocked and ready. Tony raised his hands. "Just take it easy," he said. "I'm leaving." Jimmy watched him closely, moving aside so that he could go out the door. On the porch he said, "Miranda, read the material I have left you."

She was shaken. When he had ridden away she assured Jimmy and Wynema that she was fine. But she sat there for a long time before she picked up the packet which Tony had left on a table. It was a small, leather-bound book. She opened it and there was a loose piece of paper. It was in a rough, masculine handwriting.

Miranda

The enclosed diary gave me several shocks. When Lilah Girondin was killed by Rupert Glendower, I lost a mother. Or, at least, I thought I had. Actually, on reading the enclosed, I discovered that it was you who lost a mother.

I know little of Glendower's motives in shaming you, only that he hated you. I'm sure in my mind that it was a part of his plan to hurt you to lure me, whom he thought was your own half-brother, in debauching you. So you are, I'm sure, hiding a great guilt within yourself, thinking that you participated in incest with, at times, great joy. Read page twenty-two and your mind will be relieved, at least of one worry.

If you read this it means that you have not listened to me. Perhaps, having read it, you will then be willing to meet with me and talk about a very warm and good woman, Lilah Girondin. She was a prostitute, Mindy, but she was a human being and a lovely person. I'm only sorry that you did not get to know her.

If you read all of the diary, remember that Lilah was led into her life by circumstances beyond her control, and that to the end she loved me as if she were my real mother. If you do not choose to read the memoirs of a lady of pleasure, read only those passages which pertain to you. Page twenty-two and page seventy-nine. If you wish to discuss this further, and it would give me great pleasure to get to know you in a decent way, please write to me General Delivery, Chetopa.

Tony Girondin

Her heart was pounding as she picked up the diary. The first page was labled in a flowery feminine hand as the journal of the life of Lilah Girondin, age fifteen, New Orleans. She quickly thumbed to page twenty-two and began reading. The date was April 10, 1850.

At the age of not quite sixteen, I am a mother! I am so excited. I have named the boy Tony. He is only one day old and such a little dear. My how he goes after the food from the breast of the wet-nurse. How I came to be a mother is a story which I will, someday, tell to my little Tony. So, in order to remem-

ber all the details, I will set them down here,
where all my secrets lie, locked always in my
trunk.

My dear little son, I love you already. At
last I have something which is all my own,
something I can love without fear of hurt in
return. Someday, my little Tony, you yourself will read this, and you will wonder, I'm
sure, how you came to be my son. Your
mother's name is Mimaud de Arlous, and she
is a fine lady of New Orleans society. Your
father? Mima would not tell me this, although
we are dear friends, but gave me hints which
make me think grand and glorious thoughts
for your future, for if my suspicious are correct, you have royal blood in those tiny veins.
The time elements works out perfectly, for
when that august personage visited here in
New Orleans, he stayed with my friend,
Mimaud de Arlous, and, a few months later
she began to swell. It is quite likely that your
father is none less than Louis Napoleon of
France, son of Napoleon Bonaparte's brother,
Louis, who was once King of Holland. Thus,
my little one, if it is true, your father is now
President of France and, I am told, is likely
to be elected Emperor and to be as great as
his uncle without, I pray, the disastrous
results.

Ah, my little prince. What will you think
when, one day you will inevitably discover
that, although you have noble parentage, you
have been given into the hands of a courtesan?
I will try to make it up to you by loving you

as I never have loved and never will love again.

The words blurred with Mindy's tears. Not her brother? He was not her brother? Ah, God, then what she had done in the dead of winter in that log cabin in the Unassigned Lands had new meaning. She had not killed the damned and hopeless product of incest, but had killed a child in whose veins flowed the royal blood of France. Stunned, she fluttered pages and saw a name which leaped out at her. Danny O'Lee.

Lilah Girondin had met Danny O'Lee in Texas and had fallen in love with him and, from her writing, he with her. She had given up her profession for a time and had lived with Danny O'Lee. Many pages were devoted to their travels, to her love for him. And then, with great interest, Mindy was reading of her own birth and the heartbreak felt by a young girl when she was told that her lover was to leave her and go back to his family in California.

How cruel, how hard. And yet he told me from the beginning that he would have to leave. For a while it seemed that I would be always happy, that in addition to my little son, Tony, I would have another child to love, a child of my own loins, a love child whose father has named Miranda. But he is to leave. And, to my great sadness, he is to take the little girl. It is the hardest decision I've ever had to make, and yet I know I am right. He will be able to give her a home with this

*wife of his whom I have never seen and about
whom he rarely speaks. I pray that she will
take my little girl into her heart and love her.*

She spent a day with the diary, secluded in her
room. She could watch the development of her
mother from a near child of fifteen, already a kept
woman, but a young courtesan who was kept by
men of great riches, to a woman in love with
Danny O'Lee and then, finally, into out-and-
out prostitution. As the years passed, the thoughts
put down into the diary became less and less
sensitive, and it stopped completely several years
before her death.

Mindy could feel a great sadness for the
woman who had died on the red carpet of a house
of prostitution, but she was more saddened by her
own actions. She had not even looked at her
little girl baby. Strange, her mother had borne a
girl child and had given it up. She had given
birth to a girl child and had killed it.

She was red-eyed with weeping when Wynema,
wondering, having stayed to talk with Chota
about Mindy's strange behaviour following the
visit of the unknown man, came into the room
and insisted on speaking, asking her what was
wrong. Since Wynema knew, and since she felt
a great need to speak of her guilt, she told
Wynema the contents of the diary.

"Ah, now I understand," Wynema said. "You
thought the child was the son of your own
brother, and now you know that she was not."

"Oh, Wynema, if I had only known," she cried.
"It would have been difficult to explain to those

who know about Grand, but, oh, if I had only
known."

"Yes, it is a shame," Wynema said, thinking
hard.

"Was she pretty?"

"A very pretty baby."

"Did she—did she suffer?" She could barely
speak the words.

And, to her shock, Wynema laughed. "Maybe
her toes got cold as Jimmy carried her to a house
where a childless couple took her in gladly."

Joy leaped up in her. She seized Wynema by
the arms. "Don't build my hopes falsely, please.
She is alive? You didn't drown her?"

"I couldn't, Mindy. I just couldn't. She was so
healthy, at least after I threw creek water into her
face and started her breathing, and so pretty. I
could never have killed anything so helpless, so
sweet."

"Oh, bless you, bless you. Do you know these
people?"

"My Jimmy knows."

"Bring him to me. I must know. I must go
there. Oh, hurry, Wynema. Hurry."

Part Two

1

When one looks back, from the ripe old age of thirty-five, over one's life, it is easy to see that life is quite often directed by coincidence. Miranda Woodrowe seldom had time for speculation about what might have been, but now and then the thought did enter her mind. What if she had not overheard her mother and her brother talking, thus learning that she was not the daughter of a powerful California woman but of a prostitute of mixed blood? What if she had not promptly run to the bed of Grand Woodrowe?

She sometimes felt that she would have found her way into the Choctaw Nation had she not met Grand, for after eighteen years there she felt that she would never have been happy living anywhere else. Eighteen years. And the first two filled with tragedy and violence. How swiftly they had passed. How much things had changed since she came into the Nation a young runaway, living in sin with a man much older than she. The change was all around her, in her personal life, in the growth of the Crossroads community into the booming town of McAlister, in the development of her two children.

During those eighteen years she had lost much, her husband; her beloved mother-in-law; a woman she might have enjoyed knowing, the woman who gave birth to her; a possible sweet love in James Allen. But she had gained much, too. Although his father, prematurely aged, still secluded himself in his studio, a man half-mad with his regrets and his losses, working endlessly on that huge canvas which had been altered so many times that Mindy could not remember the original form, her son, young Grand, was alive as a wildcat in a hornet's nest, an endless source of pride for her. And Tandy. Ah, that Tandy.

Tandy had been an early bloomer. She had zipped her way through the very good schools of the Choctaws, had learned not only Choctaw but Chickasaw, Creek and Cherokee and a good smattering of French, and in the process she had broken the hearts of many young men.

Possibly because she had lost her and then regained her, Miranda doted on her daughter. Mother and daughter looked much alike. If anything, the daughter, and not only because of her youth, was more beautiful. But there was in her a streak of wildness, of rebellion, which both angered and worried Mindy.

Wynema's husband, the Seminole Jimmy Bemo, had named the girl for the creek beside which she was born, the creek whose icy waters, when sprinkled in her face, caused her to begin to breath and to wail in protest. When Miranda recovered the infant from the Seminoles with whom Jimmy had placed her, the child given up reluctantly, she did not change it. She was Tandy, and she was her mother's pride and her cross.

Grand was a solid-minded lad. He had helped in the construction of the new store. Always dependable, always protective of his mother, he also helped look after his father who, as he aged, became more and more absent-minded, more and more withdrawn. And he often visited the studio to sit in awe and stare at the grand design of the life-time of labor which was his father's mural of the history of the Choctaws. The colors, the action, the stories it told—he could never see enough of it.

Although he was only a fraction Indian, he felt as much a part of the Choctaw Nation as Miranda did, and early on began to understand the problems which faced it.

One of the continuing problems was the railroads. The Act of 1871 gave Congress the right to grant building permission to railroads, regardless of the wishes of the Indians. Now they speculated in townsites, in coal land. Indeed, it was coal which had built Crossroads into a new town. Coal, good grazing land, the railroads, and the people brought in by each, the pressures for opening the assigned Lands to white settlement, all concerned the Indians.

Mindy, respected, open with her advice and always ready for a fight, had been active in all the losing battles through the years. When, in 1880, a man named David Wayne led several hundred families into the Unassigned Lands, crossing the Cherokee Strip in secrecy, sending out the message that it was no longer a question of when the lands were going to be settled, for they were settled as of then, she was among the first to send protesting telegrams to congressmen, the president, and the Bureau of Indian Affairs.

When Federal Troops removed the "Boomers", she breathed a sigh of relief.

"We might as well face it, Mother," Grand told her. "It's only the beginning. They'll be back. There's active lobbying in congress to get the Unassigned Lands opened."

"I know, I know," she said. "But for years I've been fighting to postpone the inevitable. After the Unassigned Lands what next? Individual allotments? The Nations become a part of the United States?"

"Well, at least maybe there'd be some excitement around here then," Tandy said.

Miranda had made up a convincing story as to why Tandy had been born in the Unassigned Lands, and in her telling of it she remembered the beauty of the Tandy Creek Valley, talked about it often. Out of curiosity, Grand rode there, saw the place, and returned to tell his sister and mother that his mother had not overstated the beauty of the place.

"If they ever throw the lands open for settlement, I'll be there first," Grand said.

"And leave me?" Miranda teased.

"No, I'll just leave Tandy," he grinned. "But

I'll warrant you, it's the most beautiful piece of land in the world."

None of them knew that they were not the only ones who thought often of the Tandy Creek Valley. A man who called himself David Wayne also thought of it, for he had seen it more than once, had camped beside the clear creek. When he led his Boomers into the Unassigned Lands he, himself, staked out his claim to enclose the valley and to sit astride the creek. And when he was removed by the soldiers, he vowed that he would come back.

He was a strange man, was David Wayne. He had a huge, bushy red beard, let his auburn hair, as yet untouched by gray, hand down his shoulders. He was a man of curious fire and intensity, a man with a mission. He preached the beauty of the Unassigned Lands to anyone who would listen and his hatred for all things Indian often made his blue eyes seem to blaze with a pale light. His fire, his persuasive ability, took two dollars from many a man, a fee he charged to become a part of his Boomer organization and to have the right to stake a claim, and twenty-five dollars from many who wanted to claim townsites in the capital city he had staked out inside the Unassigned Lands. This money, in addition to payments of gold from a certain railroad executive, allowed him to live well. His setbacks at the hands of the federal soldiers only strengthened his resolve.

When, as many people had expected, the federal government gave in to the clamor for news lands for settlement, when President Har-

rison, during his third week in office, issued a
proclamation for settling the Unassigned Lands,
David Wayne had already organized a new invasion force and was ready. But he refunded the
fees gladly. He had won. He felt that he had been
instrumental in striking, at last, a body blow to
the damned Indians. After the Unassigned Lands
it would be easy. The Cherokee Strip would be
next, and then, soon, the so-called Indian Nations
would be only a memory and white men would
live in that land west of Arkansas, south of
Kansas, and north of Texas. And he, himself,
would be sitting atop the finest land of all, that
land which lay in the Tandy Creek Valley.

Thus, the stage was set for the climactic encounter between the family called Woodrowe
and their old nemesis, for David Wayne was not
the auburn-haired Boomer's legal name. The man
who had led expeditions of settlement into the
Unassigned Lands, the man who had his eye on
the beautiful land around Tandy creek, the man
who had camped there while fleeing the Choctaw
Nation after shooting Caleb Woodrowe in the
back, was Rupert Glendower.

2

It was spring when President Harrison issued his proclamation which spelled the beginning of the end of the Indian Nations, and at the Crossroads Store in McAlester there was excitement in the Woodrowe family. Immediately after the announcement, young Grand announced that he would be gone for a few days, and he came back with crude maps and the assurance that he had scouted out a route which was the quickest and most direct ride to the Tandy Creek Valley.

But the interest in the land opening was not the only cause of a stir. Grand Woodrowe was a sudden celebrity. For years the Indians had come, one by one, to sit and look in awe at Grand's mural, to comment on its composite parts which

329

showed the history of the Choctaw Indians from the beginning of legend, mystical, strange portions at the beginnings giving a version of both of the Choctaw origination legends, moving through the battle with the mounted Conquistadores in Mississippi, through the war of Red Shoes, the removal. No one who saw it was unmoved. The word had spread first in the press within the Indian Nations and that, too, spread, until Grand was visited by a small delegation of men which included reporters and photographers from the east. As a result, pictures and critiques of the work, pronounced great by a famous art critic, had been in newspapers from coast to coast. Along with the picture of the painting was a story which expressed Grand's pride in his work. He had seemed to come out of his shell upon hearing the praise of the easterners, and he had stated that the painting was the work of a lifetime, that it was, in fact, his life.

Encouraged by Grand's seeming return to reality, his son spoke with him.

"I've got a problem, dad," Grand said, "and I need your help."

His father had been seated in front of the mural, musing, for there remained only one problem, and that was the completion of the work. He could not, of course, see into the future and he had a feeling that his years were numbered, and he felt a tremendous need to put on the finishing touches. Leave it open? A question of the future of the Choctaws? That was one solution.

"I want that land along Tandy Creek," young Grand said. "I know how to get there fast. I think

I can beat anyone there, but here's the situation. I'm not twenty-one, and the eligibility rules state that those who can file claims are limited to male citizens of the United States twenty-one or above, unmarried women twenty-one or over, and widows or legal divorcees. You see, you're the only one around who is eligible to file. I'd like for you to come with me, file the claim for me in your name."

At first Grand was reluctant. It would mean leaving the only thing which had meaning for him, but then, like a small ray of sunshine peering through dark clouds, he began to think that it might be good to get away for a few days, to come back and look on the work with new eyes. Perhaps then he could come up with a way of finishing it. He nodded his agreement. And at dinner he even shared some of young Grand's excitement.

Mindy, pleased by her son's interest in Tandy Creek, was heartbroken for her good friends, Wynema and Jimmy Bemo, who as Indians, and not citizens of the United States, were not eligible to make the run and to file claims.

Jimmy took it with an Indian stoicism. "Well, if I can't have it, I can't think of anyone I'd rather see on it than Grand," he said. He offered to make the ride with Grand, and was accepted. Wynema immediately objected, saying that if Jimmy went, she went.

"My God," Grand said. "What's this going to be, a family outing? I warn you, I'm going to be riding fast, just slow enough so as not to kill a good horse. If you fall behind, that's too bad."

"I can outride you any day," his sister said, and a spirited and laughing argument broke out.

Noon of April 22nd was the time. And for weeks in advance people came from all over the east, hungry for land, full of hope. The area to be opened, shaped like an anvil, was bordered on the south by the South Canadian River, by the Creek and Seminole Nations on the east, by the Strip on the north and by the Cheyenne-Arapaho Reservation on the west. The area was about thirty by fifty miles, with Tandy Creek being in the southeast corner. Thus, Grand planned to make his run from near Purcell, on the southern bank of the South Canadian.

Two railroads cut through the Unassigned Lands, the Atcheson, Topeka and Santa Fe would send trains in at the sound of the starting gun from the north, at Arkansas City, and from the south, starting in Chickasaw country at Purcell. And for weeks people made their way through the Cherokee Strip to the north and across the Chickasaw's lands. West-liners approached through the Cheyenne-Arapaho Reservation.

Unwilling to wait, Grand led his little family delegation into the booming Purcell clutter three days in advance and they set up camp outside town. His father made no attempt to be the leader, content to leave the orders and suggestions to his strong young son. Federal troops were on hand, and they were kept busy trying to keep "Sooners" from jumping the gun and staking claims before the official start of the run.

Tandy was in her glory. She had never seen so many people. With her brother, she attended a festive barn dance, dressed in her finest, young, vibrant, the target for all men, young and old. She danced until she was breathless.

Of the many Indians present not all were Chickasaw. It was a festive time, and there was in the Indians' blood a love for celebration, for mingling and listening to the spirited hoedowns played on fiddle, banjo and guitar. Tandy would have admitted that she was showing off when she used her knowledge of the Indian languages to speak with them in the native tongues. She had been conversing in Creek with a charming young man.

"You speak our language well," he said. "Almost as well as I, and I spoke nothing else until I was twelve, although my father is white."

"It's probably one of the most beautiful of all," Tandy said.

"I find it so. In fact, in my limited way, I have tried to put down on paper some of the beauty."

"Oh, you're a writer," Tandy said. "What do you write?"

The young man smiled. "Verses."

"May I hear one?"

"Remember, you asked for it," he said. "Would you like blood and thunder or pathos!"

"Your selection," Tanda said.

He smiled. Around them the dancers swirled. They stood against a wall and the boy, for he was only sixteen, mused for a moment and then began.

Why do trees along the river
Lean so far out o'er the tide?

Very wise men tell me why, but
I am never satisfied;
And so I keep my fancy still,
That trees lean out to save
The drowning from the clutches of
The cold remorseless wave.

"Why that's beautiful," Tandy said. "Do you have more?"

Young Alexander Posey shrugged. "Yes, but this is not the time."

"It's time for dancing," said a slim and handsome young man of mixed blood. "And I claim this prize." So saying, he swept Tandy onto the dance floor.

"Who are you," he asked, "who speaks all the languages so well?"

"Gentlemen first," she said.

"I am one of the infamous Starrs," he grinned. He had a strong face, black hair which shaped his head like a lion's mane, piercing eyes. He was, she felt, quite the most exciting man she'd ever seen. "You can call me Luke."

"And why are you infamous, Luke Starr?"

He laughed. "Actually, I'm still working on it. Some of my kinsmen have already made the grade. Don't you know Cherokee gossip?"

"Oh, those Starrs," Mindy said, for she had read of the battling Starr family, who had engaged in bloody feuds in the Cherokee Nation.

"And what manner of blood flows through those lovely veins?" he asked.

"Choctaw."

"Ah, the tame and docile ones."

"No more tame than you," she said.

The music ended and he led her off the makeshift dance floor. "We're all far too tame," he
said moodily. "Look, we're letting them take us
bit by bit. We let them cross our lands to set up
a white bastion here at our heart."

"Would you fight them?" she asked.

"God, I would. If I were a thousand, a hundred, I would fight. I would bring out the ancient war chants, the weapons, and I would drive
them from our land."

His intensity startled her. She laughed nervously.

"We cannot even go into the lands ourselves,
to claim a small portion of what was ours," he
said. "But we will have our share. I promise you
that."

"Oh?" she asked. "And how will we have our
share?"

"With this," he said, patting his Colt .44 in
its holster. "But enough of this. The music has
begun."

And for the rest of the evening he monopolized
her, snarling at young men who tried to take her
from him. She contrasted him with her bemused
and distant father, with her gay and fun-loving
brother. She had never known such a man. The
touch of his hands seemed as fire.

And, when it was late, and he had asked and
received her consent to see her again, he again
broached the subject of the white takeover. "They
will build their cities and the gold and silver will
flow to and from them," he said. "It will be there
for the taking." He laughed. "Isn't that amusing
to you, that an Indian should profit from the
white's industriousness?"

"It would be fitting," she agreed. "But they will also bring the white law."

"Bah," he said. "I have roved this territory since I was a boy. I know every rock, every stream, every tree. An army could not find me if I wanted to hide."

"Well, when you have made yourself rich and infamous by looting the white man's gold, come to me," she teased, "and I'll help you spend the money."

"Not unless you help me gather it," he said. He took her hand. "You have spirit. You don't like this any better than I do. We'd make a fine team."

Her heart leaped. Silly, she thought. She'd only just met him, so why that uncontrolled beating of her heart?

"I can show you places no man has seen," he said, "wild rivers and undisturbed woodlands, caves in the mountains of the east, in your own Nation, wide valleys, hidden nooks."

"Well, I'm not too wild about living on a horse," she laughed.

"And I can show you something else," he said, taking her suddenly into his arms. Before she could protest he had kissed her, his lips hot, wet, and she felt a weakness in her limbs which she had never experienced.

Miranda and her son spent the evening walking through the assembled peoples, hearing the music of the fiddle, watching as men prepared for the run, talking with men and women from Arkansas, Alabama, Mississippi, Texas. It was an exciting variety. A tent show was in progress

with girls in glittering costumes. And, in a brush
arbor on the outskirts, the voices of good people
raised in hymns praising God. She was walking
with Grand near the arbor when the preacher
began his sermon, and she was struck by the tone
of the voice, took Grand's hand and led him
closer.

Hellfire and brimstone rained down on the
heads of the assembled worshipers, who sat on
crude benches. And the man at the make-shift
pulpit was tall, thin to emaciation, his hair wild
and his eyes wilder. He was preaching the sin of
greed and his voice rose to near hysterical levels.
And she knew that voice. Brother Alphonse, who
had come to the room in which she was being
imprisoned. And for the first time in years she
shuddered with the memory of it, and of Rupert
Glendower. Surely, she thought, he was dead by
now. And yet the sight of Brother Alphonse
brought it all back and she clung to her tall son's
arm and led him away. But while they were still
in the glow of light cast by the lanterns of the
brush arbor she came up short as Tony Girondin
stood before them, taking off his hat to make a
low bow.

"Mrs. Woodrowe," he said. "It is a pleasure
to see you."

The years had been kind to him, as they had
to her. He was in the prime of his manhood, tall,
solidly built, very handsome. She introduced her
son and watched as the two shook hands, thinking of Tandy, seeing that she had Tony's eyes.
It was, indeed, a peculiar feeling to look at him
and remember that he was the father of her

daughter, that she had, for days, yearned for his touch, had been brought to tremendous heights of desire by his kisses.

"Here to make the run?" Grand asked him.

"You bet," Tony said. "I've had my eye on some fine land out there for years. You?"

"I've had my eye on some fine land, and I intend to have it," Grand said. He laughed. "Don't get in front of me or my horse will just go over the top."

Tony, too, laughed. It seemed that there was a feeling of mutual liking between them. "I just hope that we're not after the same quarter section."

"Me, too," Grand said. A girl was waving to him. "Hey," he said. "Will you two excuse me?"

Tony laughed. "Fine looking boy," he said. "You must be very proud of him."

"I am," she said.

She walked and he was beside her. "You're looking quite well," he said. "Life has been good to you?"

"Yes," she said. "And you?" Once she would have run away from him. Now she had to admit to some curiosity.

"Ups and downs," he said. "I waited for a letter from you."

"There seemed to be nothing to say," she said.

"I am eternally sorry for what happened," he said. "And had Lilah known it would never have happened."

"Did you ever find Glendower?" she asked.

"He seemed to vanish off the face of the earth," he said.

"I suppose it's just as well," she said. "I thank you, incidentally, for leaving me the diary."

"It was the least I could do."

"Would you like it back?"

"Oh, someday, if you'll allow me to visit, I'd like to read it again, but it's more yours than mine."

"She loved you very much. She was so proud of you."

"Yes," he said. "Well, it's all past now, and she's at peace. Is Grand your only child?"

She flushed, but under the cover of the darkness he did not see. "No, I have a daughter."

"As beautiful as her mother?"

"Much more so," she laughed, "but thank you."

It was surprisingly easy to talk with him. And for a moment she had a wild urge to tell him, but she was silent. He was nothing more than another reminder of an unpleasant part of her life. In a way he was as much a victim of Glendower as she.

"Miranda," he said, when they had reached the area of the Woodrowe camp, "may I visit?"

"My husband and I would be pleased if you did," she said.

"Ah, yes. I've read of your husband's great artistic ability. I'd like to see that painting."

"Come when you can," she said. "Now I must go in and check on the artist, as a matter of fact. Good night."

He kissed her hand. "Once we both thought you were my sister," he said. "For Lilah's sake, I would like to be your friend."

"Yes," she said.

Grand was sleeping. She worried a bit about

Tandy, the wild one, but she was tired. She was soon in her bedroll, and sleep was quick in coming, but it did not come totally until, in a drowsy state of comfort, her memories rose up like fire and her body, so long without love, seemed to burn with the memory of Tony Girondin. She woke and pushed the thoughts from her mind. That part of her life was past, gone forever.

3

They started lining up on the evening prior to the opening, jostling for positions. Wagons, surreys, fancy carriages, men and women on horseback and on foot. As noontime of the fateful day approached trains stood by, engines puffing steam, to travel into the Unassigned Lands from the north and south, traveling slowly so that landseekers could leap off at their chosen locations. In addition to the rich farm lands available, there were town lots to be claimed in several locations.

Tents and camping equipment left behind, stripped of all unnecessary weight, the Woodrowe group of six, Miranda and Grand, young Grand and his sister, Jimmy and Wynema were positioned to make a dash. The signal, carefully coordinated at several locations, was the firing of pistols by the soldiers. Trains puffed into motion, men shouted at their horses, fired their own guns into the air, riders quickly outdistanced the vehicles as the rush was on.

And it was Grand the younger who took the lead, racing away from the small group just down the river from Purcell, Tandy, riding astride like a young demon, close on his heels. The elder Grand, puffed with his obesity, thinking mostly of his painting, stayed with Mindy and soon the two youngsters were out of sight.

It was a wild and glorious ride, with others in sight at first, and then the crowd dissipated, some falling out to stake their claim for one hundred and sixty acres.

Tony Girondin had started from a different point, and his goal was, by coincidence, quite near the sweet and fertile Tandy Creek Valley. He had a good horse and appeared to be out in front of everyone.

Grand had chosen his animal with care, selecting a horse built for distance. After the initial burst of speed he settled down into a mile-eating gallop, looking back now and then to see, with a smile of amusement, that Tandy was keeping within sight of him and, indeed, as he crossed an area of buffalo grass in smooth, rolling country, she pulled even with him.

"Go, big brother, go," she yelled, putting the heel to her horse.

"Way to go yet," he called after her. "Better not push him too hard."

They topped the last rolling hill and there below them was the Tandy, meadows green with uncropped fresh grass, the small creek a jewel in the bright sunlight. With a whoop, Tony kicked his horse onto the downslope. And his heart fell when he saw a freshly cut stake with markings. He saw the campfire then, down by the creek under a cottonwood.

"Sooners," he told Tandy. "Damned Sooners. No way they could have beat us here and had time to put out stakes and build a fire."

"Oh, Grand," she cried. "What will we do?"

"I'm not letting any cheating Sooner steal my land," he said.

He pulled his horse to a violent stop near the tree and a tall man with a mane of auburn hair and a huge, fiery beard stood there, rifle in hand.

"Friend," said the red-haired man, "you're a little late."

"Friend," said Grand, "you know and I know that you're a Sooner. You've been here God knows how long. I'm going to file my claim and then we'll see what happens."

"Now look, sonny," Rupert Glendower said. "You've got it wrong. And I'll tell you something. Nobody's going to jump my claim." He hefted the rifle and levered a round into the chamber.

"Grand, there's other land," Tandy said, a bit frightened. "We can take the next section down the creek."

Glendower grinned. "Well, I wouldn't mind having you for a neighbor, little lady, but I think you'll find that claim taken, too. Me and my friends, we took the whole valley, as a matter of fact. All two full sections of it up onto the western slope, but there's good land on beyond. You can get it if you hurry."

"You've cheated, sir," Grand said. "And I will file a counter claim." He whirled his horse and rose to the end of the piece of land he'd picked out in advance, Tandy following worriedly. They got off their horses.

"Don't, Grand," she said. "Let's move on and find another piece."

"This is mine," Grand said. "I've wanted it ever since I saw it. And no cheating Sooner is going to have it."

He picked up a rock and started driving his stake into the ground. The rifle slug took him high in the shoulder and he pitched forward.

"I didn't shoot to kill," Glendower yelled, from fifty yards away. "Now I'd advise you to get that claim jumper off my land."

With fire in her heart, Tandy ran to her horse, yanked her Winchester from the boot.

"Don't do it," Glendower yelled, going into a crouch, his rifle pointed at her. "I don't want to have to shoot a woman." With a sob, Tandy let the gun slide back into the scabbard. She ran to Grand, who was moaning, his eyes open.

"Go for help, Tandy."

"They'll be here in a few minutes," she said. "I'll stay with you."

Meanwhile, in the excitement, Miranda and the elder Grand had been pushing hard, catching and passing Wynema and Jimmy, who, having nothing at stake other than the race itself, did not want to harm their horses. Mindy burst over the rise and started down, Grand just behind. She saw the fiery-haired man standing with his rifle pointing at the forms of her children, Tandy kneeling over the fallen son, and she cried out. She reined in and leaped from the horse, running to fall onto her knees.

"He's not hurt bad," Tandy said. "That man—"

"What's happened?" the elder Grand asked, puffing as he ran to join them.

Rupert Glendower could not believe his eyes. There they were, both of them. They were his for the taking, after all these years, the two people who had always turned up in his life just in time to cause him to lose something he valued, his herd, his girls, his house.

It was the elder Grand who turned his head to see Glendower raising the rifle, his beard and hair flowing in the wind. He threw Miranda and Tandy down with one arm around each, rolled to pick up his son's long-barreled revolver, and even as the sound of Glendower's rifle broke the stillness, he was firing. Glendower hit the dirt rolling and made cover behind a small rise of the earth.

And Miranda had seen him. "Glendower," she gasped, and it was all back with her now, all the shame, all the heartbreak. She ran to Grand's horse and seized the rifle, hearing the whizz of a round going past before, rifle in hand, she was on the ground and crawling for cover. Meanwhile, having heard the shots, the men Glendower had hired to file claims on the piece of land he'd wanted from the first time he saw it were running from three directions.

Young Grand, his shoulder tied with a scarf, ran to get a rifle and, as a man came running, firing, he dropped him with a well placed shot.

And to Glendower history seemed to be repeating itself. He had seven men out there, one for each quarter section of the two square mile valley, and he saw first one and then another turn and run. "Come back, damn you," he yelled. "I paid you."

"You didn't pay us to fight no war," the man yelled, disappearing down a small rise.

Well, Rupert thought, it was only a boy, a half-man and two women. And he wanted that man and that woman, wanted them badly, wanted to see them die before his eyes. He settled into it and saved his shots, firing only when one of them showed himself to fire his way. He had time. He would circle slowly to the left and then he'd have them in sight, for the slight rise would not hide them anymore. He crawled, Indian fashion. He was just getting into position when he heard a horse coming fast and looked up to see the rider top the edge of the valley's bowl. He'd have to work fast. He was just getting into position. He had her in view, that damned Miranda. He was going to gut shoot her, get her in the side as she lay, a rifle extended in front of her.

She heard the horse and looked up, recognized the figure as he came riding hard. "Tony," she yelled, "be careful. It's Glendower."

He heard. Tony. Damn. The Woodrowe family he could handle, but that boy had sworn to kill him. And he was no Grand Woodrowe, no half man. A black rage flew through him and he began firing at the horseman, who threw himself off the horse and rolled for cover. And his position had exposed him so that Woodrowe's fire was coming close. He couldn't see Tony in the tall grass.

His impulse was to charge, to get as many of them as he could. He rose to one knee and a slug took off his hat and he was reminded that he was merely mortal and that a bullet would rip and tear. He fell to his belly and started crawling for the trees, where he'd left his horse. Hell, it was only land. He had a good bank account, money from the railroad, money from the settlers who had paid him fees. He could have his revenge later. Once again the damned Woodrowes had robbed him of what was his.

Tony crawled to them carefully. He was near when Glendower's horse broke from the trees, the rider leaning low over the horse's neck to make a small target. Grand Woodrowe was on his knees, levering and firing as fast as he could, a snarl of hate on his lips.

"I'll go after him," Tony yelled, running for his horse, but the animal, spooked by the gunfire, was hard to catch. The sound of hoofbeats had faded by the time he was mounted.

"Oh, God, Mindy," Grand moaned. "I had him. I had him in my sights and I missed."

"It's all right," she said. "We must get young Grand to a doctor."

"I'm going to the claims office," her son said. "I'm all right."

"You're sure?"

"Yes. You stay here. See that nobody jumps." And he was gone.

It was an hour before Tony came back. "Lost

him," he said. "And I think I've lost the piece of land I wanted. Saw men there on the way back."

"There's land here," Mindy said.

"It's a sweet place," he agreed. He staked the quarter section next to Grand's choice, and left them to ride to the claims office.

"I'm sick, Miranda," the elder Grand said. "I want to go home."

"Can you make it alone?" she asked.

"I can't leave you here."

"He won't be back, knowing that we're here, that Tony is here."

"Yes," he said. He seemed to have withdrawn again. He did not speak again as he mounted and rode slowly into the distance. So it was mother and daughter who stood guard and when two riders came, held rifles at the ready. There was no attempt at claim jumping. Soon the men, her son and Tony, would be back. And as she thought of them, of their having staked claims side by side she was bemused.

4

Grand did not ride easily for long. As he turned toward the south and east, heading for home, he began to think of his painting. It was if his mind were protecting him from the near madness he'd felt when he had been so close to being able to kill Rupert Glendower, the man who had killed his father, the man who had made him less than a man. And so he began to canter and then to race and it was only when he realized that he was about to kill a good horse that he slowed, allowed the animal to drink deeply from a creek and rest.

Nor was Grand Woodrowe the only man heading for the south and east with hate in his heart. Once he was in the clear, Rupert Glendower regretted not staying, not fighting. He promised himself that the next time he got any of them in his gun sights it would be the last of them, Tony Girondin included. And then an inspiration came to him. He had read of Grand Woodrowe's fancy painting, how the man had said it was his life. And there, down in the little town of McAlister, the Woodrowe place was left with maybe a couple of Indians to look out for it. That was one blow he could strike immediately. And so it was that they rode parallel routes, Glendower slightly in the lead, not pushing his horse for he felt, with all of them back in the valley with a wounded man to worry about, that he had plenty of time.

It was a long, long ride. He rode into the night and was up with the dawn. By late evening, with shadows beginning to fall, he was near and he approached the town cautiously. It seemed almost deserted. He imagined that a lot of them had gone up to the border to see the festivities. So much the better. The store sat in its old location, the town having grown up leading away from it on one side, so that he was unobserved as he approached from the road. There was the new store building, the old house, the shed-like building at the back. When he left, all three would be ablaze.

But first he wanted that painting. Maybe it would be better not to burn the shed, maybe a harder blow to his hated enemy would be to destroy the painting and leave the remains for him to see. So, judging that the painting would not be in the house, but in the big building, he came up and peered into a window and saw it in the fading light. It was a big one, stretching down one side of the huge room. He found the door locked, but it was a simple thing to break a pane in the window next to it and reach in and unlock the window and crawl in.

Inside it was dim. He walked to stand in front of the painting. It was really something. Almost a shame to destroy it. But, hell, it was just a lot of muck about Indians.

He still had a desire to see it, so he lit a lamp and walked along it, the light reflecting vivid, bold, slashing color. One hell of a lot of work, he thought. One hell of a lot of Indians.

Grand saw the light in the window from a distance and rage grew in him. No one was supposed to be in there. He'd locked the place. His first impulse was to ride up in a hurry and kick out whoever was there, but something in him urged caution. He left his horse and approached on foot, looked, saw *him*. *He* was standing in front of the precious painting. *He* had a long knife in his hands and his teeth showed as he looked at the painting and then he drew back his arm and slashed down, making a huge rent there toward the unfinished end.

Glendower, to work better, put down the lamp.

The sound which came from Grand's throat was more animal than human, and the door gave before his weight with a crash of sound and he was moving faster than he would have thought possible with the fat he'd accumulated over the years and he saw Glendower going for his gun, picked up a heavy stool, flung it with all his might. It came at Glendower out of the darkness so that he couldn't ward it off, smashing the gun

from his hand, sending him flying, his head ringing from the blow of the stool and then there was
upon him a wild, sobbing, snarling thing, a thing
of such maniacal strength that he felt himself
going, giving way before it, arms wrapping him,
his head hitting the floor with a crash which
brought a dimness through which he could still
feel the fierce pain, see the knife descend again
and again, through dying eyes.

Having buried his enemy by the river, he went
first to the well, drew fresh water, drank deeply,
then washed himself. Inside the house he changed
from his muddy clothing and walked to his studio. He sat in a chair in front of his creation. The
damage was in a non-critical place, at the unfinished end. He could replace the slashed canvas. But that was not the prime problem. The
question was, how to end it?

The labor of lifting, digging, the long ride had
tired him. He had a faint ache in his chest, the
result, he felt, of overexercise. He had been almost totally sedentary for years. But the ache
was nothing. The painting was all. He looked at
it and the section which depicted the ancient
Choctaw blood revenge, which required life for
life, caught his eye.

"Well, father," he said, speaking to the dead
Caleb Woodrowe, "it's done."

He needed rest, thought of his bed, but could
not tear himself from the painting. He sat there,
sometimes dozing, as the day lengthened and, to
the north, spring storms dumped inches of heavy
rainfall, their thunder a background rumble in

his mind. It was late in the day and the light was fading, but he lit lamps and, mixing onto his pallet the most crimson red he could make, dipped a large brush, thinking to add just one final scene there at the end, then maybe he'd have a clue about how to finish it, to end it.

And yet he could not touch brush to canvas, indecisive, but tormented by the need to end it.

Grand Woodrowe reached toward the canvas just as the smashing pain in his chest seemed to squeeze him from all sides. He screamed once, reaching out for support, the brush still extended.

"No, no," he was thinking, "not before it's finished."

But the pain became as huge as the world and he felt his stomach begin to heave and a black roaring was in his ears as his chest threatened to explode. With one gasp of pain and anger he reached out. As he sank to his knees the crimson-laden brush raked the canvas, following almost exactly the route of Rupert Glendower's slashing knife.

"Oh, mother," Tandy wept. "Before he could finish it. Before he could finish it."

He lay on his side, face at peace, paintbrush still clutched in his hand. Young Grand knelt beside him, felt for the non-existent pulse in his father's throat. Mindy was weeping quietly.

"Oh, it meant so much to him," Tandy was weeping. "If he could only have finished."

Grand rose to his feet. "Look," he said, pointing to the slashed canvas.

Mindy saw. It was at the very end of the long, powerful mural, a slash of blade covered by a slash of crimson.

"Yes," she said, but it was Grand who put it into words.

"I think he saw that it was over when the rush sent all those people into Indian Land. I think he knew it and it was too much for him. There may be a little more time, but that's it. It's over. It ends just like that, with a sudden slash and an overlay of crimson."

5

"Luke Starr, you're as crazy as a bedbug," Tandy Woodrowe said, slapping his hand away from her breast, but sighing deeply as it returned.

He had come riding up to the new store on Tandy Creek as if he owned the place. "You're hard to find," he said. "They told me you lived in McAlester and I go there and find you've moved, lock stock and barrel."

And, indeed, they had. Because McAlester had coal and was a growing town, Miranda got an excellent price for the store and house, enough to build the new store and a new house on the creek, the store already becoming a gathering place for settlers all around. And her son had become quite the farmer, running a few head of cattle and plowing the virgin soil to plant the grains to feed the cattle, the fruits and vegetables to feed the family. Moreover, there'd been enough money to buy the rest of the valley from those who had followed them in to stake claims. Miranda now owned seven-eighths of the land within the rim of the valley, the other quarter section in the hands of Tony Girondin, who was turning out to be a good friend for Grand and a good neighbor.

"Ain't crazy," Luke Starr said, closing Tandy's mouth with his. "I want you to come with me now. It's fifty-thousand dollars, Tandy. Fifty-thousand in silver dollars. They're taking it from Caldwell to Tahlequah to pay the Cherokee grazing rights."

"With about a million guards," Tandy said.

"A half dozen," Luke said. "We can take them easy. I've got twelve good men."

"Well, don't count me in," Tandy said, but her words were not forceful, for his hand was inside her blouse, fingers warm on her breast, his face close to hers.

"I'll marry you, if that's what you want," he whispered.

"Well, that's generous of you."

"I know you want me."

"You're pretty sure of yourself."

"Shouldn't I be?" he teased.

"Oh, damn you," she said, reaching for him.

They boarded the train in Chetopa. Luke Starr knew five men in the car, but he didn't so much as nod at any of them. Tandy was dressed in a dark brown dress, made of a tough worsted. She had a heavy gun in the carpet bag she carried.

One by one, as the train rattled to the south, the five men drifted toward the rear of the train. Luke and Tandy followed suit, acting as if they were merely taking a stroll through the passenger cars, through the dining car, past the pullman sections. At a signal guns blasted and the door leading into the baggage car flew open. Tandy was standing back around a section of compartments, heard the blaze of gunfire. When it stopped, heart pounding with excitement, she ran to the door and looked in.

Already the men, led by Starr, were gathering the bags of silver dollars. The door flew open. The spot had been selected because the train had slowed in going upgrade. A bag of silver went shooting out the door, the tough, triple thickness of canvas keeping it from bursting. A barrage of gunfire from the doorway caught three of Luke's men by surprise. The other two returned fire, but Luke, seeing armed men moving toward them, leaped for the open door, calling on Tandy to follow.

She felt a tug at her skirt, would later see that it had been holed by a bullet, went flying, landing on the embankment to roll hard and finally stop, battered but only bruised and scratched. Luke jerked her to her feet and pulled her into the trees. They ran back down the track. The bag of silver was there.

He cursed. "Only a thousand," he said. "Jesus, where did they all come from?" And as he talked he was running back for the woods, Tandy close behind. The other men were moving up.

"We won't be needing five of the horses," Luke told them.

"Where's the money?" a young, mustachioed man asked.

"It's here, what there is of it. They were waiting for us, seems like," Luke said.

"All that trouble, all those big plans for a thousand damned dollars," the mustachioed man said.

Luke Starr dropped the money bag. "George," he said, "if you don't like things the way they are around here, here's your chance to change it." His hand hovered over his gun belt.

"Now take it easy, Luke," George said. "I'm just disappointed, that's all."

"You think I ain't?" Luke asked, relaxing. "But let's get the hell out of here."

They rode south. The posse picked them up just south of Tahlequah. It was a pretty good posse, following the trail of eight horses easily.

"We're gonna split up," Luke told them. He took time to divvy up the thousand silver dollars. No one complained when he took double shares for himself and Tandy, four hundred dollars.

"You all know where I'll be," he said. "Give it a couple of weeks. Let things cool down, then ride in one at a time and be damned careful you're not followed."

Seven different trails split the posse, and, as Luke suspected, a small party followed the double trail made by him and Tandy. He stopped, in the edge of hills, with pine trees giving cover, and picked off two of the four men following them. The other two didn't seem to be too eager after that.

Streams and mountains. Cool air. And up the side of a mountain, leading the horses around huge outcrops of rocks. The cave was large and cool and relatively open so that it didn't seem gloomy and dark. He built a fire and Tandy roasted a rabbit.

"How long will we stay here?" she asked.

"Couple of weeks. Till the boys show up."

"Well," she said, "you promised me San Francisco and New Orleans and bales of money, Luke Starr, and now instead I have my own private cave."

"The money will come," he said. "Next time we'll be more careful. And as caves go, this ain't a bad one, is it?"

"Not bad," she said. "What's it called?"

"Hell, I don't know," he said. "Does it have to be called anything?"

"I think I'll name it Robber's Cave," she said.

"How about calling it our little love nest?" he asked, wiping his fingers on the side of his pants and reaching for her.

She did not know it, for such things were never discussed, but she was in many ways her mother's daughter. In the arms of the man she had loved from the first night she saw him in Purcell at the barn dance, she was a shameless wanton.

6

The year of 1889 was an eventful one for Miranda Lee Woodrowe. From April, when she'd ridden into the Unassigned Lands to once again meet Rupert Glendower, events had come thick and fast. The successful claim for the land along Tandy Creek, the death of her husband, his burial followed closely by the sale of the McAlester property, the move to Tandy, the excitement of seeing a new home and a new store take shape. And then a bitter blow to show her, once again, that happiness does not last forever.

The note had said: "I am going away to marry Luke Starr. He is a good man and will take care of me. Will write."

But Tandy had not written and now there were

disturbing stories about Luke Starr and a wild, black-haired girl who rode with him. Young Grand had ridden into the Cherokee Nation to Starr's home to see if they were there, returning to tell his mother that no one had seen them or heard from them.

Ah, she thought, will my sins never cease to follow me? For she had done the same thing to the woman who loved her.

Through her sadness, her worry, there was the joy of her son Grand. He loved the new life, worked so hard at it that it worried her. And she worked hard, too. When she saw the possibilities of the place, and was able to buy the claims which gave her the whole valley, she sent for Wynema and Jimmy. Wynema was heavy with child, but she worked to help build a new home, happy to be back near Miranda.

Around them the new Territory of Oklahoma was booming, population exploding. The new towns grew almost instantly. There was a clamoring for the opening of even more territory, and Miranda knew that it was only a matter of time.

Christmas was a family affair, Miranda and her son, Wynema, her new baby, Jimmy and Tony Girondin, for Tony had become not only a good neighbor and a friend of Grand's, but a welcome guest in Miranda's house. He was there often, willing to sit with Mindy in the store and chat with customers. He was there on Sundays when the meal was special and neighbors often dropped in to sit on the porch and spit tobacco juice and talk about the good old days or to tell the ghost stories which seemed to be the chief form of entertainment in the territory.

Not once did Tony ever refer to that time in their lives when they were more than friends, and she was grateful, although she, herself, found herself thinking of it now and again.

She thought often, too, of her home, the place where she'd spent so many years in Choctaw country, and often felt as if she had betrayed a people. But the white wind of which Grand had spoken was blowing a hurricane now. There were over sixty-thousand whites in the heart of Indian Territory and, as the new year established itself, a legislature, a government. Grand's mural, which had been moved to Tandy Creek, decorated the walls of the new store, and it seemed more and more prophetic. She had offered it by letter to the new state capital, to be built at Guthrie, and men were scheduled to come for it. She knew that it was too good, too important, to be moldering away in a country store, wanted to share it with others, wanted it safe so that when the Nations had, at last, been swallowed up by the white wind there would be the statement made by a man who was only part Indian to tell the story.

She received the telegram from Tandy in the dog days of August when the valley baked in a white heat and the breeze had deserted them.

THINK OF YOU OFTEN.
LOVE YOU. AM FINE. TANDY.

Just that. From Paris, Texas. Oh, God, she didn't even know where that was. Alone in the store she wept and was trying to dry her eyes when Tony came in, wiping perspiration from his forehead with a red bandana.

"I'd pay a dollar for a cool drink," he said, then looked at her. "Hey, what's this? Tears?"

She handed him the telegram without comment. "Damn that girl," he said. "She doesn't have a lick of sense."

"Takes after her mother," Mindy said trying to be light and stop the flow of tears, but her voice caught.

"Now don't you go downgrading a fine woman," Tony said. He stepped close, took the handkerchief from her hand and tried to dry her tears.

"You're just making it worse, feeling sorry for me," she sobbed, turning away. He put his hands on her arms and turned her to face him.

"One good cure for a woman's tears," he said. "And that's a good secure hug." He suited actions to words and, feeling small and helpless, she put her face on his rough shirt and let the sobs come. His hand patted her back gently. "There, there," he murmured. "It's all right. That silly girl will come to her senses. She'll be home. But, boy, if she were here and if I had the right I'd warm her behind good."

If I had the right. The words seemed to haunt her, and she wept more heavily, distressing him, worrying him, and as he lifted her face, his hand under her chin, he saw how beautiful she was. He'd tried to ignore it, for what he had done to her could never be forgiven. But there she was, eyelids swollen, eyes red with weeping, and he could feel her in his arms and without thinking, with a sigh, he began to kiss the tears from her cheeks.

"Can't stand seeing you cry, Mindy," he said. "Now you stop it."

His lips on her cheek, on her softness just below the eye, tasting the salt of her tears, feeling the smoothness, the sweetness. And she gulped, the sobs halted, an old and familiar feeling threatening to sweep through her like wildfire. He sensed the change in her, drew back slightly to look into her eyes.

"Mindy?" he breathed, not daring to believe what he saw there. "Mindy, can it be true?"

"I don't know," she whispered, her words barely discernible.

"Oh, damn, Mindy, if only we'd met under different circumstances."

"But we didn't," she said. "And there's nothing we can do about it."

"Yes, there is," he said, drawing her to him, resolved to find out, once and for all, if that look in her eyes meant what he thought it did.

She resisted slightly, but only at first, and then, with a moan of mingled sorrow, regret and some other, happier, feeling, she let her lips melt into his and there was a heady feeling of rightness, a joy which built in her until she pulled her mouth from his and burst into glad laughter.

In his arms, where she had been before under entirely different circumstances, she was her daughter's mother, for Tandy had sprung from the passions they'd once known. Her daughter's mother, shameless wanton, endlessly loving.

In the wake of the Civil War . . .

THE BUILDERS

THE BUILDERS is the sixth novel in the series THE MAKING OF AMERICA and immediately precedes in time THE LAND RUSHERS. This is the story of the epic forging of the Union Pacific—and the mystery woman in the great railroad war.

Passions ran high in the 1860s as men and women struggled, sweated, fought and often died in the race to build the great transcontinental railroad.

Eastern money, Eastern muscle and Eastern logrolling was winning the race, aided by a ruthless killer hired as a "Consultant."

Meanwhile, those building from the Western end of the country—the "Big Four," Huntington, Stanford, Crocker and Hopkins—were bogged down in private feuds, labor strife and sabotage, until a mystery woman named Liberty Lee and her even more mysterious "friend" took a hand in the deadly race to the Golden Spike.

Sixth in the series
A DELL BOOK ON SALE NOW